———————————— ★ ————————————

"Damn." Willie let his breath go with a whoosh. "Bird, dead bodies have given me nightmares ever since 'Nam." He took a deep breath. "But I guess I better check this out."

Moving closer to the brambles, Willie leaned over and pulled some of the stalks apart, painfully snagging his fingers in the process. Above the shoe, a strip of black sock led to the bottom edge of a black pant leg. Willie dropped the brush back into place.

Good place to hide a body, he thought. A raspberry patch picked clean of berries wouldn't get any attention before next year's berry-picking season. And if this patch had been pulled and stacked up for burning, or hauling, the body might never turn up.

Willie shook his head in disbelief. Why did this keep happening to him?

———————————— ★ ————————————

THE
PRAIRIE GRASS
MURDERS

Patricia Stoltey

WORLDWIDE®

TORONTO • NEW YORK • LONDON
AMSTERDAM • PARIS • SYDNEY • HAMBURG
STOCKHOLM • ATHENS • TOKYO • MILAN
MADRID • WARSAW • BUDAPEST • AUCKLAND

In memory of my dad,
Harry L. Swartz
1921–1982

Recycling programs
for this product may
not exist in your area.

THE PRAIRIE GRASS MURDERS

A Worldwide Mystery/February 2010

First published by Five Star.

ISBN-13: 978-0-373-26700-2

Printed in U.S.A.

Acknowledgments

I am so grateful for the contributions of:

Brian Kaufman, author of *The Breach,* who put a great amount of time and energy into guiding his "student" writers into print.

Dee Cheatwood, the best first reader any writer could hope for.

April Joitel, Bev Marquart, Melissa Pattison, Sidna Rachid, and Carolyn Yalin, members of the Raintree Writers critique group, as well as former members Cara Hopkins, Danielle Johnson and Naomi Rockler; their honesty and willingness to share ideas are deeply appreciated.

And Denise Dietz, author and editor, who was willing to advise and teach as well as edit.

ONE

WILLIE NARROWED HIS EYES against the sun's glare as he watched the huge bird circle overhead. From a distance, he'd thought it was a hawk. Now he was closer, and he could tell from the six-foot wingspan that it was a turkey vulture, the first he'd seen in this part of Illinois.

The species had once inhabited the central prairies in large numbers. Now the birds weren't so common. Even so, there was hardly a soul alive who didn't know what function these scavengers performed in the earth's food chain.

Willie watched the buzzard float overhead, then turned to study the run-down farmhouse and neglected yard of his former home. After a moment he continued his trek toward the western edge of the property. He would stop by the house on his way back to Sangamon City.

A combine clanked along the narrow road behind him, raising a cloud of dust that slowly deposited a pale gray coating on the nettle and milkweed growing along the fence. As the farmer guided his massive machine past, he glanced at Willie, clean-shaven and neatly dressed. Willie raised his arm and waved, and the farmer nodded in return.

With a tug on the straps, Willie adjusted his new backpack and followed the combine toward the narrow bridge just ahead. A creeping film of perspiration on his forehead threatened to bead and form wet trails through the dust settling on his skin. He pushed his Marlins cap back and used his sleeve to wipe the sweat from his face and neck.

It had been over thirty years since he last visited this part of the country and even longer since living here. He'd forgotten how hot Illinois could be in September and wished he'd waited to take this nostalgic journey in October, when the air was crisp and the trees wore their flamboyant red and orange uniforms.

The trip provided a much-needed break from the unusually active hurricane season which had selected Florida as its primary target. After two back-to-back stints as a volunteer at one of the Red Cross storm shelters, Willie definitely needed this holiday.

As he approached the bridge he picked up his pace, eager to see one of his favorite old haunts. A few minutes later, he stood on the sun-bleached wooden planks and looked over the waist-high, rusted railing into the drainage ditch. Then he turned to survey the countryside. He whistled as he glanced around, observing the flat terrain, the straight rows, the order. Illinois was so different from the semi-tropical excesses of South Florida. He gazed at the wheat fields, soybeans, and a cornfield off in the distance. Some crops were already harvested but all had taken on the color of dried cornstalks.

Gripping the top of the railing as he leaned forward, Willie peered as far as he could see under the bridge. *Clear as a mountain stream,* he thought as he watched the water moving swiftly over sandy loam.

Higher along the banks, and meandering here and there down toward the water, were patches of prairie tallgrass. Butterprint and milkweed flourished on the untended slopes. A few yards away from the bridge, a dense stand of wild raspberry brambles threatened to spread into the field.

As Willie considered the satisfying memories triggered by the images and smells of the countryside, he also noticed the vulture tightening its circular patrol over the bridge. *Keeping an eye on me,* Willie thought.

He looked back at the water to see if a dead muskrat or snake might have attracted the vulture, but saw nothing. Late August had been unusually rainy in Illinois, so the fast-flowing water in the ditch measured at least a foot deep, a sure sign it was cold. If the carcass the vulture sought had died in the water, it was probably well-preserved. In spite of his grown-up concern about dead animals and toxic field runoff, he was tempted to splash his face and cool his hands and feet in the ditch as he had done so many times as a boy.

Willie scrambled down the bank and ducked under the bridge. This was familiar territory. The flat rock where he'd scratched his initials still rested there, the WG now barely visible. Willie dropped his backpack to the ground, pulled out his shirttail, and unbuttoned his plaid flannel shirt, flapping the edges for ventilation. Then he plopped down at the edge of the water, rolled up his pant legs, and took off his boots and socks.

The silt quickly turned the water to a muddy soup when Willie thrust one foot into the stream, held it in the water until numb from the cold, then stretched his leg out so his foot rested in the sun.

Scooting even closer to the ditch, he rolled up his sleeves and pulled a red print handkerchief from his pocket. When the dirt settled and the stream cleared, he wet the cloth and washed his face. After rinsing the kerchief, Willie started to hang it on the bridge to dry, but changed his mind when he thought of the dust cloud raised by the combine.

He stood up and stepped into the stream, shivering a little at first, but feeling good inside because the old ditch had come through for him again, just like it always had when he was a kid. Stomping in the water and swirling the muddy silt as he walked, he made his way toward the raspberry brambles. About ten feet away from his destination, he halted as the vulture abruptly landed at the top of the bank between Willie and the raspberry canes. There it sat, still as a statue, even when Willie took another step forward and waved his arms.

The two stared at each other, motionless. *Maybe this isn't a good sign,* Willie thought. He sniffed the air, expecting the stench of dead animal, but smelled nothing except fresh harvested wheat and sun-baked straw.

"Go on," Willie yelled. He waved the handkerchief at the vulture. It backed up a couple of steps and stopped, its unblinking eyes now focused on the red flag.

"I mean it. Get on out of here." Willie picked up a few pebbles from the ditch bank and tossed them toward the bird. It sidestepped the missiles and backed closer to the brambles.

Willie decided to hang the bandanna on the other side of the brush. Antagonizing his unwelcome companion didn't seem the best way to handle the standoff. The creature was far too ugly not to have an equally unpleasant disposition. Willie edged past the raspberry patch and waded farther up the ditch. The bird thrust his head forward and two-stepped his way along the bank in an obvious effort to stop Willie's approach. They stopped again and stared at each other for several seconds.

Willie looked away first. The bird's blank gaze gave him the creeps. Avoiding eye contact with the vulture, Willie nervously studied the huge raspberry patch again. He noticed a few wilted leaves, and bits of damp soil clinging to the roots. The rambling plants had clearly been ripped out of the ground and dumped into this field—and not so long ago, either.

At one edge of the pile, near the ground, a black shape

poked through the green and brown vegetation. Willie ignored the buzzard and climbed farther up the bank to get a better look.

A shoe—a man's black leather shoe.

He reached out and gave it a sharp tug, but couldn't pull it free. He let go, stepped back, and then stood very still. *The shoe is most likely attached to a foot.* Fear crawled down his spine, leaving a wet streak that soaked through his shirt.

"Damn." Willie let his breath go with a whoosh. "Bird, dead bodies have given me nightmares ever since 'Nam." He took a deep breath. "But I guess I better check this out."

Moving closer to the brambles, Willie leaned over and pulled some of the stalks apart, painfully snagging his fingers in the process. Above the shoe, a strip of black sock led to the bottom edge of a black pant leg. Willie dropped the brush back into place.

Good place to hide a body, he thought. A raspberry patch picked clean of berries wouldn't get any attention before next year's berry-picking season. And if this patch had been pulled and stacked up for burning, or hauling, especially if a killer did the burning or hauling, the body might never turn up.

Willie shook his head in disbelief. Why did this keep happening to him? During his homeless days in D.C. after the war, he'd stumbled across an elderly street woman who'd been set on fire and burned to death, most likely by some gang of hoodlums. In his attempt to shove the ugly vision back under its rock, Willie unwittingly let another escape: the old fisherman whose waterlogged remains had washed up under the pier at Deerfield Beach. *This bad habit of finding bodies will have to stop.*

He glanced back at the vulture whose secret he now shared, then looked around to see if anyone approached. The farmer on his combine was no more than a cloud of dust on the horizon. No one else could be seen.

Willie turned back to the bird and spoke. "You know, even if I did stop at one of those houses, there might be someone there who wouldn't be too thrilled about our discovery. You understand what I'm saying?"

Moving down the bank to the water, bent low so he couldn't be seen from the fields, Willie crept back and picked up his pack. He stuffed his socks and boots inside, tied the wet handkerchief around his neck, and climbed up close to the ditch bank. Uneasy, he decided not to return to the road where he might be seen. *South along the ditch is definitely the way to go,* he decided. *More trees and hedges for cover.* He waded into the cold water and began his barefoot trek, turning only once to look back at the vulture.

"If I were you, bird, I'd hit the trail. It might not be safe around here."

Twenty minutes and one mile later, Willie reached old Route 10, a busy two-lane highway leading west from Sangamon City through prairie farmland and small towns. The heavy traffic made him nervous, so he sat down with his back to the road and stared north, ignoring the hum and clank and sputter behind him, thinking instead of the peace and calm he'd experienced before his discovery of the body.

The tall stands of prairie grass by the ditch swayed hypnotically in the breeze. Sparkles of sunlight bounced off the water like silent fireworks, distant rockets, gunfire... Willie shook off the notion and searched the sky. A mile away, near the bridge, a tiny speck circled. The vulture had obediently taken to the air.

"Hey, buddy!" The shout came from behind. Willie jumped up, then dropped back into a crouch as he turned toward the man's voice.

A deputy sheriff stood less than ten feet away, his car parked at the edge of the highway with the driver's door hanging open. After seeing Willie's defensive reaction, the wild look in his eyes, and his disheveled appearance, the hefty deputy took a step back and raised his hand to place it on the butt of his holstered gun.

At the same moment, Willie realized he faced a lawman, and he relaxed his shoulders and stood up. He grabbed the cap off his head and ran his fingers through his sweat-matted gray hair, replaced the cap, and started to button up his shirt.

"Yes, sir. Wow, you really scared me. Whooee!" Willie shook his head.

"How about some ID, buddy?"

"Yeah, sure." Willie bent over his backpack and unzipped the inside pocket which held his identification. He located his billfold and handed it over, noticing the officer had unsnapped his holster when Willie reached into his bag.

"Mr. Grisseljon, you're a long way from home." The deputy's voice sounded neutral enough, although not exactly friendly.

Willie watched the lawman as he studied the voter registration card which contained little to explain Willie's identity. Squinting to read the small print, and then deepening the crease in his forehead with a frown, the lawman glared at Willie. "Don't you have a driver's license?"

"I don't drive."

"Why not?"

Willie shrugged. "Don't have a car," he answered.

"What are you doing out here in the middle of nowhere with no car?"

"Vacation. I like walking."

The deputy digested the response for a moment then motioned toward Willie's feet. "You go walkin' with no shoes?"

"I was down in the ditch, in the water. I have boots and socks in my pack."

The deputy nodded and closed the billfold, hesitating as

he examined the worn leather. "This here looks like blood," he said. "Do you have blood on your hands, Mr. Grisseljon?"

"Scratched my fingers on some thorns." Willie held out his hand as though to show the deputy his wounds. "But…I found a body back there," he suddenly blurted out. He pointed north along the ditch then raised his finger to point toward the sky. After a glance at the name tag pinned above the deputy's badge, Willie continued. "See that big bird, Deputy Morris? Right where it's circling, there's a dead man down on the ground. Somebody covered him up with a lot of raspberry brambles—trying to hide the body, I'll bet."

The deputy stomped back to his car without a word and returned with a pair of binoculars which he trained on the distant speck, then down toward the ground, slowly studying the landscape as though he thought the body would suddenly jump up from the bushes and wave.

Turning abruptly, and again without a word, the deputy took Willie's billfold and strode back to his car. He got in, picked up the radio mike and held it close to his mouth as he talked, watching Willie through the windshield. When he finished, he lumbered out of the car and called Willie over. "Let's go. You can show me just where this body of yours is."

Willie grabbed his pack and hurried to the deputy's car, where he climbed into the secured backseat. The deputy tossed Willie's billfold onto the front passenger floor, and climbed in behind the steering wheel. After pulling his door shut and starting the vehicle, Deputy Morris turned and looked at Willie through the wire grill. Then he pulled onto the highway and sped toward town with his lights flashing, ignoring all Willie's directions to the body.

Twenty minutes later, the deputy shoved his barefoot

prisoner through the door of the Lincoln County Hospital. Morris gave the intake clerk instructions to admit the vagrant to the holding facility for a psychiatric evaluation.

As Willie heard the deputy tell it, he suffered from hallucinations and confusion, had blood on his hands and forehead, and didn't seem to know who he was. No one paid attention to Willie's insistence that he had identification, or his demands to use the telephone, until long after Deputy Morris had left the premises, still in possession of Willie's billfold.

"I'm here on vacation," Willie protested to anyone who would listen. "I live in Florida. I have family there. My parents. My sister. Call my sister," he insisted. "She's a circuit court judge. She'll tell you."

The intake clerk transferred him into the custody of Dan, an amiable but imposing six-foot nurse with well-developed biceps. The grip he applied to Willie's elbow implied Dan was the usual custodian of patients with violent tendencies. He escorted Willie to a sparsely furnished room where he left the door open but parked himself on a chair in the hall. After much cajoling and explaining, Willie finally convinced Dan that not only was he perfectly sane, but that he deserved to have his case presented to a higher authority.

"It's just a vacation, a visit to the old homestead," Willie repeated to the grim woman who served as the hospital's night administrator. "And this is involuntary commitment, which, by the way, probably isn't legal. I know it's not legal in Florida. Would you call my sister now?"

The supervisor nervously shuffled papers into a yellow manila folder as Willie talked. However, when Willie explained who his sister was, and questioned the legality of his continued presence at the facility, he received her full attention.

"Yes, yes, I don't know what the deputy was thinking," she mumbled as she nodded her head and shoved the folder to one side. "I'll talk to the sheriff tomorrow and let him handle the problem. Dan will take you to your room, but if you give me your sister's phone number, I'll call her now, then personally come and tell you what she says."

I know exactly what she'll say, Willie thought. He shrugged and blew a little puff of air through his lips as he imagined Judge Sylvia Thorn's reaction.

TWO

"Ow, OUCH! Blast it, Tak!" I shouted.

"Jus' one of those distal points. I tol' you before, it'll be good. I promise."

"You twisted the needle, didn't you?"

"But the pain's fadin' now, right? You are so uptight, Judge. This won' do you any good if you don' relax and let the needles work. Look, your foot is drawin' the needle in. See how it's puckered?"

Yes, I could see how it puckered, but I wasn't impressed. For six months now, I'd been giving acupuncture a chance to work on my unbalanced chi, but I've never managed to quietly ease into and through the pain. I tended to blame Tequila Picon's sadistic side more than my own body's sullen resistance. She also pushed a vile herbal concoction she claimed was Chinese. More likely an obscure Puerto Rican ritual poison with African origins. Yes, I'm still taking it. No, I don't know why.

Tak and I hit it off from the beginning at least two years ago, long before I agreed to let her use my body as a pincushion. As Judge of the Fifteenth Judicial Circuit of the State of Florida, I'm usually treated with a certain amount of respect and courtesy, so when a prospective juror, a certain Miss Tequila Picon, spoke to me personally during voir dire, I was somewhat taken aback.

"Judge, your Honor," she began, "who cut your hair?"

"Shhh," cautioned the prosecuting attorney. "Don't talk to the judge."

"Why not?" Tak asked indignantly. "She like a goddess or somethin'?"

"Excuse the juror," said the defense attorney.

"Excuse me? Why? Did I do somethin' wrong?"

I stopped the bailiff as he stepped forward to escort Miss Picon from the courtroom. "No, Miss Picon, I'm not a goddess or something. I cut my own hair. And for now, it's important you concentrate on the attorneys' questions."

"Okay, your Honor, but let me just say you need to find someone to give you a good haircut."

In an involuntary response to Tak's observation, my right hand reached up and smoothed the uneven wispy strands I'd left in the back. *Damn, what a stupid move. Everyone in the courtroom saw me do it.*

Since Tequila made it through the entire process and was accepted as juror number five in a civil case involving bank fraud, she managed to enlighten and entertain the court for three weeks with her unorthodox, irreverent, and often impertinent observations. She got away with it because she was smart, wise, and utterly charming. None of us wanted to throw her out. A few days after the trial ended, I was enjoying a solitary lunch in a restaurant near the courthouse when Tak audaciously plopped herself down in the empty chair across from me, eyed my new hairstyle, and nodded approvingly before launching into an entertaining explanation of how her Mexican mother and Puerto Rican father met, married, and decided to name her Tequila.

"Thanks God, they didn't call me Rum," she'd told me.

Now here I was, two years later, totally at her mercy, unable to hop up and run away since she'd been kind enough to come to my condo and needle me unmercifully before we enjoyed an evening of beer, pizza, and a new British version of *Jesus Christ Superstar* on DVD.

The sensation of melting muscles that often washed over me once the needles were in place had just begun when the phone rang and a call from the Lincoln County Hospital in Sangamon City, Illinois, changed my evening plans as well as those for the weekend.

Shit! My chi had really looked forward to Saturday's walk on the beach. I also needed several hours of practice in accessing and using the new database recently installed throughout Florida's legal community. The computer, and my chi, would just have to wait. Willie needed me.

After the early Friday morning flight from West Palm Beach to Indianapolis, including a speedy plane change in Cincinnati, the two-hour drive from the Indy airport to Sangamon City unfolded without mishap in spite of my near-zombie state. Even so, the countryside still snagged my attention, reminding me there were interesting alternatives to the manicured lawns and stately palms of Boca Raton, Florida, or the wild tropical growth of the Everglades. The warm weather and vibrant fall colors of Illinois could persuade an unsuspecting visitor to linger too long and find the world had turned frigid and gray, or worse, bone-chilling white. None of that yet, thank goodness.

I left this part of the country for good when I turned twenty-five and haven't been back in the thirty-four years since. My brother Willie wanted to come back, mostly, I think, to find out if the safe, comfortable places he remembered from his childhood still existed—or if they had become as mean and tough as South Florida. He flew to Indy and took a Greyhound bus to Sangamon City with plans to stay at the Ramada Inn for a week while he took daily hikes to visit favorite haunts: the old farm, our country grade school, the greasy diner a block from the high school. But something had gone wrong.

As I turned into the hospital parking lot, I was distracted by vague memories of visits to ancient relatives when this building had been the county's first nursing home. It was majestic then, the original redbrick mansion standing alone in its hundred-year-old splendor. But there'd apparently been a need for expansion. New one-story wings, covered with yellow vinyl siding, now stretched from each corner like long tentacles, giving the hospital a disjointed and inconsistent look. Now the complex served as a county hospital and shelter for indigents and generally confused souls, so perhaps the building's personality suited its clientele well.

Willie waited patiently in the lobby, writing in one of the notebooks he always carried. He looked up when I strode through the front entrance, conducted a visual inspection of my appearance, and returned his attention to the book. I wore khaki slacks with a brown leather belt, a long-sleeved silk blouse with a geometric pattern in brown, black, gold, and cream, and new brown loafers. Apparently my outfit met with Willie's approval. He hates it when I run around in public in T-shirt, jeans, and running shoes. Willie also encourages me to keep my curly hair short and naturally gray because he feels it looks more distinguished. He insists I get regular manicures but wear only clear polish, and he nags me if I wear any jewelry other than tiny gold earrings and medium-length gold chains. My brother has very definite ideas on how a judge should look and act.

I wouldn't get nearly as much flak from my free-spirited, eighty-five-year-old mother, who was currently dragging my dad around Key West for the umpteenth time since they'd retired, just because she thought it the only place on the mainland to get a decent piña colada.

Our parents, Peter and Kristina Grisseljon, threw off their conservative and morose Norwegian heritage and adopted a what-the-hell way of life when they retired and moved to Florida a good twenty years ago. They continue to maintain a level of activity easily rivaling that well-known, frantic pink bunny, although I've occasionally seen my father slowly amble toward a destination while my mother darted back and forth to examine every shop window or flower bed on the way.

While Mom works on convincing me to examine my wild side, Willie, still the morose Norwegian, tries to keep me grounded. But my brother doesn't know what my mother quietly applauds—I have a tattoo of a butterfly above the bikini line of my left hip. This may seem like a very small rebellion, especially since I no longer wear a bikini, but it was a significant triumph for me when I acknowledged the sense of freedom I felt after divorcing my second husband, Ronald Grant, the verbally abusive, overly competitive shyster who nearly ruined my life in two short years. Re-establishing my identity as Andy Thorn's widow, and gritting my teeth through the pain just to get a tattoo, which my sweet Andy would have loved, put me back on the right path. In this case, the right path involved going into therapy to help me complete the mourning process I'd tried to skip after Andy's accident. There are no shortcuts to the other side of grief.

I sat down next to my brother. "Hi."

In answer, he raised his hand. "Wait a second."

I waited.

He flipped back a few pages, and then handed the notebook to me. "I wrote it all down."

"Am I supposed to read this right now? Shouldn't we get you out of here first?" I looked around for the hospital administrator who'd called me the night before, full of apologies as she told me she would make sure the county sheriff heard all about his deputy's actions.

"You have to sign me out because the officer who brought me in said I was crazy...so go on, sign me out." Willie spoke impatiently, as if I'd been holding him back from a mad dash toward the door.

A lot of our history is based on Willie being the older sibling and feeling very much at home bossing me around. In reality, I look out for Willie and have since 1968 when I found him in a homeless shelter in Washington, D.C., after the VA hospital abruptly released him, proclaiming him as cured of war as he would ever be. No one had thought to notify Willie's family, so he wandered the streets until I tracked him down.

It was disconcerting to think we were about to replay that ancient experience, so I was very relieved to find Willie fully functional and ready to roll. Able to spring him with a minimum of effort, I couldn't understand exactly why he'd been dumped at the facility in the first place, since the deputy sheriff whose name was listed on the paperwork as Stoney Morris had only noted that Willie seemed confused, thought he'd seen a dead body, and had no identification. I requested a copy of the sign-in form and tucked it away in my bag, hustled Willie out the door and to the car, honestly thinking we would be on our way back to Florida before noon the next day. Willie straightened me out before I could fasten my seat belt.

"Read it now. It tells how I found the body."

I turned to look at him, figuring I was expected to read a poem he'd written, or one of the mystical essays that creep free of the dark shadows protecting him from images too vivid to confront directly. Willie today is very different from the Willie I'd known while we were young, but not in the ways you would expect. Even as a child, he'd been serious and introspective. It surprised no one when he elected to abandon his accounting career and join the Marines, rather than patiently wait for the United States Army invitation to visit the other side of the world. Love of country, taking responsibility, and a sense of duty were character traits firmly ingrained in people like us. My mother's father, a first-generation Norwegian immigrant, had served in the army during one war and in the navy during a second. He came back unscathed.

Willie didn't fare so well. In less than three years he returned home on a medical discharge. The Marine ahead of him had stepped on a land mine and his body had shielded my brother from serious injury, but not from shock. According to the doctors' reports, Willie suffers from hearing loss and an inability to tolerate prolonged agitation or sudden loud noises. This translates into a fear of long trips on South Florida's Interstate 95, especially between Miami and West Palm Beach, or fireworks, or rock concerts. He also won't watch movies or television where anything gets blown up, especially people.

"No, this is real," he said. "I didn't make it up."

Willie is a poet in his own world. Most of the time, however, he's a resident of my world. He's established a small public accounting firm, which he's now in the process of selling. In his spare time, which will increase significantly with his retirement, he provides perceptive observations of people and events related to my cases, regularly volunteers at a Delray Beach homeless shelter, and spends a few hours every week fishing off the Deerfield Beach pier with a few of his veteran cronies who manage to talk for hours without ever once telling a war story or discussing politics, religion, or death. Willie tunes in, listens, and hears what others overlook. Sometimes his thought process seems more intuitive than deductive, but he is rarely wrong. I always listen, and so does everyone else who knows him.

Distinguishing between reality and fantasy had never been a problem, so when Willie said this was real, I couldn't ignore him. I cocked one eyebrow at him anyway, just to test his reaction. Willie shook his head vehemently and led me through it like a teacher describing a complicated concept to someone who has only a basic knowledge of the language.

"I found a body in the country. I got scared and ran away. When I got to the highway, a deputy stopped to talk to me. I told him about the body but he didn't believe me. He brought me to the hospital and left me here. He forgot to leave my billfold. Now we have to get it back, and we have to make someone go out there and take care of that dead man." Willie grabbed the notebook from the car's center console where I'd placed it and thrust it at me, practically in my face. "Read it," he said again.

I knew when I'd lost a battle. I leaned back to think a minute. As soon as I'd received the call from the hospital, I claimed a family emergency and had my clerk clear the docket through Monday. The schedule had included clean-up on several hearings, mostly trust matters, and all were easily moved to Tuesday. I booked an early flight for this morning, hoping we could return tomorrow, but I'd checked Sunday and Monday availability just in case. If I called the airline this evening, I could probably still get the seats changed to Sunday morning.

"Okay, but we have to fly back no later than Monday, no matter what. I have a case coming up that won't get postponed or bargained. And Willie, I hate to tell you this, but there's another hurricane headed for Florida. Should make landfall next Thursday or Friday."

"Syl, we have more than enough time. Read this first."

I slid the car seat back and retrieved a pair of reading glasses from my bag, took the notebook, and started to read. Willie's style is usually poetic, even when his essay concerns the ugly side of life. This time proved to be no exception.

After I'd read his words through once, I turned back to the beginning and read them again. I was hooked. I had no doubt everything happened exactly the way Willie wrote it down. He sometimes has a problem with verbal communication, gets flustered and appears to be confused or forgetful. As a result, he tends to keep his spoken comments short and to the point.

Even so, he has a phenomenal memory and no trouble getting his thoughts down on paper. The other thing he's good at is reading people—feeling vibes and sensing when something isn't right.

I suppose there was no reason to assume the dead man Willie found was murdered. I suppose there could be a perfectly natural explanation for a man to die in a field with raspberry canes piled on top of him. And I suppose it was perfectly logical a deputy sheriff would believe a man to be nuts if he claimed he'd found a body. But I also knew neither Willie nor I would be able to walk away until we figured out what happened and why. We needed to talk to a few people before we could head back to Florida.

THREE

THE RAMADA INN near the Prairie Community College campus would have been the next logical stop if I hadn't been itching to get out to the country while plenty of daylight remained. Driving through town, I could see how Sangamon City had changed. Even though the historic dwellings still lined the narrow downtown streets, and the imposing Carnegie library looked as solid and indestructible as ever, the city's perimeter now sprawled in every direction like the uncontrolled expansion of an agitated amoeba. When we reached what used to be the edge of the city, I could see how extensively civilization had invaded prime Illinois farmland.

Willie pointed the way as though he thought I'd forgotten how to get home. An odd thought, since this had not been my home for many years. I felt Willie's eyes on me. What was he thinking? How hard I'd cried when he went off to college, even though it took only an hour to drive there? Or when I'd baked and frosted the cake for his eighteenth birthday, and then tripped and dropped it upside down on the floor? I cried then, too. Willie treated me so well, even though I was nearly six years younger and a royal pain in the ass. I reached over and patted his hand. He ignored me, of course.

"It took over two hours for me to walk out here," he said. "I figured it would be an all-day hike since it's at least ten miles from the motel, so I left as soon as it got light."

"You didn't tell me you made it all the way out here. Is this where you found the body?"

"Remember the ditch on the west side of the farm?"

"Sure."

"That's where I went."

"Then the body's on our old place?"

"Yep."

"Well, Willie…oh, look. There it is." I slowed the car as we drove by the one-story, dingy white house. *So much smaller than I remember.* I didn't say anything, and I don't think I changed expression, but Willie caught my mood.

"You're disappointed."

"Now, how could you know that?" I glanced at him, saw him shrug.

"I was disappointed," he said. "Why wouldn't you feel the same? They've stripped off the porch, the barn is gone. Looks like they ripped out the apple orchard. The place doesn't have a personality anymore. I stood out in front for a minute, and I felt like I'd lost something important. Which is why I decided to go down to the ditch. I figured they wouldn't mess with that."

I nodded. "Looks like no one lives here." I studied the old place as we drove by, and then returned my attention to the road ahead. "Okay, back to business. Keep on going straight?"

"To the bridge. There's room to pull off on the south side. What I saw is about twenty-five feet in, close to the ditch."

"Why would a body be dumped so close to the road? Why not buried out there in the field, or stashed underneath the bridge?"

"Wasn't necessary, I guess. You'll see. It's hidden just fine." Willie pointed toward a huge mound of debris. Only when I heard him start to mumble profanities did I turn my attention away from the field and stare at my brother. He never uses bad language.

"What's wrong, Willie?"

"Someone's been here. They piled more stuff on the body."

It sure looked like a lot more than the tangle of raspberry canes Willie had described in his notebook. As I drove closer, I could see rubbish dumped in one huge heap—a couple of tree trunks, what looked like a section of hedgerow, and lots of black soil. I pulled over and parked the car. Before I could remind him about footprints, tire marks, and other evidence we shouldn't disturb, Willie scrambled out the door and headed across the field.

The temperature had eased down since the sun had dropped lower, but Willie was dressed appropriately for the occasion. Envious of his jeans, flannel shirt, and hiking boots, I pulled my brown leather travel bag to the front seat and yanked out a gray sweatshirt, stuffed the car keys in my pocket, and hurried to follow my brother with only a brief thought of the damage I might do to my new loafers.

The burial mound stood nearly twice my height of five feet six inches. Willie looked it over, shook his head, and walked around to the other side. "Syl, come here."

As I carefully made my way across the rough ground, I looked for any sign of a body. I saw nothing. Nothing, that is, until I joined Willie, who stared down at a clump of dark gray feathers. He turned the carcass over with his foot, exposing a huge gaping hole smeared with blood. The naked red head flopped to one side as though to stare incredulously down at its mutilated body.

Willie walked a few steps away, pulled out a handkerchief, and reached down to pick up something. He stuffed whatever he'd found in his pocket.

"Don't touch anything else," I cautioned. "There's

nothing we can do here. We need to call the sheriff's office."

When I turned back toward the car, I saw we had company. An official county vehicle had pulled up tight behind my rental, and a beefy country boy in a brown-and-tan uniform was checking out the inside of my car.

"Willie, take a look."

He peered around the pile of dirt. "It's the deputy who took me to the hospital." Willie frowned and the determined expression I knew so well swept over his face. He started a grim march toward our car.

"Wait, Willie. I want to hear what he has to say."

Willie didn't wait. I walked faster to stay close behind him.

I wonder if it's possible to find one unique character in this world. I guess I'll have to keep looking. This deputy fit a classic Southern mold, even to the jowls and the cigar hanging from the corner of his mouth. I was trying to figure out how he'd strayed so far north when he turned on us with all the fury of a bull separated from the object of his affections by the electric current charging through a barbed wire fence.

"What are you people nosing around for? This here's private property. Ya'll are trespassing. Get on out of here."

Willie didn't back away, which is certainly what I felt like doing. "You forgot to give me back my billfold—with my identification in it. Maybe you dropped it inside your car." Willie turned and started toward the deputy's vehicle. I hadn't a doubt in my mind he meant to search it as thoroughly as the deputy had been searching my glove compartment.

"Whoa, there. What are you talking about?"

"You know, when you picked me up on the highway and dumped me off at the hospital. You forgot to give me back my billfold."

The deputy frowned at Willie, then turned and looked me over pretty good. When he thoughtfully refocused on my brother, he had the look of a suddenly illuminated lightbulb. Maybe he'd assumed Willie was alone in the world. Now he had to deal with the vagrant's well-dressed accomplice. Whether being offensive was his normal state or merely an attempt to intimidate us, the deputy gave it his best shot. He tucked his thumbs in his belt and struck a tough-guy stance, then fixed his eyes on me and squinted in an obvious effort to look official and in control.

"Who are you? What are you doing with this crackpot?"

I felt a crawly sensation on the back of my neck. The pores under my arms released a load of anger pheromones. I was pissed off, but decided to hold back.

"I'm Willie's sister, Sylvia." I stuck my hand out and smiled. "I sure want to thank you for helping Willie the other day."

The deputy's attention was caught by Willie's shout. "Hey. Your car doors are locked."

"Ah, hell! What's going on here?"

Willie and I started talking at the same time.

"Willie and I used to live around here…"

"I need to get in your car to look for my billfold. You forgot…"

"All right, that's it." The deputy's face turned red and saliva began to dribble out around his cigar. He grabbed it from his mouth and spat, the glob landing about two feet from my right shoe. If I looked as disgusted as I felt, it could explain the deputy's satisfied expression.

"Go on, both of you. In your car."

"But my billfold…"

"My brother's billfold…"

"I don't know what in hell y'all are talking about. I do

know you're trespassing, and I do know I could arrest you if I had a mind to. Now get on out of here."

While the deputy glared at me, I glanced over at Willie, who shushed me and waved me toward our car. I looked back at this caricature of a lawman, shrugged my shoulders, and walked away. I could only hope the rest of the county's law enforcement officers were nothing like this one. Otherwise, a dead body would never get officially reported and Willie would never recover his property.

Once again I'd underestimated my older brother. We no sooner got in the car and snapped the locks when Willie tapped me on the arm and showed me his billfold, before he shoved it under his leg.

"My God, Willie, where? You said his car doors were locked."

"They are—now. Hurry up. He's watching us. Get out of here before he sees what I've done."

"The keys are in the car?" My voice took on the high sound that ranks just one level below shrieking. "You locked his doors with the keys inside? Oh, my God!"

"Hurry up! He'll think he did it himself until he sees the billfold's gone. Let's go."

I started the car, did a sharp three-point turn to get headed back in the right direction, and got the hell out of there. One last glimpse in my rearview mirror as we sped away revealed the deputy standing where we'd left him, still watching. I didn't want to be around when he finally realized he'd been locked out of his car. My foot pressed down on the accelerator just a little harder.

FOUR

"WILLIE, YOU'VE GOTTEN us into a whole lot of trouble. He probably has a spare set of keys." I glanced in the rearview mirror again and sighed with relief to see no car behind us, especially one with blue and red flashing lights.

"Keep going, Syl. The sooner we get back to town, the better. Anyway, he doesn't have a clue where to find us."

"It won't take much if he wrote down our license number. And the hotel name is on the rental agreement. The way he rummaged around in this car, he probably inspected my bag, too."

Willie shook his head. "It doesn't matter. He'll look like an idiot if he makes a fuss about the keys. No one will believe he didn't do it himself. And how can he complain about me retrieving my own billfold when he had no reason to keep it in the first place? I think he wanted to chase us away for good so we wouldn't report him."

My shoulders relaxed a little. I wasn't easy to intimidate, so I'm not sure why I let this particular deputy sheriff get to me. Obviously, the deputy's bluster and bullying were suspicious. Those were behaviors used to hide a mistake he'd made, or maybe a secret.

"He tried to create a diversion," said Willie.

I hate it when he reads my mind. It gives me the creeps.

Willie turned and looked at me until I glanced over to acknowledge his perceptive observation.

He grinned like a Cheshire cat. "He can't be as stupid

as he acts. I mean, refusing to investigate the report of a body found in a country field? Even if he did write me off as loony, he must have noticed that you look like a fine, upstanding citizen. He should have listened to you."

I shrugged. Those were my thoughts exactly. "So you think the yelling and posturing were intended to scare us off and make us forget about the body? If that's true, then he must have had something to do with…well, with whatever happened here."

"Or he knows who did. Or maybe he received instructions to keep people away from here but wasn't told why."

"Any of those reasons could make him dangerous." I frowned as I thought about this deputy tracking us down. "Should we cancel our rooms at the Ramada and stay somewhere else? Maybe we could get a flight out of here first thing in the morning."

"Wait a minute. We can't leave before we report this. You're a judge. You know you have a duty—"

"Okay, Willie, it was just a suggestion. We'll call the sheriff's office or the Illinois State Police. I'm out of my jurisdiction, so my only duty is to report what I know. I don't have enough information to accuse this deputy of anything, and I don't have any way to protect us if he's a murderer."

As we drew closer to the city limits, I breathed a sigh of relief and glanced at my watch. Nearly five—a little early for the intense hunger pangs gnawing away at the lining of my stomach. But, after all, it was almost six in Florida. I turned north on Cole Avenue to see if the old Hong Kong Restaurant had survived the years.

"You up for Chinese, Willie?"

"Now? We need to report the body."

"Once we get inside any lawman's office, we won't be eating for hours. Why don't we order something and take it with us?"

"Okay. Sure. Anything's fine."

I pulled into the run-down parking lot of the shabby block building with some misgivings, but brightened up to see a major renovation had taken place indoors. I could still smell the sharp fumes of fresh paint and new carpeting. The interior was spiffily decorated in red, black, and gold with faux ebony tabletops, excellent Chinese watercolors on the walls, and a large, empty bar in a quiet area opposite the sparsely populated dining room. I tossed two quarters on the counter and tucked a newspaper under my arm.

"Willie, this way." I directed him toward the bar.

He stopped, focused beyond me to see the row of bottles reflected in the wall-to-wall mirror, and raised his eyebrows as he silently changed direction. I sensed his disapproval, which wasn't hard because I know him so well. He wasn't concerned I'd drink too much, nor did he think I had a drinking problem. Willie just couldn't tolerate the idea that I continued to put unhealthy things in my body. He thought the same way about sugar, fast food, caffeine, or anything else I really liked.

We picked a booth near the door, hoping our location would encourage fast service. I put my bag on the seat and placed the newspaper on the table. The waitress brought a bowl of peanuts and took Willie's order for green tea and mine for a very dry, double gin martini with two olives. Willie glared at me until I placed the takeout food order, and then he pulled the front section off the newspaper and began to scan the first page. He looked up briefly when his tea arrived, glanced at my drink and then at me just long enough to make eye contact, then coolly returned to the paper.

Refusing to be intimidated, I sipped the martini while trying to read the upside-down headlines. Not very successful at this effort, I studied Willie's hands, read the menu, stared out the window, and finally zeroed in on

Willie's increased tension level and the intensity with which he studied the lead article. He flipped the folded paper over and continued to read.

"What is it?" I asked.

He mumbled something and tried to shut me up with a wave of his hand. About to voice my indignation at this inconsiderate behavior, I hesitated when he unfolded the paper and turned it around so I could read the headline: "SANGAMON CITY BUSINESSMAN MISSING."

Willie tapped the article. "Read this."

I pulled the paper closer and studied the professionally posed photograph of a distinguished-looking guy in a business suit. He looked familiar. I turned my attention to the article and discovered his name was Clayton Taylor. Clay Taylor, a boy I'd gone to school with, had even dated for a while. After studying the picture again, and in spite of the gray in his hair and the weathered lines in his face, I recognized Clay. The article stated his wife Marella had reported her husband missing on Thursday evening, after he failed to return from the afternoon farm visits he'd scheduled. He was described as a farm manager, also active in farm real estate, farm appraisals, and related ventures. His company, Taylor Agricultural Services, had been transferred to him in 1975 upon the retirement of his father. The article continued,

Taylor is on the boards of several organizations, but is best known for his work with the Park District and Forest Preserve of Lincoln County. He's an environmentalist and naturalist, and has pushed hard for preservation of Illinois prairie lands. A recent attempt to acquire two hundred acres for a nature preserve has met with serious opposition from landowners who want to subdivide the property for residential

development. As board president, Taylor threatened
to start condemnation proceedings on behalf of the
PDFP.

I thought about the Clay Taylor I remembered from
high school—a very nice person, as well as bright, athletic,
and handsome as all get-out. I dated Clay my junior year,
and if I'd been one of those stay-at-home girls with
marriage on my mind, I probably would have tried hard to
hold on to the boy. But I had my heart set on college and
law school. Clay and I weren't meant to be, and we developed other attachments during our senior year. Anyway, I'd
found my true heart's desire after college and married him.
Lost him, too. I didn't like where these thoughts were
going, so I shook them off.

"Do you think I might have found Taylor's body?"
Willie asked me.

"I don't know. It makes sense, though. Does it say
where he was going yesterday?"

Willie shrugged, so I bent over the paper and scanned
it again. The reporter had interviewed two other PDFP
Board members in his pursuit of newsworthy quotations.
Louise Branson, of the wealthy Alvin Branson family, if
my memory served me correctly, said she hadn't seen Clay
since the August board meeting. The reporter noted
Branson owned property adjoining the two hundred acres
Clayton wanted for the nature preserve, and she'd ada-
mantly opposed his single-minded crusade to establish yet
another stand of prairie grass in the county.

I remembered the exact location of the Branson Farm.
It consumed the four hundred forty acres to the south and
west of our old place, completing the tidy square mile
characteristic of rural divisions in that part of the country.
I did not, however, remember Louise from grade school

or high school. I'd ask Willie later, after I finished the article.

The other board member interviewed was Brian Kelso, a local attorney. I didn't recognize the Kelso name, but certainly understood from the article that he eagerly sought publicity and recognition. He'd told the reporter that Clayton Taylor was obsessed with the prairie grass project, and anyone who tried to remove Class I agricultural land from production, just to preserve some useless grass, wasn't acting in the public interest. Then he suggested Clay should immediately resign from the PDFP Board. I would bet this lawyer was some kind of hotshot in the courtroom. You can say lots of interesting things if you don't make the mistake of confusing the issues with facts. Had he even understood the press solicited the interview because Clay was missing?

I read to the end of the article and found no mention of the farms Clay intended to visit on Thursday. To the best of my recollection, most farm managers handled whatever farms they could get, regardless of their geographical proximity, especially since banks had entered the farm management business and now provided serious competition to independent farm managers. He might have had contracts to manage clusters of farms in one area, or scattered farms across the state.

"Doesn't say where he was going," I reported. "But the sheriff says they went to Taylor's office and got a list of his farms. What if one of them is our old place?" I paused a moment to think it through, then continued, "The sheriff sends his deputy out to the farm. He knocks on the door, but there's no one there. He looks around the place, finds nothing. He goes back and tells the sheriff he didn't find Taylor."

"Especially if the deputy doing the canvassing is the creep who ordered us to leave," added Willie.

"Exactly."

I looked at my watch and assessed my hunger level. The two olives and the peanuts were not going to hold me for long.

"I could eat later," Willie said eagerly. "I think we should go now."

"Sheriff's office?"

"Don't even call first."

I was disappointed in Willie. I would have voted to wait for the food. Duty called, however, so I signaled the waitress by waving a twenty and dropping it on the counter as I asked her to cancel the order. From the tone of her voice, I felt pretty sure the barrage of Chinese words pursuing us out the door did not translate to "Have a nice day."

FIVE

It wasn't difficult to find the county building, sheriff's office, and jail since the four-story, brick complex was the tallest building in the downtown area. All three functions were performed in the same new construction that had been built a couple of blocks from the shopping plaza on the site of the former Sangamon City High School.

We left our car in the underground parking garage and entered the elevator at basement level after learning from the directory that our destination was on the second floor. The minute the doors opened to the sheriff's department, new building smells swamped us once again. I began to wonder if all of Sangamon City was one big remodeling project. A prominently displayed information sign directed us to the counter near the back of an expansive lobby, but the lone officer on desk duty concentrated on a handcuffed juvenile who repeatedly tried to yank his elbow from the grip of a second deputy who wasn't about to let go. Willie wandered over to sit on one of the chairs by the wall, while I waited behind the testy teenager who now demanded to call his mother. *Mama's boy,* I thought. I'd seen a few of those in my own courtroom.

The deputy finally hauled the kid away to find a phone, or to explain the facts of life, and I had the desk officer's full attention. I wasn't exactly sure how I wanted to approach the situation, but I plunged right in anyway.

"I want to speak to someone about a possible crime—

a murder." I turned and waved at Willie, signaling him to join me at the desk. "My brother went walking out in the country and found a body under a pile of brush."

The deputy looked at me for a moment without speaking, then frowned as though he didn't understand what I'd told him. "Your brother found a body?"

"We think so, yes."

"You're not sure?"

"It's a long story, Officer, but this is the real thing. Why don't you let me tell it to the sheriff, or whoever handles homicides?"

He hesitated again, probably trying to figure out if I was nuts. Or if he would get into trouble if he dumped me at the desk of one of his superiors. By then Willie had joined me and, as usual, was unable to stand back and be quiet when he thought someone had failed to treat me with proper respect.

"Sergeant Green," Willie began after a glance at the man's name tag, "my sister's a circuit court judge in Florida. She doesn't make things up. If this is too much of a bother for you, we can go to the state police."

"No, no, not necessary." Green picked up the phone and within minutes a tall, dark-haired man, whom I immediately recognized, walked into the reception area from the rear offices. He glanced at the desk sergeant, who nodded and gestured toward us. A frown creased the sheriff's forehead as he saw me, glanced at Willie, then immediately returned his attention to me and concentrated on my face as he approached.

"I think I know you," he said.

I laughed. "I should think you do, Trace. Sylvia Thorn. I used to be Sylvia Grisseljon. We spent a lot of time together our senior year of high school."

Trace Parker nodded as he looked me over. "I guess we did."

I was charmed and a little shocked. I hadn't seen Trace since the day I headed off to West Lafayette, Indiana, to enroll as a freshman at Purdue University. That was forty-one years ago. Trace hated my decision, had no desire to maintain a long-distance relationship, and quickly turned his attention to my least favorite female classmate, Cynthia the Slut. Although it was hard to break up with a devilish, sexy boyfriend who constantly tested the boundaries of the wild side, and even harder to see Cynthia draping herself all over him when I came home for Thanksgiving, I wanted college more than I wanted Trace Parker.

I couldn't believe my rakish high school sweetheart had grown up to be a cop.

Nor could I believe the way my fifty-nine-year-old body had zipped open and released a flood of sexual tension when this guy approached. I can't remember having such an intense reaction since well before my divorce. If you don't count the day a filming crew shot a scene on the courthouse steps and I nearly collided with Sean Connery as he came running around the corner of the building. I decided to blame this current attraction on the "man in uniform" syndrome. As for Sean Connery, who needs an excuse?

I've been married twice, once happy and once unhappy, but both ended in disaster. I consider myself wise enough to avoid walking into a relationship which might someday cause me more emotional pain. But I definitely felt my heart flutter and my cheeks grow warm when I looked into Trace's brown eyes. Those eyes had always been my weakness. Along with his coaxing kisses, the way he stroked the back of my neck, and the habit he had of sliding his palm across mine so gently my skin tingled all the way to my toes. *Enough of this,* I thought.

Trace smiled as though he knew what I'd been thinking.

He pointed toward the hall. "Let's go to my office. Can I get you something to drink? Coffee?"

"No, I'm okay."

Trace glanced at Willie, who simply shook his head no. My overprotective brother edged a little closer to my side so I couldn't fail to see the curled lip and raised eyebrow, his way of letting me see he'd noticed my reaction and disapproved. Willie had never liked Trace. Willie was convinced Trace was headed for trouble and wanted to drag me along with him. I wondered what Willie thought of this odd metamorphosis from pre-delinquent to lawman.

"So, Sylvia Grisseljon Thorn, what brings you back to Sangamon City?"

"Trace, you remember my brother, Willie? He came up here from Florida on a vacation and hiked out to the country."

"I found a body." Willie had a habit of getting right to the point.

Trace raised his eyebrows but didn't comment as he ushered us into his office and pointed toward the chairs sitting across from a very large and very old oak desk. The furnishings were a nice change from the utilitarian metal equipment I'd seen in the other offices and cubicles closer to the reception area. I glanced around, admiring the wood-toned blinds, the aerial photo of the new courthouse, and took a quick peek at the picture on his desk—a lovely woman and a young girl. *Oh, well*, I thought.

Willie perched on the edge of his chair and tapped his foot as he waited for Trace to sit down. Once more I listened to the story of Willie's innocent and pleasant walk through the country, his fright and flight after finding the body, and his indignation when Stoney Morris dumped him off at the county home. Willie hesitated, and then proceeded to tell about the dead vulture, how we'd been treated by the deputy when he caught us out on the farm, and how he'd recovered his billfold from the deputy's car. I noticed he left out the part about locking the lawman out of his vehicle.

"Didn't you believe Willie's story, Syl? Is that why you went out to the farm and then stopped for food instead of coming directly here?"

I decided to ignore the crack about eating and deal with Willie's credibility. "I never doubt Willie's word," I assured him. "I wanted to take a look for myself, make sure the body was still out there. Be able to support Willie's story when we came in. As it turns out, I can't provide solid verification because more junk has been piled on the spot where Willie saw the body. Brush, dirt, tree stumps—it looks as if someone bulldozed a whole hedgerow and dumped it by the drainage ditch. I'm afraid you're going to need some big equipment to move the debris. It would take forever to clear it by hand."

Trace sat back in his chair, watching and listening. "And the additional delay while you stopped to have dinner?"

"Simple. I'm starved. Knowing how the legal system works in Florida, I figured it wouldn't be much different here. If we went straight to the police, we wouldn't get a chance to eat for hours, so we decided on takeout from the Hong Kong. And then…then we picked up the newspaper and saw the article about Clay and…I wondered…"

"Yeah, it's crossed my mind, too."

"Anyway, once we saw the story, I lost my appetite. So here we are."

Trace leaned forward and turned his attention back to Willie. "You say you found a dead vulture near the brush pile?"

Willie nodded. "Dead as a doornail. On the far side, away from the road."

"How do you think it died?"

Willie stood up and reached into his pants pocket. He pulled out the bunched up handkerchief and laid it on Trace's desk, pulling the edges away until he'd exposed the empty casing of a shotgun shell.

"You found it close to the bird?" Trace asked.

Willie nodded.

We all thought for a second, knowing the vulture's presence called attention to the site, which was most likely the reason the bird had been reduced to a pile of bloody feathers. "I'll get someone to bag and label this. You picked it up with the handkerchief? You didn't touch it yourself?"

Willie shook his head. "With the handkerchief. None of my prints will be on it."

"What about the area around the brush pile, Willie? You know you've contaminated the crime scene."

"I walked all over the place earlier, before I knew there was a body. Lots of bare footprints, those will be mine. And I touched the bridge railing, rocks, sat on the ditch bank, walked in the water. Syl and I were back there for only a few minutes. We didn't touch anything, but we did walk up as far as the dead bird. I turned it over with my boot."

"Okay, let me get someone working on a search warrant, lights and earth-moving equipment, and order a car out there to secure the area before it gets too dark. I guess you both should go along to make sure we're marking the right spot. You can stay in my office while I get things organized. Restrooms, coffee, water fountain are all down the hall to the left." He glanced at me. "Vending machines, too. I won't be long."

As Trace left the office, I stood up to stretch my legs. Willie sat watching me and shaking his head.

"What?" I asked.

"Syl, do you have to look at the man like you're going to eat him alive?"

"I'm what?"

"He's married. And he has a kid." Willie pointed at the picture.

"Willie, I'm not looking at him like anything. I used to go with the guy in high school, and I haven't seen him in over forty years. I just…"

Willie shushed me, then stood up and walked out of the room. It infuriated me to feel like a little kid being disciplined by my older brother. Maybe chanting my maturity mantra, "I am a judge, I am a judge," would have helped. Or maybe a power mantra, "I am a powerful judge." Okay, for Willie's benefit, I'd try harder to be impersonal and professional in my dealings with the sheriff.

I found it difficult to stifle my curiosity, however. Trace was always a charmer, even if a bit dangerous. Having him as my boyfriend was wild and crazy conduct for an eighteen-year-old virgin with big ambitions. I'd gone off to college with my virginity intact, despite Trace's best efforts. But even now, thoughts of the emotional struggle made me blush.

Trace's behavior seemed so different—more reserved and most definitely not amused by our sudden appearance on the scene. Of course, this was a serious matter. I couldn't blame him for being preoccupied. I refocused my thoughts, reconsidered the appetite I'd lost, and headed for the vending machines.

SIX

WHILE WE WAITED, I consumed enough coffee, powdered sugar mini-donuts, and chocolate-covered raisins to keep me going for the next two days. Willie used his normal self-control and opted for water and plain peanuts. I wanted to point out the greasy coating on the inside of his cellophane packet, but restrained myself.

At the mercy of my caffeine and sugar high, I paced back and forth, using the old "stretch my legs" excuse, while Willie sat with his hands resting palms up on his thighs and his eyes soft-focused on the plain gray tiles. I don't know how he does it. Willie once tried to teach me how to meditate, but I never got past the unpleasant sensations. My feet went to sleep, my legs tingled with nervous fidgets, my hands twitched, my eyelids jumped—it just didn't work for me. I finally found Tai Chi, which can be used as a moving meditation. I clear my mind and focus on the slow fluid forms, and I never have to worry about jittery legs or wandering thoughts.

"Sergeant Green tells me you're a judge," Trace commented when he returned.

"Yes. Palm Beach County."

He gave me an amused glance, but refrained from making any remarks about hanging chads. "We can go," he said. "You two ride with me. The other cars will follow us out to the farm. I don't expect to have lights or equipment for a couple of hours, but we can get the site locked down and place guards out there to keep an eye on things."

PATRICIA STOLTEY   47

"Will that deputy—?"

"Stoney?" Trace shook his head. "Dispatch will call him and tell him to report back here and wait for me. I don't want him at the crime scene again until I've talked to him."

I sighed in relief, but Willie looked disappointed. For a long time I couldn't understand why Willie buckled under some types of stress but sought out others. I'd asked him, but he said he didn't know, either.

"Maybe I have to be in control in order to cope," he'd answered.

"But you love to fly and you're not in control when you're a passenger in an airplane."

Willie had shrugged. "There you go."

Hard to figure, I thought. Maybe Willie wanted to see the deputy get called on the carpet, knowing there would be zero consequences for us. I could picture my brother gloating, standing behind the sheriff but clearly visible to Stoney Morris. Goodness knows he'd done it to me plenty of times when we were kids. I turned my attention back to Trace as he motioned toward the door and herded us out to the elevator and down to his car.

"How long have you been the sheriff, Trace?"

"Seven years. I may not run again, though. I'm not getting any younger and there are safer and more lucrative ways to make a living."

"What would you do instead?"

"I'm not sure."

I gave Willie a dirty look as he quickly jumped in the front passenger seat, forcing me to sit in the back where I'd be unable to open my own door from the inside. I had to talk to Trace or Willie through a metal grill separating front from back. I repeated my mantra. *I am a judge. I am a powerful judge.*

It is said everyone reverts to being a child when visiting

parents, but I've never experienced that. I didn't return to their home in Sangamon City for visits once I'd moved away. Instead, I met my mom and dad in Florida during their annual winter vacations. Since they've retired, it's hard to get them to slow down long enough to meet for dinner, much less share any trips down memory lane, so I never feel they are being overly parental. Willie, however, is a different story. He'll be my bossy big brother forever.

The two patrol cars pulled in behind us as we drove out of the parking garage and proceeded through town, toward the country. Once again I watched for familiar landmarks, but after all these years there weren't many left. Storefronts sported new redwood or wood-shingled facades, parks displayed fiery red shrubs and mounded beds of gold and yellow chrysanthemums, and old schools had been razed and replaced with rambling one-story campuses. One thing remained the same. The streets were still in terrible condition.

With lights and sirens, it took twenty-two minutes to reach the drainage ditch. We piled out of the cars and gathered around Trace as he gave instructions for staking and taping a perimeter while we waited for the equipment. It was already too dark to search for evidence, but Trace gave instructions for the cars to be moved so that their headlights pointed toward the brush pile. Willie and I were sent back to Trace's car to wait. This time I sat behind the steering wheel so I could get out on my own.

Willie seemed content to sit quietly and watch the officers at work. I jiggled my foot and picked at a rough cuticle, thought of my busy court schedule, wondered how my parents were doing in Key West. *Oh, shoot,* I thought, *I forgot to leave a message on their answering machine. Maybe when we got back to the motel, I should...*

"I forgot to tell Trace about the holes," Willie shouted, nearly scaring me to death.

"Holes?" I asked.

Too late. Willie was already out the door.

The air had grown considerably cooler, and I shivered as the chilly breeze rushed into the car when Willie opened and closed the door. Grateful to be inside, protected from the night air, I leaned my head against the window and watched the deputies work. I saw Willie touch Trace's elbow to get his attention, and then direct him toward the ditch bank where they squatted down and peered at the ground. Trace called one of his deputies over and indicated an area stretching from the brush pile all the way down to the water. The deputy nodded and trotted over to the heap of supplies sitting a few feet from Trace's car. He returned with three additional stakes and a roll of yellow tape. Together the sheriff and his deputy extended the crime scene perimeter to include this new section of land. Willie then returned to the car, but instead of getting in and giving me an update, he leaned against the front left fender and watched the men complete their tasks.

Maddening. I opened the driver's door and stepped out into the brisk air. "What's that all about, Willie? What kind of holes did you see?"

"Not sure. There were a few patches of Big Bluestem and some Indian Grass before. Looked like someone tried to start a stand of tallgrass prairie. When we came back, it had all been pulled up. Seems strange. These grasses have deep, strong root systems so they grow back even when most of the plants get destroyed. If someone wanted to get rid of this stuff, he'd have to dig large holes. They did that in a few spots, dug with a spade maybe, but mostly it looks like they pulled the grass out of the ground by hand."

Big Bluestem and Indian Grass? A very long speech for Willie, but a good example of the stuff Willie knows. He has an insatiable curiosity and retains everything he learns as he studies, watches documentaries, and reads. He's always been this way, even before he went to Vietnam. Although he studied accounting at the University of Illinois and passed all parts of the CPA exam the first time, his interests range from history to natural resources and from geology to psychology. Whenever I need information or have a problem, I can count on Willie to come up with some brilliant piece of logic, little-known fact, or the precise name of a book or Web site that will provide the information I need.

"Willie, the newspaper article about Clay…didn't it say he was an environmentalist interested in preserving prairie lands?"

"It did."

"So maybe he planted the grass out here."

"Maybe."

"But then, why would someone dig the grass up after Clay was already dead, assuming this really is him?"

Willie shrugged.

"Hmmm." I got back in the car and sat on my hands to warm them up. I wasn't sure why a man would get murdered because he wanted to plant prairie grass on—what did the paper say?—Class I agricultural land. And anyway, the article had mentioned that some of Clay's opponents were more interested in subdividing property for residential use. Hardly a good alternative for the best farmland in the state. My best guess suggested missing prairie grass had nothing at all to do with his death. Then I reminded myself once again that we didn't know for sure Clay was dead.

In spite of my stimulant intake, my vision started to blur, and I yawned several times. I leaned my head back against the seat to rest my eyes.

A flash of light and a low rumbling noise brought me

fully awake. A glance at the rearview mirror revealed several sets of headlights headed toward us from the direction of Sangamon City. My watch said it was nearly ten o'clock. Had I really slept for two hours? I was sure this convoy included the lights and equipment needed to clear the rubble and expose the body. When the first truck pulled up behind the police cars, I stepped out to watch.

I'd wondered what would be used to move the pile of brush away from the body. A bulldozer would be tricky, likely to destroy more evidence than it uncovered.

The first two semi-cabs towed portable floodlights and their generators. Minutes after they were pulled into place on the north and south sides of the taped area, they lit up the site like a movie set. A group of three officers moved to the east side of the brush pile and began a slow walk back and forth from the mound of debris to the tape line, occasionally stooping down to retrieve an item with a rubber-gloved hand and place it into a small plastic bag.

Once this group completed its examination of the first quadrant, the men moved to the north side of the brush pile, opening and marking new plastic bags as they walked. A third truck, pulling an empty flatbed trailer, slowly edged close to the east side of the site which had now been released by the officers. When the flatbed's position satisfied Trace, it was immediately joined by a dump truck, which the sheriff motioned forward until it sat nearly touching the side of the first vehicle.

Except for the three deputies who continued to examine the surrounding grounds, all other activity stopped. Everyone waited.

I glanced at Willie, who still stood near the front fender as he watched the men meticulously search the ground.

"How do you think they're going to move the brush?" I asked him.

"By hand. Only way."

"Going to be a big job."

"Won't take long with several guys working at it. Worst part will be moving those two big tree stumps. They might have to pull them off with ropes and drag them away with one of the trucks."

I nodded, then decided "won't take long" could mean an hour or two. I decided to wait it out where fewer breezes would chill my bones. I got back in the car.

The next thing I knew, the door opened and Trace poked me in the shoulder to wake me up. I looked out the front windshield but didn't see Willie.

"Do you want to come take a look?" Trace asked.

"You're done already?"

"It's after midnight. It took longer than I thought it would. But Willie's been out there and verified the body is wearing the shoe he saw sticking out of the brush pile. I know Clay well enough to confirm his identity. There's not much more for us to do here except wait for the medical examiner to finish and authorize moving the body. Thought you might like to take a walk around before we go back to town."

"Sure." Although I wasn't really sure. Viewing crime scene photos was something I occasionally had to do in my line of work, but visiting crime scenes before the body was hauled away wasn't part of my routine. It had happened to me only one time, and that was an accident. I had stumbled over a little girl whose brutally beaten corpse lay abandoned in an outdoor park restroom, which I decided to visit on an early morning walk. By the time the police arrived, I was more than ready to relinquish my vigil and try to forget what I'd seen. Maybe viewing Clay's body wasn't such a good idea. After all, I'd known him well. It would be hard to see him like this, even after so many years.

I followed Trace, but stopped by the rear of the truck and quickly glanced toward the body before looking away. Funerals with viewings are sad enough, but at least by then the damage done to the dead person is repaired as much as possible. We're spared the shock of dealing with the brutality of violent crime and saved, to a certain extent, from thinking about how it happened and how the victim might have felt if he realized he was about to die.

I had no standing in this case; I wasn't a witness; I had no obligation to look at Clay's body if it would cause me more trauma than just knowing an old classmate had been murdered. I looked around the site instead, noting most of the brush was now piled high in the dump truck. Small thin pieces of broken glass littered the ground. The holes near the ditch Willie had described provided a welcome diversion as I turned my back on the body of my once-favorite beau and walked toward Trace, trying not to show how little it would take to make me cry.

"Enough?"

"Yes."

"Okay. Let's get back to town. If Stoney is still sitting in my office like he's supposed to be, he has a lot of explaining to do and it's going to take some time. I'll drive you two back to your car so you can go to the motel. I need to see Willie tomorrow morning so we can review what happened one more time. Have him in my office at nine. You're welcome to come if you want."

"Trace, Clay was married. The paper…"

He nodded. "I already radioed in and sent a deputy and the victim counselor to her place. They asked her to come in tomorrow morning to officially identify the body. She said she'd be there about eight-thirty."

Trace turned to locate Willie, shouted his name, and motioned him toward the car. Willie gave one reluctant glance back toward the crime scene, then walked briskly toward Trace's car. He made it two steps ahead of me, once again claiming the front seat. It was just as well. If Willie insisted on working this hard to keep me from getting too chatty with Trace, he probably had a good reason, or thought he did. I dozed on the way back to Sangamon City while Willie gave Trace the third degree about Clayton Taylor, farm management, and the Park District and Forest Preserve of Lincoln County.

SEVEN

"Syl, ARE YOU warm enough?" asked Trace. "You want the heater turned up?"

Willie glanced back toward his sister. "She's asleep. Guess she's okay. Sheriff, I'm curious about some things. Could I ask you a few questions about Clayton Taylor?"

Trace shrugged his shoulders. "I don't mind. Not sure I'll know all the answers. What do you want to know?"

"This controversy over the agricultural land versus nature preserves versus commercial and residential development. Clayton was a farm manager, so why did he push so hard on environmental issues?"

"According to Taylor, the two interests aren't so far apart. Clay, like his father, loved this part of the country and respected its natural history and its wildlife as much as its valuable farmland. I think you'd call the two of them naturalists more than you would environmentalists, although Clay sure could get a bee in his bonnet when a company dumped chemicals in the river or spewed foul-smelling fumes into the air. He claimed his vision was well balanced. He wanted land set aside where the prairie grass could grow and shelter pheasants and quail, and people could see what the Illinois prairie looked like before the settlers and traders moved in. He had nothing against farms or factories or houses. He just didn't want them on those two hundred acres. His dad felt the same way. The fifteen hundred acre forest preserve about thirty miles north of here had the old man's support long before the notion got popular with the rest of the country."

"Where's the land Taylor wanted to use?"

Trace glanced at Willie. "Back there where we found Clay's body."

"Our old farm?"

"What do you mean?"

"Syl and I lived there until she started high school. My dad wasn't able to make ends meet and he finally lost the farm, sold it at auction. We moved close to town and Dad went to work for the big grain terminal warehouse on Route 150. He stayed there until he retired about twenty years ago, and he and Mom moved to Florida."

Trace nodded. "I remember the little house you lived in near town, but I didn't know you grew up out here. Is that why you were hiking around the Taylor farm?"

"I wanted to get in touch with my roots," said Willie, grinning wryly at the cliché. "I had some happy memories of walking barefoot down that dusty road on a hot day, wading in the ditch in violation of my mother's strict orders to stay out of there. Sheriff, did you mean Clay Taylor owned this farm?"

"Taylor's wife. I don't know who bought it when your dad sold out, but Marella Taylor owns it now."

"His wife? But didn't he want her to sell or donate the land for the nature preserve?"

"Yep. But she wouldn't go along with it. Clay got mad and threatened to start condemnation proceedings on behalf of the PDFP Board."

"Park District?"

"Park District and Forest Preserve. Since Marella couldn't talk Clay out of his plans, she stirred up some of the other board members so they'd oppose the suit. Louise Branson is one of the county's biggest and richest landowners. As a matter of fact, she owns all the land on the south and west side of the Taylor farm, all the way to the highway on the south and to Elevator Road on the west. Owns a couple more farms east of town, land she inherited from her mom's folks.

"Marella had Lou convinced that if Clay succeeded in his project, he'd be after the Branson property next. The other board member who's riled up about Clay's proposal is Brian Kelso. He's a young guy, an attorney who represents a lot of different interests in the area. I suspect one of his wheeler-dealer clients wants to buy the farm for a more profitable venture than a nature preserve."

"Doesn't sound like the Taylors had a happy marriage."

Trace frowned. "Not one I'd want to be in the middle of if I was married."

Startled, Willie looked at the sheriff. "I thought you were married. The picture on your desk—"

"My daughter and granddaughter. My wife died five years ago."

"Oh. You must have had some rough times."

"Very rough."

"Does your daughter live around here?"

"No." Trace didn't elaborate. "What about you, Willie? Are you married?"

"Not married now and not likely to ever be. I have more than enough trouble taking care of myself and trying to help Syl when she needs me."

"And your sister? Is she married?"

"Has been. Isn't now." Willie turned to look out his window in an effort to discourage additional questions about his younger sister. He thought the sheriff showed too much curiosity about Syl already, and didn't want to encourage that interest. It was just a feeling, but he didn't think Trace Parker could measure up to the standard set by

Syl's first husband, Andy Thorn. And if that were true, then they didn't need the sheriff pushing his way into their lives to create upheaval where there was now calm.

Trace took the hint and asked no more about Syl, but instead turned his attention back to Willie. "What's your situation? You were up here on vacation. What do you do when you're back in Florida?"

Willie took a deep breath. It always came down to explaining his life in as few words as possible. "I was on disability for a while—shell-shocked. Then I got better, started my own accounting business. I'm selling it now and retiring. I spend most of my spare time doing volunteer work, helping Syl, reading, and I travel a lot. I don't usually get into trouble and have to be bailed out, though."

"Vietnam?"

"Yeah."

Trace nodded and the two sat quietly for a moment.

"What about the deputy, Stoney?" asked Willie.

"I'm not sure what to think. Stoney Morris has been a deputy for a long time. He served in the Army before that. His military record was a little shaky, but he had an honorable discharge and had no serious on-the-job complaints. He's not popular with the other deputies, but he's smart enough not to offend the people who could get him fired. I don't understand why he dumped you at the county home without your identification, and I'm confused as to why he would chase you and Syl away from the farm without initiating an investigation. I'll find out when I talk to him."

"I'd sure be curious to hear what he says."

Trace nodded but said nothing more. Willie yawned, propped his elbow against the window frame, and rested his head against his hand. He thought back over the events of the last two days, thought how quickly things can change.

As Trace guided his car into the parking lot and

followed directions to the rental car, Willie turned and tapped Sylvia on the knee to wake her up.

"Hey, Syl, we're back. Are you able to drive?"

She nodded. "I'm okay." As she stepped out of the car, she turned to the sheriff. "You want us here at nine tomorrow morning, right?"

He nodded, shut the rear door, climbed in his car, and gave a quick wave as he drove over to his own parking space.

"Looks like the sheriff's going back to work," said Willie.

"Let's go, Willie. I've had it for today. Even though we might have to sit and wait for Trace to finish up with Marella Taylor in the morning, we still need to be here by nine."

Reluctantly, Willie turned toward his sister's car. "We need to be here earlier than nine. I'd like to get here by eight-thirty."

"Why?"

"You said Taylor's wife is going to be here. I want to see her."

"Marella? Why? You can't talk to her. You can't talk to anybody except Trace."

"I know. I want to get a look at her. See how she acts. Maybe…"

"Feel the vibes? Willie, you can't get involved with this thing any more than you already have. We're going home as soon as Trace releases us. The only way you'll have any additional connection with this case is if Trace needs you to testify. And that's highly unlikely since you didn't see or hear anything that points to a suspect."

"Except the grass."

"Oh, Willie, what could that have to do with anything?"

"I'm not sure. But it doesn't make sense. First it's there, and then it's gone. And it happened right next to a pile of brush hiding a dead body. A pile of brush, by the way, which suddenly got a whole lot bigger during the few hours I spent at the hospital. It's suspicious. And I might be the only person who knows the grass disappeared."

Willie saw Sylvia roll her eyes. He pressed his lips together, then turned to her and poked her shoulder with his index finger. "How many times have I sat in the courtroom during one of your cases and told you how jurors were likely to vote? How many times have I given you—"

"Okay, Willie. I'm sorry. I'll be ready to go at eight-fifteen. But you can't talk to Marella Taylor. Just observe. Okay?"

"That's all I ever planned to do." He waved his hand toward the steering wheel. "Drive, drive, drive," he said.

EIGHT

My ALARM BEEPED me awake at six-thirty, just as I'd instructed it to do. It wasn't enough sleep for someone who cherishes her nightly eight hours. I stayed in my comfortable pajamas for thirty minutes of Tai Chi practice to get my blood moving, repeating the first basic forms over and over, alternating the right and left sides.

Using the motel's two-cup coffeemaker, I started a pot of the fully caffeinated brew and then, before stepping into the shower, I flipped on the TV and watched the headlines scroll across the bottom of the screen. At the same time, I punched Willie's room number into the phone console and hit the pound sign. As expected, he didn't answer. Willie needs less sleep than I and, like all dedicated fishermen and beachcombers, is an early bird. I knew he would return in plenty of time to make our short drive to the sheriff's office.

After a quick shower, I dressed in jeans and a T-shirt and pulled on the same gray sweatshirt I'd worn yesterday. No choice on the shoes. The new loafers were it. I knocked off the rest of the coffee and stuffed my driver's license, cash, and keys into my jeans pocket. I'd already decided the bag could remain in my room since we expected to stay over at least one more night.

I opened the door to find Willie leaning against the passenger side of the car, patiently waiting for me. "What's been keepin' ya?"

I glanced at my watch. "I'm three minutes early. How long have you been standing out here?"

"Two minutes. When I heard the phone ring, I thought you might be ahead of schedule."

I laughed. I couldn't remember when I'd ever been ahead of schedule. "If you heard the phone ring, why didn't you answer it?"

"I knew it was you."

"So you just sat there?"

"Yep."

I sighed. He probably did know it was me. I couldn't fault the logic. I unlocked the car for him, ran back into the room, and turned off the coffeepot, television, and lights. I pulled the door closed behind me and jumped in the car. My watch said eight-fifteen. Exactly as we'd planned.

As we pulled into the parking lot at the county building, Willie pointed toward an open visitor's parking place in the first row, next to a red BMW. *Nice,* I thought as I headed toward the neighboring space. A second later, before I had time to pull all the way in, the driver's door of the BMW swung open and a tall, blonde woman, elegantly dressed in black, her hair sternly pulled back into a bun, stepped out without a glance in our direction. I waited until she shut her door and walked off before I drove forward.

"Must be Taylor's widow," Willie said.

If that was Marella Taylor, I didn't remember old Clay as well as I thought I did. I took another look at the red BMW and turned to gauge Willie's reaction.

"Do farm managers make a lot of money?" he asked.

"I don't think so. But he sold real estate, too. Maybe he made a bundle on that side of his business."

"Do you remember much about Taylor?"

I laughed. "I thought I did."

"You used to go out with him."

"Well, yeah, junior year. We didn't exactly have a long-term relationship. As soon as Clay found out I wanted to go to law school, he lost interest. He wanted a hometown girl he could keep barefoot and pregnant."

"Hmmm."

"Maybe I had Clay all wrong."

"She's a lot younger than you."

"Oh, Willie, how can you know that? If they had money for BMWs then they had money for face-lifts and tummy tucks and weekly visits to the gym and spa…" I paused. "Do you mean she's not the first wife?"

"It's a thought."

I pulled the keys out of the ignition and opened the door, flipping the automatic lock as soon as Willie had his own door open. Now intrigued, I wanted to get inside and take another look at Marella Taylor. My brother was already determined to solve the puzzle, and I knew he would pull me in, drawn like a sailor to a siren's song. I reminded myself again that I had no legal standing here, not even as a witness. I needed to mind my own business.

However, I scrambled to keep up as Willie hurried inside the building. The object of our interest paced back and forth by the second floor front desk while the officer used his phone to track down the sheriff. We crossed behind her to approach the counter. Marella stopped abruptly and turned, nearly colliding with Willie. He stood his ground, but smiled apologetically and reached out as if to steady her. Marella jerked her elbow away and glared at him as if she were trying to evaluate what kind of vermin he might be, and then she haughtily turned back to the officer as he hung up the phone.

"He knew my appointment was at eight-thirty," she said. "Where the hell is he?"

The officer pointed toward the hall as Trace hurried into the waiting area.

"Mare, I'm so sorry for the delay." He reached out as though to shake her hand, but she stepped away and assumed a soulful expression, complete with downcast eyes and a pathetic pout.

Mare? A little familiar, I thought, as I peeked at my watch. It was eight-thirty-two, for God's sake. I mentally slapped my mouth. Marella Taylor had come here to identify her husband's body. She deserved a little compassion, even if she looked as if she'd kick puppies and small children out of her way.

An elbow jab in my ribs rudely directed my attention back to the widow, who had replaced her outrage with suffering. Marella dabbed at her eyes with a handkerchief. She leaned against Trace. He had no choice but to put his arm around her shoulders as he directed her toward his office. Willie and I must have suddenly become invisible because we didn't receive as much as a nod from Trace. I watched Trace and Marella walk down the hall, and I felt my jaw drop and my eyebrows hop up toward my hairline as Marella fluttered her moist eyelashes at the sheriff, then bowed her head and sniffled into the hanky.

"I wonder what Trace's wife would think," I whispered.

"Oh, yeah," Willie said. "I forgot to tell you. The sheriff's wife died about five years ago. The picture is his daughter and granddaughter."

I stared at Willie in amazement, and then disgust, as he innocently returned my look with a self-satisfied grin.

He leaned toward me so he could whisper confidentially. "I bet Mrs. Taylor has something to do with this. And did you hear what the sheriff called her?"

I shrugged my shoulders, reminded the desk officer who we were and of our appointment scheduled for nine, then made a trip to the vending machines while Willie settled himself on a bench near the door. *So he won't miss anything,* I thought. With a package of powdered donuts and some coffee to satisfy the gnawing discomfort in my stomach, I rushed back to join my brother. He found my choice of breakfast food sickening, of course, but I ignored his curled lip and wrinkled nose.

"How can you put that stuff in your body?" he asked.

"How can you go without breakfast?"

"I didn't go without breakfast. I had oatmeal, yogurt, and orange juice at the diner near our motel."

Now that pissed me off. Willie knows I hate to miss a meal. "You could have said something before you ate."

"You'd want me to wake you up at five-thirty to go out for breakfast?"

"You could have brought something back for me."

"I refuse to touch the kind of stuff you eat."

I decided to shut up. We'd argued this subject for years, and I knew I'd never win.

Trace returned at five minutes after nine. Marella Taylor was nowhere in sight, so I assumed she'd been escorted to her car on the way back from the morgue.

"Morgue must be in another building," observed Willie.

I nodded. Made sense to me. Could also account for why it had taken over thirty minutes. Trace waved us down the hall to his office.

"How'd it go?" Willie asked.

My brother is never bashful about asking questions concerning matters which are none of his business. I sat down, wondering if Trace would answer, and curious about what he might say.

"She sobbed, got hysterical, and pretended to faint."

Boy, what a surprise. "Pretended?" I couldn't help myself. After all, Trace had volunteered information.

"Yes, Judge Thorn. The Taylors acted like they hated each other, even in public. Especially when the land deal came up for discussion. I can't believe Marella was really distraught." Trace thought for a moment. "But maybe I'm wrong. You never know what goes on in a marriage when the couple is behind closed doors. Maybe they really loved each other."

"Do you think she had something to do with Taylor's death?" Willie asked.

I watched Trace carefully as he pondered the question. He leaned back in his chair and looked from Willie to me and then back at Willie again.

"I doubt it," he said. "Of course, I can't rule anyone out, not yet."

Willie persisted. "Why would you rule her out? It seems like she's an obvious suspect."

I guess this question stepped over the line because Trace shook his head. "Can't discuss it."

Willie sat back, obviously disappointed, then leaned forward again. "How about your deputy, Stoney? Was he here when you got back last night?"

"He was here. I suspended him for two weeks for dumping you at the county hospital and not following up on your story. I've got some more questions for him, but first I want to understand everything that happened." Trace looked at me. "I know you want to return to Florida as soon as possible, Judge Thorn. But I need you to stay one more day so I can take Willie back to the farm and have him walk me through the whole business, from finding the body until Stoney showed up. You can ride with us, or follow us in your car, or pick Willie up here later."

"I'll take my own car and wander around the house and outbuildings at the farm, if it's okay. Is anyone living there now?"

"No. I checked yesterday. Wanted to see if we had some potential witnesses on the place. There used to be a tenant farmer named Wayne Puckett living in the house, but now he only farms the land. He lives in a trailer on the Branson property. I'm not sure what the Taylors had in mind for those buildings, but I don't think they're in very good shape. You can take a look around, but you should be careful. Watch out for rotten boards, rusty nails, snakes…"

"I'll keep my eyes open."

"And if Wayne shows up, tell him I gave you permission."

"And Mrs. Taylor? Any chance she'd come by?"

"I doubt it. But she'd just tell you to leave."

"Which I'd do, of course."

"Okay, then. We'll drive out Route 10 and leave my car at the pull-off where Stoney first spotted Willie. You can drive us down to the bridge and drop us off before you go exploring. That way, my car will be waiting when we finish the walk from the bridge to the pull-off. Before we come back to town, we'll drive by the house and check on you. If your car's gone, we'll meet at my office. Sound okay?"

"Sounds fine…and Trace?"

"Yes'm?"

"Call me Sylvia."

He smiled and nodded. Willie ignored the exchange.

NINE

THEY WERE BARELY on their way before Willie began asking Trace more questions. "Where did Taylor meet his wife? Is she from around here?"

"They met in Chicago a couple of years ago, at a farm managers' convention. She needed someone to run the property she'd inherited when her grandfather died, so she arranged for meetings with Taylor and one or two managers affiliated with Sangamon City banks. When she and Clayton hit it off, she hired him."

"And then she married him," Willie said.

Periodically checking his rearview mirror to confirm Sylvia stayed close behind them, Trace continued to describe the relationship between Marella and Clayton Taylor. "They were married suddenly, a little over a year ago. Flew to Vegas and got hitched in one of those little chapels. I heard talk that Clay didn't want the marriage, that he still carried a torch for his ex-wife, but Marella won out. There was also a rumor Clay stood to gain financially from the marriage and couldn't resist the opportunity to live a little higher on the hog. Marella has plenty of dough, that's for sure."

"She's from a wealthy family?"

Trace glanced at Willie. "You've heard of the Vortintos? Aldono, Vincent?"

"Sure. She has mob connections?"

"She's kin."

"Ah."

"To be fair, I'm not sure she has all that much to do with them. No obvious visits from undesirable relatives, no sign of trouble. It's rumored her inheritance came from her maternal grandfather, and that she made a clean break from her father. In fact, she severed her connections with the whole clan, hoping she could then be accepted by the local country club set."

"But if there was anything funny going on, wouldn't they want to keep a low profile? It's not like they'd call attention to themselves by creating a lot of fancy limousine traffic between Chicago and Sangamon City."

"Could be. I'll have to keep it in mind during the investigation. Right now I'm a lot more interested in some of the local disagreements Clay was involved in, mostly the land acquisition dispute."

"But that was a problem with Marella as well, right?"

"She was definitely in the middle of it. But other folks were opposed to the nature preserve, too. Louise Branson shouts about the traffic a nature preserve would bring to the area, the waste of good farmland, and the uncontrolled spread of weeds and insects onto her property. What she's really worried about is future expansion of the preserve, which might scoop up part of her farm. She could care less whether the land is used for farming or residential development, or a big old factory, as long as she gets a premium price when it's sold.

"Brian Kelso also opposed Clay's project. He's hot-headed and very unpopular. Acts like he's the only smart man in a city of idiots. His verbal attacks against Clay have been well publicized."

"What's his problem?"

"I don't have a clue other than the fact that he's a jerk. I think Brian represents someone who has a financial interest in the outcome of this suit, which means Brian has a financial interest, as well."

"How much money are we talking about here? The property's only two hundred acres."

"Depends on who the buyer is and how badly he wants the land. The city is growing. The land is less than ten miles from town. We could be talking anywhere from two to six million dollars."

Willie let the air escape through his teeth in a slow, soft whistle. "This is beginning to make more sense." He pointed toward the side of the road where an access lane entered a field near the drainage ditch. "You can park your car there, Sheriff. This is where I climbed out of the ditch and where Deputy Morris picked me up."

Trace slowed, turned in, and parked.

Sylvia also signaled to turn, and pulled her car in behind.

Willie stepped out of Trace's car and gazed off toward the north, first along the ditch and then at the sky.

Trace locked his car, and both men climbed into Sylvia's car, with Willie opting to take the backseat. They all remained silent as Syl drove to the bridge on the dirt road where Willie had first stopped to enjoy a peaceful moment in the September sun.

Sylvia said, "What did you do before you became sheriff, Trace? The last time I saw you, you planned to go to the University of Wisconsin, study economics, then get an MBA."

"I wasn't a very good student. I quit and joined the Navy, where I ended up in the Shore Patrol, hauling drunken sailors out of bars in San Diego. I went back to school when I got out, and earned a degree in criminal justice with the idea of becoming a big-city cop and working my way up to homicide detective."

"Did you become a big-city cop?"

"I did. City of Chicago. Eventually, I saw the error of my ways. After four years of watching the politics and the corruption and realizing how little I could do about it, I decided to leave."

"Where did you go?"

"Small place up in Michigan, about an hour from Detroit. Fancy community full of rich people. I worked for a big security firm for a few years, then decided I wasn't making any more progress there than I'd made in Chicago. By then I was married and had a daughter, so I started looking around for a better job. We moved here because I found an opening in the Sangamon City Police Department for a liaison who could work with state police and county law enforcement. Then I ran for Sheriff of Lincoln County when the previous sheriff retired."

"Willie mentioned your wife died. I'm sorry to hear that."

"Thanks."

"And your daughter? Does she still live here?"

"No."

Willie had been half listening to the conversation, but Trace's curt answer concerning his daughter's whereabouts got his attention. Apparently, the lawman didn't like to discuss his personal life any more than Willie did.

There must be a problem, Willie thought. Why else would Trace not want to discuss his only child? Grandchild, too. He hadn't remarried, so why didn't he have a picture of his wife in his office? Unless he still mourned his loss. Willie remembered how long it had taken his sister to recover from Andy's death.

As for the murder investigation, Willie believed the sheriff had dismissed Taylor's widow as a murder suspect far too early in the case, a fact made even more curious by the familiar way he had addressed Marella at the county building that morning. But perhaps he knew something about Marella that put her above suspicion.

The more questions I ask, the more questions I have, Willie mused.

When Syl pulled to the edge of the road by the bridge, Willie still didn't have any answers. Mentally setting the conversation aside, he waved goodbye to his sister and joined Trace to prepare for their trek back to the pull-off on Route 10.

TEN

AFTER I LET WILLIE and Trace out, I drove to the house and buildings where Willie and I had spent most of our childhood. So much had changed. I could see it before I even turned into the driveway.

A yard-wide, rotting tree stump had once supported a massive oak which occasionally dropped heavy limbs with little regard for the buildings below. The porch that had extended the entire length of the east side had been stripped away. I had actually noticed that the day before, when we first drove out from town. This time, as I came from the direction of the ditch, I realized the six-foot hedges along the north and west sides were gone, as well.

The windmill looming over the water pump and tank and the old-fashioned red barn were conjured up by my memory and properly positioned in the barnyard, which was now a dried-out stretch of wasted space. Like a kid arranging the toy farmyard she'd received for Christmas, I popped in a white fence, a few cows and pigs, and a tractor. I shook my head and the picture dissolved.

When I thought of the work and money my father had invested in this property over the years, I understood why he now refused to come back. It hurts us, almost in a physical way, to look back and see a great effort wasted, especially if we made great sacrifices in the process. Dad won't ask about the farm, and Willie and I won't tell him anything he doesn't want to know.

Deep ruts grabbed at the wheels of my car as I drove up the lane. Nothing but a tractor could maneuver such a mess after a heavy rain. I stopped the car by the gate and got out, stuffing my keys in my pocket as I looked around. There were no signs of Wayne Puckett, the man who farmed the property. I gave a shout to make sure.

"Hello, anyone here?"

No answer, but I tried again, a little louder. Still no response.

The metal gate between the driveway and the yard was securely wired to the rotten end-post of a sagging fence. It didn't seem wise to mess with the rusty wire. I couldn't remember when I'd had my last tetanus shot. The whole fence, gate and all, would probably topple over if I touched it, anyway.

Since this useless barrier extended the length of the driveway and abruptly ended at a sheet-metal lean-to, it didn't prevent me from walking around the end of the structure and approaching the house from the south. Well, maybe not walk. I didn't want to destroy those new loafers. I got back in the car and parked it behind the lean-to. This time I decided to leave the keys in the ignition. I didn't think I'd stay very long.

Bits and pieces of the past popped out at me as I walked into the main yard. Thoughts of wild kittens hidden in the haymow and our childish attempts to capture and tame them; my inability to learn the fine art of milking a cow; the odor of fresh cow manure mixed with straw. It was unbelievable how vivid the pictures were, how sharp the smells.

A five-foot weathered wooden post once stood a lonely vigil at the corner of the barnyard. My father had slaughtered chickens, one by one, by grabbing the legs in his left hand and propping the neck across the post. One swift swing of a machete in his right hand and the chicken's head flew off in one direction, the body in another, and while the bird flopped around in its final frantic protest, Dad grabbed the next chicken and the cycle continued. The process from slaughter to freezer was even worse, but I wasn't eager to recall the sights and smells of that operation.

It's odd that the few unpleasant memories I have of farm life involve chickens. The big white rooster that guarded the barnyard and scared the living daylights out of me when I was young. The worst farm chore of all— cleaning out the chicken house—when I grew older. Even so, I think there's nothing better to eat than good home-cooked, country-fried chicken.

I turned my back on the barnyard and walked toward the house, passing the ragged stump of a cherry tree, a garden overgrown with weeds, and a rusted water pump on a cracked concrete slab.

A ten-by-twelve-foot building we'd used as a shop and toolshed still stood between the barnyard and the house. Surprised to see its door looked new and was secured with a heavy-duty padlock, I couldn't resist looking in the windows, then strolling completely around the building to check them all. Someone had nailed sheets of plywood over all four openings. The man who farmed the land probably stored tools and supplies there. The electrical wiring which ran from the shed toward the house seemed in good repair. With lights and functional outlets, the shed could be useful in lots of ways.

Too bad I couldn't get in. Willie and I had spent a lot of time in there, building a bird house, assembling kites, and I longed to smell the oily wood and turpentine just to see what other memories might be conjured up.

I turned and studied the sad, dilapidated ruin that had once been home. The house looked small and naked without the porch. Three concrete blocks substituted for stairs to the back door, although they were unevenly stacked and somewhat askew. I walked closer and leaned down to wiggle the blocks back and forth, testing their stability. Encouraged when the steps stayed in place, I put one foot up on the first block and slowly put my full weight on it. So far so good. I tried the same with the second block. It wobbled a bit, so I kept my weight on the lower step while I pulled the screen open and checked to see if the door was locked. I was amazed to find it opened easily, even though the hinges screeched in protest when I gave it a firm shove.

I stepped over the top block and used both hands on the door frame to steady myself as I entered the kitchen. Remnants of gray and white linoleum littered the floor. Even from the doorway, I could see broken floorboards exposing rusty nails. Torn dirty wallpaper hung in strips, huge brown circles covered the ceiling, and chunks of overhead plaster lay on the dining room floor. I wanted to explore further, see the living room and my old bedroom, but was afraid to risk it while I was alone. It would be best to wait until Willie and Trace returned.

Gingerly, I backed down the steps and returned to stand in front of the toolshed. I gave the door a couple of hard pushes and one good kick, just in case it wasn't as secure as it looked. But the only sounds I heard were my own assaults, the distant drone of farm machinery, and the occasional song of a red-winged blackbird. Until a man's voice yelled, "What the hell are you doin' here?"

I must have jumped six feet straight into the air and turned one-hundred-eighty degrees. I ended up gaping at a red-faced Deputy Stoney Morris, as I clasped my hands to my chest to still my racing heart and struggled to catch my breath.

"My God, you scared me to death. Where did you come from?"

Morris took a menacing step toward me and shook one fist in my face. He used the key in his hand to point at my nose. Concerned he would jab it in my eye, I focused on the key and took a step backward.

"What the hell are you doin' here?" he repeated.

Morris's nasty tone and menacing posture were more than enough to raise the hackles on the back of my neck. I planted my hands on my hips and widened my own stance, thrust my chin forward, and glared. "Who do you think you're talking to?" I put as much authority behind my words as a short, slight woman can muster when being threatened by a big, hostile male.

"Well, for one thing, sister, I'm talking to a trespasser. You're on private property."

"Is it your property?"

"No."

"Then how do you know I don't have permission to be here?"

"Let's find out. Wayne! Come over here!"

It occurred to me that I might have a problem. Willie and Trace would be on foot and halfway to Route 10 by now. It would be thirty minutes or more before they'd get back. Meanwhile, I'd be hauled to the sheriff's office… and then I began to wonder if these guys were a danger to me. According to Trace, Deputy Morris had been suspended for two weeks, so whatever he was doing here with Wayne Puckett wasn't official police business. And if he wasn't being a deputy, what could he be so upset about? Why would he care? I didn't like this at all.

"Listen, Deputy, Sheriff Parker knows I'm here. I just wanted to look around the place because I lived here when I was a kid. If you tell me to go, I'll go."

At that moment a short, wiry man with leathery, wrinkled skin walked around the corner of the shed and stopped short when he saw me with Morris. The man I assumed to be Wayne Puckett tipped back a dirty Stetson ringed with sweat and threw a half-smoked, unfiltered cigarette to the ground. He rolled up the sleeves of his gray flannel shirt while he looked from me to the deputy and then back at me again.

"Who's she?"

"I think she's the sister of the guy that found Taylor's body. Ain't you?" Stoney directed the question at me and I gave a sharp nod.

"What the hell's she doing here?"

"Just what I asked," said Stoney.

Wayne turned to me. "How'd you get here?"

"Drove my car."

He looked around. "Don't see no car. Where is it?"

I waved my hand toward the corner of the barnyard. "Back there behind the lean-to. I used to live on this farm a long time ago. I told Sheriff Parker I—"

"Parker." Wayne spat the name out like it left a bad taste in his mouth. "Is he here?"

"Well, no, he—"

"Open the door, Morris."

The deputy looked at Puckett as though the man had lost his mind. "Open the door? While she's standin' here?"

Wayne frowned at the deputy and silently gestured toward the shed. It seemed odd, but Wayne Puckett was clearly the man in charge. Morris stepped forward and inserted the key in the padlock, pulled the lock away, and swung the door open.

"Step inside, lady."

On the other hand, maybe I wasn't so anxious to reminisce in there. "Oh, I don't think I need to go in. It looks terribly dirty," I said, sounding like a dumb smart-ass who had no idea she should be terrified to death.

"Get the hell inside!"

Wayne Puckett was definitely in charge. I walked to the doorway and hesitated, but stumbled through when a hot sweaty hand against the middle of my back shoved me forward. The door slammed shut and the padlock clicked before I could protest. Alone. In the dark.

Crap!

I stood facing the back of the building, so I made what I hoped was a half turn to orient myself, then stood still and waited for my eyes to adjust. I couldn't see a thing— no light coming through cracks around the door and no light leaking past the plywood window covers.

Remembering the wires running to the building, I faced straight ahead and shuffled forward, knowing the door stood only a few feet away. When I touched wood, I carefully moved my hands back and forth until I found and flipped the light switch. A dim glow from the ceiling fixture was much better than no light at all, and with any luck the bulb wouldn't burn out until I escaped. Always the optimist, I assumed I would indeed escape. I chose not to dwell on the alternatives.

Slowly surveying the room, I tried to figure out why a padlock had been placed on the door and why the windows were boarded over. On the shelves of the back wall were glass jars full of nails and screws, old cans of turpentine and dried-out paint and varnish, and containers of rose dust and weed killer. A small, rusted fertilizer spreader sat in one shadowy corner, and a dirt-encrusted posthole digger with a wooden handle leaned against the wall. Four bags labeled COMPOST were stacked in one of the back corners.

Nothing seemed valuable enough to warrant this level of security. I looked up toward the rafters to see if anything had been hung from the roof or stacked on crossbeams.

Nothing. I walked over and peered inside the spreader, and then moved it to one side. Nothing. Mystified, I examined the room from this new perspective.

This time I saw streaks on the floor where the compost bags had been dragged from the doorway to the back of the room. If I remembered correctly, under those bags there was a trapdoor that accessed a root cellar. Maybe something was hidden down there.

I tugged the top bag off the stack, then the second, pulled the third to one side, and dragged the fourth to the other side, relieved the last one did not snag on the trapdoor's metal hook. The bags were coated with a gritty, but hopefully non-toxic, substance. I wiped my hands on my sweatshirt, then swung the door back on its hinges, releasing a rush of odors—musty black earth, clean dry hay. It didn't make sense. No one stores hay in a damp underground hole.

Kneeling alongside the cellar opening, I leaned over and peered into the darkness. A lantern or flashlight would have helped, but even without it I could see that the frame of the opening supported the top of a wooden ladder, and bales of hay were arranged around the ladder's base. What on earth could be down there? A worm farm? Mushrooms? What would be secret about that?

I brushed the dust off my knees as I considered climbing into the cellar and taking a closer look. Probably not a good idea. If Morris and Puckett came back, they could pull up the ladder, drop the trapdoor, replace the compost bags, and leave. No one would hear my calls for help. I shivered and decided to put things back the way I'd found them.

I dragged the first two bags back into place, then braced my legs and hoisted the other two on top. Winded, and wincing a little at the muscle spasm I felt near my left shoulder blade, I sat down on the top bag and tried to relax. What on God's green earth could I do now? I glanced at my watch, wondering how much longer it would take Trace and Willie to finish. Would they drive by without stopping when they didn't see my car? Trace would have to pull all the way up to the lean-to to see where I'd parked. If he didn't do that, I could be here for hours.

ELEVEN

TRACE AND WILLIE stood at the bridge and watched Sylvia drive away, her car raising a cloud of dust that hung briefly in the air before drifting back to earth.

"Well. Let's get on with it," Trace said. "Why don't you walk toward the bridge and retrace your steps as best you can remember. Talk me through it as you go, what you did, what you saw, what you felt."

Willie nodded and moved toward the drainage ditch, describing the weather, the chilly water, the small, cultivated plots of prairie grass, the search for a place to hang his handkerchief to dry. He described the vulture and its defensive behavior, then crouched by the ditch and looked warily around the countryside as he told of his apprehensions concerning who the killers were and whether they could be lurking nearby.

Trace glanced at his watch, then followed as Willie slid down the ditch bank and set out for Route 10.

This time, following along the edge of the water instead of wading in the stream, Willie demonstrated his original, loping stride while hunched over to remain as invisible as possible. He then slowed to allow Trace to climb back to the upper bank and observe from the higher vantage point. Glancing back over his shoulder from time to time and pointing to the ground, Willie tried to indicate where he thought someone had altered the scene as he remembered it.

Finally, Trace caught up to him. "What are you pointing at?" Trace asked. "I don't see anything."

"Exactly. There's nothing here now."

"What did you see before?"

"More prairie grass. There were patches of Big Blue-stem along the field and on the slope. Some of them were three or four feet tall. They're all gone. Seems like a strange thing to dig up."

Trace took off his hat and wiped the sweat from his forehead with his sleeve. "Maybe Puckett cleaned it out when he finished picking corn. Probably thought they were weeds."

"No reason to do that, though. The grass hadn't invaded the cornfield. Fall plowing would keep plant migration under control. There's more to the story. It has to mean something."

"I'm not sure what it would be, Willie, but we'll keep all this in mind when we talk to Wayne and Ms. Branson."

"Is this field part of Taylor's farm?"

"No, we're on Branson property now. The dividing line's about halfway back to the road, where the row of hedges cuts between the two fields. Ms. Branson's farm runs from the hedgerow up to Route 10 where we left the car and includes everything on the west side of the ditch all the way to Elevator Road."

"Didn't you say Ms. Branson is dead set against putting a nature preserve out here?"

"She's very vocal in her opposition."

"But someone had to plant the grass by hand. Why would she allow that?"

"Maybe she didn't know. If Clay managed the test plots, it would have been easy for him to continue all along the ditch."

"Trespassing?"

"Yep. She or Wayne probably found the grass and figured out what Clay was up to. Neither one of them would hesitate to take matters into their own hands. They're well within their rights to dispose of anything planted or deposited on their land without their permission."

"So you think Louise Branson pulled up the samples?"

"Or Wayne," Trace said. "And with him farming both the Branson and Taylor properties, I bet he's the first man Ms. Branson would call if there was a problem. I'll send someone out to talk to Wayne today. I need to get back to town, Willie. Let's go on, see if we spot anything else."

Willie glanced back from time to time to make sure he wasn't too far ahead, just in case the sheriff had any questions. When he saw Trace bend over, pick something up from the ground, examine it closely, and put it in his pocket, Willie frowned and scrambled up the side of the ditch bank. "What did you find?"

"What?" Trace asked, a startled expression on his face.

"I saw you pick something up and put it in your pocket."

"Oh." Trace chuckled. "I found a quarter, Willie. I thought it might be an old one, but it's not."

"Okay. Thought maybe you found something interesting." Willie turned away and slid down the bank to continue his trek along the ditch toward Route 10.

Over an hour from the time they'd started their walk, the two men reached the car. Trace backed out to the berm, where he pulled onto the highway to return to the Taylor farm. A few minutes later he cruised past the house, turned around at the bridge, then accelerated and headed back toward Sangamon City.

Sylvia's car wasn't in the drive.

After a few minutes of silence, Willie cleared his throat, started to speak, then changed his mind and turned to look out the window. Finally, he squared his shoulders and looked at Trace.

"You seem to know Mrs. Taylor pretty well," he said.

Trace kept his eyes on the road and didn't answer. Finally, he said, "Not really. Why do you say that?"

"You called her Mare."

"I felt sorry for her. She seemed upset."

"But you said you knew she was faking."

"Sure…after I thought about it for a few minutes, I knew. But right at the beginning, she got to me. Can't stand to see a woman cry."

"But calling her Mare?"

"Willie, does this have a point?"

"Just curious. I thought maybe you were old friends or something."

"No."

"Were you close friends with Clayton Taylor?"

"Willie, I'm beginning to wonder who's in charge of this investigation. Do you help your sister this much?"

"Sometimes. She likes it when I help."

"I'll bet."

"You can ask her."

Willie sensed he'd obtained all the answers he'd get for the moment, even though he had lots more questions to ask. The sheriff hadn't sounded angry, so maybe he'd be more receptive later. He wished he'd brought his notebook so he could write things down as he thought of them. He would have to concentrate and remember and be ready.

It was obvious from Trace's sarcastic tone that he thought Willie more likely a nuisance to Sylvia than a help. Willie smiled. After Syl had rescued him from the homeless shelter in D.C. and moved him to Florida, she'd insisted on his full participation in the lives of his family. She made sure he used the library, set him up with a computer and Internet access in his apartment, and then she gave him real research assignments and even some writing projects. He knew he had emotional limitations, and there were stressful things he couldn't handle, but he also knew the part of his brain that comprehended and analyzed ideas and numbers was the part of his brain that worked even better now than it had before he got injured in Vietnam. His sister also understood this. As a matter of fact, she figured it out sooner than he did. Syl had been the first one to suggest he establish a small accounting service, a venture which had grown into a full-time business with two employees.

He forced his thoughts back to Sheriff Trace Parker. Why did the sheriff make Willie feel so uncomfortable? Except for the brief incident with the fawning Marella Taylor, Trace had not done or said anything wrong. He acted properly concerned about his deputy's odd and perhaps unethical, if not illegal, actions and had therefore suspended Morris. Trace had treated both Syl and Willie with respect and had responded quickly and professionally to their report. He seemed eager to solve the murder and had already initiated interviews with key people.

So what bothered him so much about Trace?

Back to Marella Taylor. And Syl. Did Trace want to renew his relationship with Syl? Or was he already involved in a flirtation with Clayton Taylor's widow. If that was the source of Willie's discomfort, it made a lot of sense. Syl was deeply wounded when Andy Thorn died. And when the rich attorney, Ronald Grant, swooped in and dug in his talons, he captured a wounded rabbit with no strength to resist. It wasn't until Grant turned his verbal tirades on Willie that Syl's spirit regained consciousness and allowed her to flee the marriage.

In Willie's opinion, Trace had not been a suitable match for Syl in high school. With his charm and daredevil antics, he could have lured Syl into a lot of trouble. Willie had no idea how much Trace might have changed over the years, but he didn't want his sister to take a chance. She'd come too far.

Willie decided he'd keep his eye on Syl, and if it looked like Trace planned to make a move on her, Willie would intervene.

TWELVE

I SAT ON THE STACK of compost bags for no more than five minutes before I felt an overwhelming urge to beat on the door with my fists and yell until my voice gave out. It was important, however, to keep my cool and save all my noise-making skills for the right moment, since it was too soon for Trace and Willie to return. And besides, beating on the door and yelling was way too wimpy for the tough broad I imagined myself to be.

On the other hand, staying locked in the old building didn't feel like an acceptable alternative. There had to be something in the shed which could be used to pull plywood off the windows, or perhaps pry the door open at the padlock. The sill was only a couple of inches high, so the lock should be even with my chin from inside. I searched for a crowbar, a hammer, or a heavy screwdriver. I found nothing. *Rats.*

Ooh, nasty thought. Huge rodents, as large as cats, used to scurry through the barn, foraging for loose grain. Those ugly creatures could have moved to the shed when the barn was torn down. The very idea made me shiver. After another look around, I felt reassured to find few hiding places and little evidence food had ever been stored there. As much to calm my jitters as to exorcise the picture my fertile imagination had summoned, I jumped up and paced back and forth between the door and the compost bags.

I heard a whispery sound, and tiptoed to the door, unsure

whether I heard words or just the sigh of breezes swirling through the tall, dry weeds surrounding the shed. After a few minutes, when nothing had changed, I resumed my pacing.

Another look at my watch confirmed I had been locked in the shop for twenty minutes. It felt like two hours. A muffled thud brought me back to full alert. Had someone slammed a car door? But there'd been only one thump, not two. Maybe Willie had jumped out of Trace's car to look for me. Or Stoney Morris. Or worse, Wayne Puckett. Now why did I think Wayne would be worse than Stoney? Because a deputy sheriff would exhibit signs of restraint, while Puckett had already shown his mean streak? Planning for the worst, I looked around the shed for something I could use as a weapon.

The posthole digger was the only thing heavy enough to do sufficient damage, yet small enough for me to lift and swing. It was about four feet long, with a short, crossbar handle at one end. The other end had two dull, curved metal blades to cut and hold the soil in a rounded clod. I figured I could swing the tool pretty hard if I gripped the handle end and got a little momentum going. A brief vision of the digger whacking into Trace or Willie by mistake crossed my mind, but was quickly dismissed as unlikely. They didn't have a key to the lock and, anyway, they would call out for me when they arrived, especially if they saw my car.

I positioned myself in front of the door and took a practice swing with a generous head start, nearly throwing myself off balance when the business end of the posthole digger swung past the door. Satisfied that even the bulky Stoney Morris would be knocked off his feet by a direct hit, I stepped into position, and waited. And waited.

Five minutes later, after leaning the posthole digger against the wall by the door and returning to my compost-bag roost, I absentmindedly wondered how Morris could have been so stupid as to expose his complicity in a crime to a total stranger.

Of course, he didn't know I was a judge, but even so, he'd created suspicion where none had previously existed. It didn't make sense.

Another noise interrupted my train of thought. One thud, then one more.

I returned to ambush mode with both hands gripped around the digger handle.

A new sound—someone had started a car.

I didn't get it. It couldn't have been Trace and Willie. Either Stoney or Wayne, or maybe both of them, must have been lurking. What had they been doing? And if the engine was loud enough now for me to hear, why hadn't it caught my attention when they first arrived? Unless… they'd started my car. I took my right hand off the digger handle and patted my pocket to see if the keys were there. Then remembered. I'd left them in the car. *Damn! Stupid move. What was I thinking?*

Maybe one of those creeps was sitting in the driver's seat of my rental car, putting his sweaty hands on my steering wheel— ugh. With any luck, there would be some of those dandy little antiseptic wipes in my glove compartment. On the other hand, maybe my car was about to disappear. Maybe I would disappear, as well.

A surge of fear jumped on top of my adrenaline-fueled anger. Beads of sweat popped out on my forehead, while a cold chill crept down my back. It was hard to take a deep breath in the stuffy room, but I didn't want to hyperventilate. Remembering Willie's lectures on deep breathing and biofeedback, I slowly brought the panic under control. Then I dried my clammy hands on my jeans and wiped the digger handle with the sleeve of my sweatshirt. After a few minutes, when nothing more happened, I leaned the tool against the door by the wall and returned to my perch.

I had been locked in for over an hour and was up pacing the floor for the third time, when I heard the thump of the padlock against metal. As I grabbed the posthole digger, I thought, *I need to be in the dark.* I jumped forward, switched off the light, and assumed my attack position. My hands tightly gripped the digger's handle. My legs were solidly planted and my stance wide. My whole body braced to clobber whomever came through the door.

With a creaking noise, the wooden door swung open. Stoney Morris stepped inside, feeling for the light switch. With full knowledge that I planned to assault a police officer, I lifted my weapon. I had some pretty good momentum going by the time I swung the blades in a direct line toward Morris's belt. The impact took his breath away. He dropped to his knees and clutched his side, the padlock and keys bouncing against the wall as he fell. A string of obscenities spewed from his mouth ending with, "You bitch. You stupid bitch."

That really pissed me off, so I gently whacked him again, this time on the side of his head. He collapsed into the shed, his face bouncing against the floor with a dull thud guaranteed to give him a bloody nose. He'd have a tough time explaining his bumps and bruises to Trace.

The posthole digger dropped out of my hands as I crept past the motionless heap of lawman and ran far enough into the barnyard to confirm my car's disappearance. Dashing back to Stoney's side, I struggled with his snapped holster and removed the gun. A wild race toward the driveway in the foolish hope the deputy's car waited—keys conveniently in the ignition— provided my second disappointment. Puckett must have dropped Morris off, after they'd disposed of my car.

Alternative escape paths flashed through my mind so fast I couldn't sort them all out. I thought of running to the drainage ditch by cutting through the cornfield, but the crop between the drive and the ditch had already been harvested. Anyone running across the fields could be clearly seen from the road or the driveway.

The nearest neighbor lived in the opposite direction from the ditch and more than a mile away. If Wayne came back and caught me running down the road or crossing the pasture, I'd be a sitting duck.

I wouldn't be any better off if I were inside the house, especially if Morris regained consciousness and had access to another gun. The turkey vulture had been reduced to a pile of bloody feathers, probably by a shotgun blast. I didn't want to suffer a similar fate.

After a cautious approach toward the house, I examined the foundation on the south side and found it pretty much the same as it had been when I was a kid. Morris was still out cold, so I edged around the corner to the east side to stare at the opening that led under the house. Two cement blocks leaned loosely against the foundation, blocking the hole.

The last time I had squeezed into the crawl space, I'd been twelve years old. Getting under there now shouldn't be a problem. How to do it without leaving a clear trail that even an idiot could follow could be a challenge. Most of the ground leading to the hole was covered with powdery dust. My footprints would point the way as clearly as a flashing red arrow.

Beyond the entrance to the crawl space, weeds and dried grass stretched all the way to the frontyard fence. The time lost covering my tracks, and the risk I'd run while visible from the road, were chances I'd have to take. As long as Puckett didn't show up, or Morris didn't regain consciousness, I'd make it safely to cover.

I turned and ran through the dust toward the barnyard and around to the driveway. Sprinting down the drive to the road, where my footprints wouldn't show, I dodged pebbles and ruts. A fall could be disastrous, especially if I sprained an ankle. Dried vegetation provided a safe walking mat from the road, through the sagging front gate, and across the yard to the north side of the house.

Something odd caught my eye. The windows of the parlor and the door that had opened onto the now-extinct porch were…what?

I had no time to figure it out. I had to hide. Swinging out just far enough to confirm Morris hadn't moved, I swerved back toward the east side of the building and knelt down to pull the cement blocks away.

Struggling to wriggle through the opening into the dark, musty space, I thought for a moment I'd grown too large to fit. There wasn't much head room, which forced my elbows and feet to work overtime, scooting me around so I could reach out and pull the blocks back into place. So much for the new loafers.

And the stress overload was whacking the hell out of my psyche.

Shoving the concern for my shoes out of my mind, I concentrated on the task at hand. If I hunched into the space backwards, the motion would force dirt up my pant legs, so I dug my toes in and turned again. With the gun pushed along ahead of me, and my elbows and shoulders working in ways they hadn't in years, I propelled myself as far back into the space as I could go. Then I stopped and edged around again, so I could see the light that crept through and around the cement blocks. Hopefully, I had crawled beyond the kitchen and hid under the west wall of the dining room, almost at the center of the house.

I dropped my forehead onto my hands and took a deep

breath, promptly filling my lungs with mold spores and a musty odor I could taste. Dirt coated the inside of my mouth, along with… I told myself not to think about it. Feeling incredibly dim-witted and a little nauseated, I tried to spit the gritty mud into the dust without making any noise. My sweatshirt proved useful again, this time for cleaning my lips and tongue. With my head carefully turned to one side, I rested my cheek on my hands and waited.

It was quiet outside. I assumed Morris remained unconscious because I felt sure he'd bellow like a castrated calf when he finally came to. I thought about it for a moment and wondered if I'd hit him hard enough to kill him, but discounted the thought. His midsection was too well padded and I had deliberately held back when I tapped him on the head.

The quiet and dark of the crawl space, mixed with the familiar musty smell, triggered another memory. The last time I had crawled under the house, I'd inched my way to the warm space under the kitchen where our brown-and-white pointer had hidden her eight newborn puppies. I brought them out, one at a time….

A sharp and abrupt sound—the slam of a car door—brought me back to the present. I snapped my head up to listen and hit one of the floor crossbeams with a dull thud. A muffled *ooof* sound escaped before I could stop it. I dropped my head back to my hands and prayed no one had heard.

Nothing happened. No one came. There was no sound. It was too dark to see my watch. I carefully raised my head and propped my chin on my left fist, my right hand resting on the .38. *Wait a minute…why did Deputy Stoney Morris still carry a gun if he'd been suspended?* Could this have been an oversight because the sheriff was preoccupied with the murder investigation? Hardly likely. Maybe

Morris had his own pistol, which he'd decided to carry even though he wasn't on duty. I'd have to ask Trace when I saw him.

Again, I heard a car. It seemed to slow, then accelerate. Then silence.

I corrected myself. I'd have to ask Trace *if* I saw him. Trace and Willie had probably cruised by, assumed I was on my way to town, and driven back to the county building. Too much time had passed for any other possibility.

What in holy hell am I going to do now?

THIRTEEN

EVEN THOUGH SYLVIA'S CAR wasn't in the county building parking lot, Willie saw no reason to be alarmed. She could have stopped by the motel to change clothes, gone for coffee, even decided to drive past the high school.

He followed the sheriff into the elevator and stayed on his heels as they walked into the department lobby. Marella Taylor was pacing the floor near the counter and didn't see them come in, but a well-groomed older woman, who sat on the edge of her chair by the hall, abruptly jumped up and charged toward the door.

Trace frowned and glanced toward the desk sergeant, who shrugged and leaned forward on the counter to watch. Willie moved a step closer, hoping the sheriff wouldn't notice.

"I need to talk to you right now," the older woman demanded, as she tried to push ahead of Marella Taylor.

Trace removed his hat with his left hand and extended his right. "Ma'am."

She shook his hand impatiently. "Right now, Sheriff Parker."

"Ms. Branson, I need—"

"There you are, Sheriff," Marella interrupted. "I've been waiting to see you. Have you found the man who killed Clay?" She turned to glare at Willie. "Is this the man?" She reached her hand out to touch Trace's arm and tried to move between him and Ms. Branson, but the older woman held her ground. Trace was forced to step back so Marella wouldn't end up wedged between them.

Ms. Branson raised her eyebrows and pursed her lips, brusquely pointing toward Trace's office.

Marella clutched at Trace's arm and appeared to stumble toward him when he stepped backward. Suddenly, she covered her face with her hands and sobbed. Then she tried to lean forward again, as though expecting Trace to put his arms around her. Instead, he moved out of her way and headed toward the counter, leaving Willie to stop Marella's forward momentum. As she felt someone grab her elbows, Marella dropped her hands to level a teary, soulful look at Trace—and found herself looking at Willie instead. She jerked her arms up and staggered to regain her balance while glaring indignantly, first at Willie, then Trace. Finally, she turned and promptly collided with Ms. Branson.

"Shit!" Marella shouted, causing Ms. Branson's eyebrows to jump even higher.

Sergeant Green nodded at Trace, then came around the counter to stand in front of Willie and the two women while his boss escaped down the hall, toward his office.

"You all need to have a seat right over there," Green said.

At the same time, Ms. Branson said, "I need—"

A red-faced Marella said, "I was—"

"Sit down," ordered the desk sergeant.

Willie obediently walked to one of the chairs. Both women started to protest but changed their minds when they saw Green put his hands on his hips. The two selected chairs at opposite ends of the waiting area.

"Sheriff Parker needs a few minutes before he can see anyone," Green said. "He'll call me when he's ready and tell me who to send in. Both of you ladies will have your chance, but you may have to wait awhile, so try to be patient. Can I get anyone a cup of coffee?"

The next fifteen minutes were uncomfortable and the atmosphere downright hostile in Willie's opinion. He studied the two women at length as they thumbed through old magazines and pointedly ignored each other. He noticed Marella had changed her clothes since this morning and now wore a red pantsuit, a low-cut white sweater, and red shoes with very high heels. Willie wondered if her outfit matched her BMW. Her shoulder-length hair, released from its upswept hairdo, fell in wild, curly waves, and her makeup suggested meticulous application with a generous hand. Her tears had smeared her mascara, leaving kohl-like rings around her eyes.

He turned his attention to the neatly dressed Louise Branson and watched her turn the pages of *People* magazine with a haughty expression, as though the celebrities pictured were representatives of an untouchable class. She dropped the magazine on a nearby chair and wiped her hands on a lace-trimmed handkerchief pulled from the pocket of her suit jacket. Ms. Branson had short white hair, combed away from her face in waves and tight curls. The hairdo looked to Willie as if it couldn't be displaced by even the strongest wind. Her tweed suit, brownish-orange blouse, and brown shawl suited the season, and sturdy walking shoes gave her the appearance of an elegant English woman just in from a stroll around her country estate.

When he heard Sergeant Green call his name, Willie started in surprise.

Marella Taylor jumped up and stomped to the counter. "I was here first."

"Sheriff Parker needs to see Mr. Grisseljon for a few minutes."

Marella turned around and glared at Willie. "Who is he, anyway?" She frowned. "Hey, weren't you in here this morning?"

"Ma'am, please have a seat," Green said. "It won't be much longer. Mr. Grisseljon, you can go on in. The sheriff needs to see you before starting these interviews."

"Interviews?" Marella scowled. "Excuse me, but I'm not here to be interviewed. I'm here to find out what's been done to catch the person who murdered my husband."

"I'm sorry, Mrs. Taylor, I didn't mean to imply anything." Green sighed as the woman mumbled under her breath and stalked back to her chair.

Willie hurried out of the waiting area and down the hall to Trace's office. He found the sheriff sitting at his desk, his hands cradled around a mug of coffee. A dusting of powdered sugar and a crumpled cellophane wrapper revealed how the sheriff had spent part of his fifteen minutes. *Trace and Sylvia may have more in common than I thought,* Willie mused.

"Sit down a minute," Trace said. He drained the mug and set it to one side. "Sergeant Green tells me Sylvia hasn't come back yet."

"No."

"I wanted her to sit in on the interviews, especially with Marella Taylor."

"For protection?"

Trace developed a sudden interest in refilling his coffee mug from the insulated pot on the credenza behind his desk. He took a couple of sips, then leaned back and looked thoughtfully at Willie. "Seems prudent. I could call in one of the other officers, but…would you mind?"

Willie shrugged, as though the thought had never crossed his mind. "Stay in here while you conduct your interviews? No, I wouldn't mind."

Odd, though, thought Willie. *Why would he ask me instead of having one of his deputies present?*

"Good. Stay right where you are and try to look official." Trace picked up the phone and told Green to send Marella Taylor to his office. When she stormed into the room, Trace stood up and waited until she stopped in front of his desk.

"Have you found out anything?" she demanded.

"We're still gathering evidence, Ms. Taylor. If you'll have a seat, I'll tell you what we know so far."

Marella waved toward Willie without looking at him. "Who's he? What's he doing here?"

"Mr. Grisseljon is the person who found Clay's body. Won't you have a seat?"

She sat, adjusting her jacket so her generous cleavage became clearly visible. She laid her red purse on the edge of the desk.

Willie scooted his chair back a few inches and turned it slightly so he could easily observe Marella. She glanced back and gave him a dirty look, but turned her attention to the sheriff without comment.

Trace folded his hands and placed them on the desk, then leaned slightly forward and frowned as though seriously considering what he wanted to say.

"Ms. Taylor—"

"Oh, for Pete's sake, call me Marella," she snapped. After a quick glance at Willie, she lowered her eyelashes to squeeze out one more tear and start it rolling down her cheek. "I'm sorry if I was rude out there. I've been so upset. Have you found Clayton's murderer?"

"We don't have a suspect yet. We're still investigating. I hope you'll have some information that could help us."

"Like what?"

"Did your husband mention anything about meeting someone when he went out to the farms?"

"No. I never knew his schedule. He conducted his business outside of the office half the time, so if I needed to get in touch with him, I'd call his cell phone."

"Did he keep the phone in his car?"

"Yes. Or in his briefcase. Sometimes on his belt."

Marella reached for her purse and shoved it into the narrow space between her left hip and the chair. Willie frowned, but said nothing.

Trace ignored the action. "We didn't find the phone, or his briefcase, and, as you know, the car hasn't turned up, either. Did Clay keep an appointment book?"

"He usually carried it in his briefcase."

"Ms. Taylor, did your husband ever talk to you about the nature preserve, or prairie grass, or disagreements about land use?"

"No." She shrugged. "I don't know very much about Clay's business. It's kind of boring. I'm a city girl."

"So I've heard. You grew up in Chicago?"

"Yes."

"Ms. Taylor, does anyone else in your family have an interest in your husband's business?"

She sat up sharply, looking astonished and a little apprehensive. "What do you mean?"

"I mean, does anyone else in your family own a share of your husband's business, or sell products or services to your husband or any of his farm owners or tenants, or buy products or services from your husband or any of his farm owners or tenants, or own property your husband manages?"

She looked puzzled, turned her head slightly toward Willie, and then visibly relaxed. "No, nothing like that."

"Any other ties?"

"What else could there be?"

"Why don't you tell me? Does anyone in your family have a connection with Clay's business in any way?"

Marella shook her head vehemently. "No."

"But you own the property where we found Clay's body?"

"Yes."

"Can you tell me what you were doing all day last Thursday?"

"Me? What the hell are you saying?"

"I'm not saying anything, Ms. Taylor. I need to know where you were last Tuesday. It's for the record. Please start with first thing in the morning and include anything Clay might have told you before he left the house."

"I don't like this one bit. I came here for information, not to be grilled like a common criminal. I want to talk to my lawyer."

Trace leaned back in his chair and sighed. "Ms. Taylor… Marella…these are the same questions we'll be asking everyone. You haven't been singled out; you aren't being treated like a criminal. I need your help. Won't you cooperate?"

She folded her arms across her chest and glared at the sheriff. "Not until I've talked to my lawyer."

"Okay. I'm going out to the lobby to talk to Ms. Branson for a few minutes. You can call from here." Trace pushed the phone across the desk. He motioned with his head for Willie to follow him out of his office.

The lobby was quiet. Louise Branson was nowhere to be seen.

"Green. Where's Ms. Branson?" He motioned the sheriff over to the counter and handed him a note. "She got a phone call, then came up here and said she had to leave."

"Sound like an emergency?"

"I don't know. She talked pretty soft so I didn't hear much. But her face got real red and it sounded like she chewed somebody out. The only words I heard her say for sure were 'I'm on my way,' right before she hung up."

"Sheriff Parker!"

Willie turned around and saw Marella enter the lobby

from the hall, her jacket buttoned up and her purse tucked under her arm.

"Ms. Taylor," Trace said, "I need to talk to you some more. Come on back to my office."

She looked around the room. "Where's Lou?"

"She had to leave. An emergen—"

"I have to go. My attorney said he'd come with me tomorrow morning. We'll be here at ten-thirty." With that, she ignored Trace's protests and strode resolutely toward the elevator.

Willie watched her leave, puzzled by Trace's lack of follow-up when it came to the land disputes. Trace knew Marella owned the land, knew she and her husband disagreed on how that land would be used.

Confused by the way Trace had effectively cut the interview short by antagonizing the woman, Willie began to form a new list of questions. Why hadn't Trace asked Marella for her husband's cell phone number, even though he obviously wanted to find the missing phone? And why he hadn't picked up on the fact that Marella had moved her purse when the phone was mentioned? *Too late to do anything about it now,* Willie thought, as he watched Marella savagely jab the elevator call button.

When the doors slid closed, Trace turned away and shrugged. "Didn't go too well, did it?"

Willie nodded.

FOURTEEN

ACCORDING TO MY best guess, twenty minutes or so had gone by since I'd heard any sounds from outside my hiding place. Would I have been better off out in the open? I'd never know. The crawl space seemed secure at the moment, but if Puckett and Morris figured out where I was, they'd have me trapped. My safety depended entirely on their stupidity. Granted, they hadn't shown flashes of great intelligence so far, but they might be savvy in a street-smart sort of way. Hopefully, they were dumber than…well, dumber than the person who thought it smart to hide under the house.

My heart was beating slower, my blood pressure surely normal, when a series of noises sent everything haywire again. A shot of adrenaline coursed through my body. I tried to quiet my breathing and relax my muscles, tensed for a fight-or-flight response. I could neither fight nor flee. Raising my head so that I could hear and see better, I watched the tiny slivers of light that were my only windows to the outside world. If an eye had suddenly appeared in one of those little spaces between the concrete and the foundation, it would have scared me shitless. Would I actually use the gun if that happened? I didn't have a clue.

First, I heard men talking, but couldn't understand the words.

One voice grew louder and more agitated. "Wayne, you don't know what the hell you're talkin' about!" Morris shouted.

"Well, whose fault is that? You're the one who let the little broad knock you senseless. Marella Taylor and her daddy ain't gonna like this one damn bit. You're a lot more likely to end up at the bottom of the gravel pit than getting a job with the Vortinto mob."

Was Puckett suggesting he already worked for the Vortinto family and Morris wanted a job in the organization, as well? Did Trace have any clue that his good-old-boy deputy had such lofty ambitions?

"You better keep your mouth shut, asshole."

Morris again. His voice sounded loud and a little shaky. I wasn't sure whether he was angry or just scared.

"What? Keep my mouth shut and let them think I'm the one who's stupid and sloppy and can't do my job right? I'm not taking the rap for your mistake, you dickhead."

"Wayne, I'm warnin' ya."

"You threatening me? What, you gonna kill me?"

There were scuffling sounds, a *thunk,* a groan, and then silence. I held my breath. Was one of the men unconscious? Dead?

After a few minutes, a new set of sounds triggered my internal alarm system: a *shooosh* combined with an *unhh,* a pause, followed by another *shooosh* and *unhh,* and, occasionally, a *whump.* I couldn't figure out what the hell that noise could be…unless one of the men was injured and being dragged along the ground.

The noises seemed very close. I grabbed the gun, pulled it forward so I could grip it with both hands, and pointed it directly at the opening to the outside. But instead of coming along the side of the house, the source of the noise mounted the block steps and opened the squeaky kitchen door. There was one loud *thunk,* then the sound of someone going back down the steps. I heard grunting and mumbling and then more *shooosing* noises over my head, toward the direction of the living room. There was a muffled *thunk,* then silence.

It must be a tremendous challenge for the blind to inter-pret sounds in an unfamiliar place. I tried to concentrate on the noises inside the house, hoping to figure it all out before I was subjected to any unpleasant surprises.

A faint jingling reminded me of the sound a key chain makes when someone's trying to find the right key. A grating sound like wood on metal followed. Had the person in the house removed another padlock? I remembered what had disturbed me as I walked toward the front of the house. The back door had been unlocked, but the front door into the old parlor had been secured with relatively new locks. The sliding door inside was probably locked as well. What was going on in there?

There were two more *shooshing* sounds, another door opening—the closet by the front door?—and then a screech followed by a *clunk.* Oh, God, I'd forgotten about the other entrance into the crawl space. Dad had installed a door in the closet floor to make it easier to access the wiring at the front of the house. Now the trapdoor was open and light flowed into the crawl space from behind me.

My heart leaped into my throat, threatening to choke me right there on the spot. I couldn't take a deep breath, probably a good thing since I'd dropped my face into the dirt again. Wriggling around so I could see was out of the question. To avoid making any noise, I had to get my breathing under control and then change my position very slowly. Meanwhile, I turned my head to the side and twisted my shoulders and neck as far left as I could. That put me in a position of total vulnerability, but I was able to see if someone stuck his head down through the opening.

The trapdoor into the crawl space remained open, so

the next two *shoooshing* noises were much louder than before. The light suddenly dimmed as a large shadow filled most of the space. Expecting someone to crawl through the trapdoor and come after me, I swallowed several times, closed my eyes, and decided this would be a good time to pray.

Please, God. Please, God. Please, God.

Another muffled *whump* prompted me to open my eyes. Light shone through the trapdoor again, but now a rounded heap of darkness filled the space directly under the light. I wondered if that rounded shape might belong to Morris and if it was about to move, and then I saw something else thrust down from the room above. A bundle wrapped in a heavy gray flannel shirt.

Oh, shit!

I dropped my head and yanked both hands to my ears, but only the left hand did what it was supposed to do. With my right hand, I clunked myself in the head with Stoney's gun. At the same time, someone fired a shot through the make-shift flannel-shirt silencer, into the dark shape.

My head throbbed and my ears rang. I'd never hear again. Analyzing my reactions reassured me. My brain hadn't turned to mush, not that it mattered if I were about to die anyway. Had the shot been fired into the crawl space to scare me out? Was the person above me going to start firing into the floor?

I was petrified.

At that moment, the trapdoor dropped into place and the odor of violent death rushed over me, a revolting assault on my senses. My stomach made a few tentative ripples, which threatened to lurch out of control if not quickly subdued. I pulled the neckline of my sweatshirt up over my mouth and nose, hoping for a good mixture of perspiration and musty, crawl-space dirt.

I was now trapped under the house with a body, and I had no idea how long I would have to stay there.

Willie! Tune in right now! Big Brother, I need you.

It probably wouldn't do any good, but I wanted to explore all options. The one time Willie deliberately tuned in to my frequency happened right after Andy died. I'd slipped out of the house while my mom and dad and Willie were sleeping, driven up to Delray Beach, parked my car in a public lot, and walked north along the ocean to watch the sunrise. Willie's voice rang loud and clear in my head when he asked me where I was. And he heard my answer.

Unfortunately, my brother wouldn't be worried about me yet. I hadn't been missing long enough to raise any alarms. He wouldn't know I was in danger unless he received vibes so strong he couldn't fend them off. My brain wasn't capable of that kind of effort.

What in the world was I thinking when I frantically worked my way under the house? I definitely didn't qualify as a private eye. McCone would never get herself into this kind of a fix. And Warshawski sure wouldn't! She'd have stood her ground and used the gun to protect herself.

Not that I couldn't use a gun if I had to. My dad taught Willie and me to handle everything from a shotgun to a bow and arrow, as soon as we turned thirteen. Then the FBI put me through basic firearm training in order to qualify for a desk job. I'd met Andy Thorn there.

But would I have fired a gun from under the house, even if Wayne Puckett himself had decided to crawl under there? I had my doubts. The semi-muffled explosion had seriously shocked my senses, but it would have been much worse if I'd fired the gun myself.

I had to find a way out of the crawl space, and fast. And I had to do it without getting caught.

FIFTEEN

"NO, IT'S NOT GOING well at all," the sheriff repeated. As he turned away from the elevator where Marella Taylor had just made her hasty exit, he looked at his watch and frowned. "Willie, what time did you expect your sister to return?"

Willie shrugged uneasily. "I was surprised she wasn't back by the time you started talking to Mrs. Taylor, but then I figured she stopped to eat or maybe changed clothes at the motel. Now I'm not sure. If we drove out to the country to look for her, she'd probably turn out to be on her way here, and then you would've wasted a lot of time."

"But if we sit here and wait for her, and then it turns out she's had a flat tire or fallen through some rotten boards in the old house, we're going to wish we'd acted sooner."

"Don't you have any deputies out there? Could you have them stop by the farm?"

Trace shook his head. "That was Stoney's patrol. I don't have anyone else closer than twenty miles. Listen…right now I need to make a bunch of calls…try to get Brian Kelso in here for an interview, track down Louise Branson and reschedule her appointment, and see if I can get a message to Wayne Puckett that I want to talk to him again. Why don't you have a cup of coffee or something? If your sister hasn't come back by the time I'm finished, we'll go out and look for her."

Willie nodded and strolled down the hall to the break room, where he found a chair by a window so he could watch for Syl to drive into the parking lot. He felt uneasy, but chose not to tell the sheriff quite yet. Sometimes Willie knew something was wrong, but not what that something was. It was difficult to explain, especially when he talked about intuition versus acute perception versus direct telepathy versus prescience. People tended to look at him as though they expected to hear the theme song from *The Twilight Zone*.

This ability to sense life's disruptions and undercurrents didn't apply only to his sister. He had a funny feeling about a lot of things related to Clay Taylor's murder. Ms. Branson and her mysterious emergency, for example. Something about the woman caught his attention. What was it? Maybe the way she moved. She looked so elegant and reserved, grim even, but she had a lift to her step and a swing to her hips that led him to think she might have a relaxed, down-to-earth side to her personality.

Marella Taylor, on the other hand, seemed outspoken and straightforward in the words she used, but her body language was out of whack with the things she said. Willie was uncomfortable in her presence, anxious even, because he got mixed signals. She seemed to be acting out some part she'd created for herself, rather than just being natural.

Willie shook his head. He'd meant to tell the sheriff about how Marella had moved her purse when her husband's missing cell phone was mentioned. But why hadn't the sheriff seen it for himself and asked her if she had the phone? Had he really not noticed? Maybe Trace wasn't a very good detective. Willie wondered what the rate of solved versus unsolved crime statistics were for Lincoln County. Marella Taylor had to be a prime suspect in her husband's murder, but she hadn't been subjected to a serious interview. Of course, she had escaped before Trace could finish, so maybe he'd been working up to the tough questions.

There's too much I don't know, thought Willie. He hoped Trace would let him sit in on the other interviews. Especially Louise Branson's. And Brian Kelso, too. But there was no logical or legal basis for Willie to be included. The only reason the sheriff had wanted another person in the room when he talked to Marella Taylor was to divert any suggestion of impropriety. She was a blatant flirt, even though she'd just lost her husband.

Trace Parker is an interesting character, Willie mused. He stood up and walked to the water cooler, where he filled a tiny cup and drank, then refilled it several times until he'd quenched his thirst. He stopped by the window and looked for signs of Sylvia or the rental car, then walked out to the hall and looked both ways. He could faintly hear the sheriff's voice. Apparently, he was still on the phone.

Now that he knew Trace was single, Willie wondered again about the attraction between Sylvia and her old boyfriend. *Maybe it hadn't been right to try to squelch that interest,* Willie thought ruefully. But surely Trace didn't have the kind of money it would take to sustain a relationship with someone who lived halfway across the country. And anyway, what did Syl need with a guy who lived so far away? She could do a lot better. Willie wasn't sure he liked Trace Parker any better now than he had when Syl was in high school.

Willie shook his head, knowing he had to be open-minded but honest. He'd tell Syl what he thought, whether she wanted to hear it or not. But at least Trace didn't seem to be wild and reckless. It was unlikely he would have succeeded in his job in a conservative Midwestern town, and then been elected county sheriff, if his image and reputation had been tarnished by inappropriate behavior. Local newspaper reporters enjoyed exposing the indiscretions of public figures, so it was hard for officials to misbehave and survive.

Just as Willie returned to the window for one more glance, a man with tousled, blond hair pulled his black Mercedes sedan into the lot, parked in one of the visitor spaces, and stepped out of his car. He straightened his diagonally striped, gray and burgundy tie and buttoned his dark, pin-striped suit jacket as he strode toward the building. He glanced up toward the window where Willie stood watching. The two briefly made eye contact.

The man projected a surge of energy—not an altogether pleasant experience for Willie. He shivered and took a step back. He hadn't sensed menace or threat, but he had felt something disturbing in that brief instant. Eyes reflected the accumulated feelings and emotions that were the result of a person's experiences, both good and bad. Pain and suffering, love and compassion, hatred, frustration—all could be revealed in a person's gaze. This man's eyes, although they were electric, revealed…nothing. Since it wasn't likely a man who appeared to be in his mid-thirties had no life experiences, he had to be proficient at masking his thoughts. From Willie's point of view, that made the man suspect before he ever opened his mouth. If he hid things that well, he must have important things to hide.

Willie walked back to the door of the break room and stood outside where he could see the door to Trace Parker's office. Within minutes the desk officer came down the hallway with the man from the parking lot. The officer knocked on the door, then opened it and leaned in. "Mr. Kelso's here, Sheriff." He stepped aside and motioned the attorney into the office, pulling the door closed as he headed back down the hall toward the reception area.

Fast work, thought Willie. If this visit came as the result of one of Trace's calls, then either Trace was very persuasive or Brian Kelso had things he wanted to talk about. The man's identity also helped explain Willie's perceptions gleaned from the brief eye contact. Brian Kelso was a lawyer. He knew secrets. The law required him to keep those secrets. Willie thought he was probably very good at his job.

Although he could hear the sound of voices from where he stood at the break room door, Willie couldn't hear what the voices were saying. He walked down the empty hallway and strolled by the sheriff's office door, then turned and went slowly back. Still nothing but muffled sounds. As much as he wanted to eavesdrop, he did not want to get caught lurking in the hall.

Willie walked back to the break room and sat down on one of the straight-backed chairs. It was the right height for him to sit up straight, both feet flat on the floor and his hands resting palms-up on his thighs. He noticed the hum of the refrigerated vending machines, the heat from the window, the occasional sound of a stapler or pencil sharpener. His softened view of the room melted the pale green of the wall into the mottled brown of the floor tile, and those colors became the background for the images that flowed in and out of Willie's mind as he accepted, greeted, and then sent these intrusive thoughts on their way.

It was as though Willie had dialed his sister's number and fully expected her to answer. He focused on his mud-colored screen and waited.

SIXTEEN

FOOTSTEPS SHUFFLED, doors banged—someone moved through the old house above me. Then the jingle of keys, followed by the sound of wood scraping against metal as the heavy parlor door slid back into place. Footsteps tracked over my head, then away to the west toward the bathroom.

The first time I saw that bathroom, I was only six years old. The tiny room originally contained a claw-footed tub and a sink with an orange hand pump perched at one end. After a few uncomfortable trips to the outhouse during winter, my father made the installation of an inside toilet top priority.

Now someone had decided to use those facilities while I cowered beneath the house, wishing I'd thought ahead and done the same. Only seconds later, footsteps passed overhead again. No flushing. No water running.

I suppressed that train of thought and concentrated on what had happened in the parlor. After the killer dropped the trapdoor and closed off the entrance to the crawl space, he had immediately walked away. As best I could remember, the opening hadn't been fitted for a lock, so it might be possible to enter the house from below and get inside the mysterious locked room.

Then I remembered the dead man who lay directly underneath the trapdoor. I wasn't strong enough to pull him out of the way—which, in any case, would be tampering with evidence and contaminating the murder scene. The alternative was to crawl over the body and somehow manage to get the leverage needed to push the door up and pull myself through without tromping all over the corpse.

There had to be a better way to satisfy my curiosity.

I turned my head to the other side in order to rest my neck, but lifted it up to listen when I heard another noise. Apparently, the killer also heard something. He ran through the room just above my head, slammed the screen door, and rattled down the steps. The outside din became louder—a large motor, shifting gears. The machine, whatever it was, seemed to stop, its engine revving in short bursts as though the driver's foot repeatedly pumped the accelerator. There were male voices, a shout, shifting gears, and then a terrible racket. The roar vibrated through me and my teeth clicked together with an annoying staccato beat. The truck had to be in the yard by now, after surely mowing down the fence like a tank in a war zone. Suddenly the noise stopped.

A door slammed. The voices again. This time I could hear every word.

"You made good time." Sounded like Wayne Puckett's voice.

Obviously, Puckett wasn't the corpse under the house.

"No sweat. Stoney here?"

"No. He had to leave."

No shit. It was now quite clear whose body lay crumpled up under the parlor trapdoor.

"Ain't that his car in the drive?"

"Somebody picked him up. He'll be back later."

"Well, now, I'd feel a lot better if Stoney was here. You sure he knows we're hauling this stuff away? I don't want no trouble."

"There's not gonna be any trouble. Stoney knows we're

here. Anyway, he doesn't give the orders. You know who's in charge, don't you?"

"Yeah. I know."

"And you know why we have to get this stuff out of here?"

"Sure. In case the cops start snooping around. They found the missing guy's body out here."

"Exactly. We got to hurry. I'll get the lock. You go down in the cellar and throw those bales up here."

"Hey, why me?"

"Because you're bigger and stronger, you idiot. I can drag them over to the truck a lot easier than I can push 'em up through that hole."

"Don't call me an idiot, Wayne."

"Oh, shut up."

It was a relief to hear the other man give up his protests.

Maybe he already knew how dangerous Wayne Puckett was. If so, the driver also understood he was extremely vulnerable while he remained alone in the root cellar and Puckett stayed aboveground. Accidents had a way of happening to expendable people who let themselves get backed into a corner by killers. I grimaced as I thought about how I'd done that very thing. Trapped under the damned house with a dead man—you can't get much more cornered than that!

Better to focus on the activity outside. The two men had been ordered to pull the bales of hay out of the cellar, load them onto a truck, and haul them away. They called the bales "stuff" and they referred to someone in charge. All I could think of was drugs.

The bales weren't marijuana; I would have recognized the smell. The drug awareness classes given by the West Palm Beach police department were thorough, and the cops always liked to burn a little of the stuff and wave it under a judge's nose. The bales in the root cellar had their own distinctive hay smell, like dried leaves and brisk air on a sunny, fall football afternoon.

I flashed back to the Frampton concert I'd attended in my younger days, my one and only exposure to concert culture. High up in the cheap seats, I sat surrounded by the odor floating in a sweet haze, giving the massive arena a dreamlike quality.

Definitely time to get a grip on my thoughts and concentrate. *Focus, Sylvia, focus!*

Anyone who stored marijuana in a cellar would be real stupid. Weed would mildew in no time. There could be no logical reason to hide the bales themselves, so there had to be something valuable or illegal hidden inside. Could they be running a meth lab upstairs in the parlor? Surely there were distinctive and potent chemical fumes associated with the process. I hadn't smelled anything except musty crawl space and dead body.

An angry skunk, I thought. That's how bad it smelled in the crawl space. If my gag reflex kicked in from that distance—although the distance wasn't all that great— then how could I get close enough to climb over the body and up through the trapdoor?

When I was a kid, I lured a skunk into the house, hoping to keep it for a pet. No one told me a skunk had to be deodorized. It let loose at the first unfamiliar noise and sprayed everything in the house.

I couldn't believe the way my mind wandered...stress overload.

"Hey, you asshole, be careful." The boys were at it again.

"Wayne, you're not working fast enough. I can throw three of these bales up there while I'm waiting for you to stroll over and lift one out."

"Throw 'em, then. Just hurry. We got to finish before someone shows up. It's damn suspicious to store hay in a cellar."

"Yeah, yeah."

Maybe they had raw cocaine hidden in the bales. Coke usually shipped in plastic bags. If so, it wouldn't be damaged by the damp cellar air. Where would cocaine come from? Most illegal substances entered the United States through Mexico or Miami. Illinois was a long way from both those places. But then, I knew drugs were everywhere, and they had to get there from somewhere else. Why not routed through an abandoned farm in central Illinois?

Aagh. Something crawled rapidly up my neck and onto my cheek. I brushed it away, this time remembering to use the hand that wasn't holding the gun.

"Okay, Wayne, that's it. I'm coming up."

The next thing I heard was the grind of the truck's ignition, shifting gears, more banging and rattling as the vehicle moved away from the house, then the fading clatter as the bales were hauled away. Best of all, I heard another motor start, followed by the rattle of loose dirt and gravel on metal as, I hoped, Wayne Puckett accelerated out of the driveway.

I had to make a decision and make it fast. To get the devil out of the crawl space and hide somewhere else, or try to get away before Wayne came back…or somehow get around and over what I thought were the remains of Stoney Morris and find out what was in the parlor.

It didn't take long to decide. Using my elbows and toes, I propelled myself toward the light. When I reached the cement block, I pushed it away and wriggled out into the fresh air. It was a struggle to get to my feet, not as easy a task as it had been ten years ago. Gripping the .38 with both hands, pointing it at the ground and to the side, I checked to make sure everyone was gone. I sucked in more fresh air and tried to decide what to do next. Taking off across the field or down the road would expose me to the world. Since I had no idea which direction Wayne and his partner had taken, or how long they would be gone, I didn't think I had enough time to reach help or get to the drainage ditch.

The locked room presented the biggest problem—or, more accurately, my nosiness about the locked room. I carefully climbed the blocks and stepped into the kitchen, then gingerly walked on through the dining room. Wayne had moved through the house as though confident the floors would hold, but I worried about rotted boards underneath. One wrong step could result in a broken leg or sprained ankle. I'd be trapped again, but would have no way to call for help. My stubborn refusal to carry a cell phone began to look like a bad mistake.

A few baby-steps carried me through the living room to the double-width, wooden panel that opened into the parlor. The left side of the door slid between the walls when opened, and the right side fit snugly against the doorjamb. There was a keyhole just below the door's handle. A padlock hung from a steel device that had been securely screwed into the doorjamb on one side and the door on the other.

I stood back and looked at it for a few minutes, remembering the time I'd found an old key on a closet shelf when I was nine, maybe ten years old. I had managed to turn the key in the lock. Unfortunately, the key didn't work in reverse. My father finally used a crowbar to lift the door from the bottom and scoot it off its track, ripping the whole mechanism out of the doorjamb in the process. The complete sliding-door portion of the fixture had to be removed while the door and jamb were patched and painted. The door itself was so heavy it took my father, my uncle, and the hired man together to set it back in place.

No crowbar this time. Not enough muscle to do the job with ten crowbars, for that matter. If there were any tools in the house, they were probably locked away in the parlor. I bent forward and peered closely at the padlock, grabbed hold of it, and gave it a couple of sharp tugs. Ever the optimist, I had hoped the door or the jamb was rotten enough so that one end of the lock would pull out, but neither side gave an inch.

However, the deputy's .38 still rested firmly in my grasp. Even though I hadn't fired a gun since I'd worked at the FBI, I felt sure I could hit the padlock from across the room. Stepping back a few paces, I lifted the revolver to shoulder level and brought my left hand up to steady my aim with a two-handed grip. My feet apart, my knees slightly bent, my elbows locked, I studied the angle at which a bullet would strike my target. Obviously, that trajectory could give me some trouble. A bullet would do serious damage if it ricocheted off the wall and hit me.

The floor squeaked a split second before a forceful and authoritative woman's voice shouted, "Don't fire that gun! The way you're aiming, you'll probably kill yourself."

I kept the two-handed grip on the revolver, but dropped my arms so the gun pointed toward the floor. How the hell had this person gotten in here? Had I been so engrossed in Wayne Puckett's activities that I'd missed the sound of a car? Or did she show up after Wayne and his buddy left? Was she part of the Wayne/Stoney/truck driver gang? If so, I was in a terrible fix. Again! Who the devil could she be?

"I have a shotgun," she said. "Gently put your gun down on the floor. Then turn very slowly toward me."

A shotgun, huh? Who would argue with a woman holding a shotgun?

I did exactly as I was told. As I turned to face her, she said, "Slowly. I mean it."

I complied.

"Now use your right foot and slide the revolver over here."

Okay, no argument. She did, indeed, hold a shotgun, but it hung through the bend of her right elbow and pointed toward my feet. What a relief!

The woman had a few years on me—maybe in her late sixties. Her overalls and manure-flecked cowboy boots contrasted in a big way with her well-groomed hair and nails. Tan lines on several fingers of both hands suggested she often wore rings. A silk, burnt-orange blouse with three-quarter sleeves seemed a strange type of shirt to wear with overalls, but I guessed this lady had her own sense of style.

"Who are you?" The woman's tone threatened me far less now that she'd disarmed me.

"My name's Sylvia Thorn."

"What are you doing here? Do you know you've got dirt all over your face?" She looked me over. "On your clothes, too." She curled her lip to show her disgust.

And this from a woman with manure on her boots?

"I lived here when I was a kid," I said. "I wanted to look around."

"With a gun?"

Well, yes, how to explain that? What would justify the gun? Telling this woman about Stoney Morris, Wayne Puckett, and the bales of hay might be a stupid move since I didn't know her identity, nor whether she was involved with these other people. As long as she didn't know I'd seen anything, maybe she would let me go. Changing the subject seemed like the best plan.

"Who are you? I know you're not Mrs. Taylor." She considered my questions for a minute, then shrugged.

"Lou Branson. I own the next farm over. I'm looking for the tenant farmer who works my place and this one. He called me earlier about an injury to my horse."

"You were looking for him with a shotgun?"

"I intend to shoot the son of a bitch. I told him to call the vet and wait at my place until I arrived, but when I got back to the farm all I found was my horse limping around with a big open cut on his leg."

"Is the horse okay?"

"Yeah, vet says she'll be fine. But Puckett doesn't know it. I intend to scare the little weasel so he'll do what I tell him next time."

Ought to work, I thought, and could provide me with a way out of my predicament, as well. "Ms. Branson, I'd like to call the sheriff and have him pick me up. Could I call from your place?"

Lou Branson squatted down to pick up Stoney Morris's gun, then quickly stood up. I stared at the woman and wondered if legs that strong come from horseback riding. Even regular yoga and Tai Chi practice didn't give my body the ability to squat easily, and I sure as the devil couldn't stand back up without using my hands to push off the floor.

"Outside," she said. "I'll follow. Don't stop until you get to my car."

Maybe that meant yes. Still worried about the rotten floorboards, I walked gingerly back through the house. As we passed through the dining room, we heard the crunch of tires on gravel. *This could be good,* I thought, *or it could be very bad.*

"Ms. Branson, I think we should find out who that is before we walk outside."

She looked at me curiously. "Wait here," she ordered. She stepped into the kitchen and disappeared off to the right.

The bathroom, I thought. *There's a window that looks out on the driveway.*

"It's that little asshole," she yelled as she charged through the kitchen and out the door, leaving me in the dining room with no gun and nowhere to go.

"Wait," I called after her. She kept going, oblivious to my concern. I stood still, expecting to hear Lou Branson's outraged commands and Wayne Puckett's explanations and the shotgun explosion. But there was only silence, followed by the tentative squeak of the screen door, a couple of footsteps, and the startled face of Wayne Puckett peeking around the corner from the kitchen.

Puckett's face turned scarlet when he saw me. A spray of spittle accompanied the question he threw at me in a soft, menacing tone. "What the hell are you doing in here?"

He carried Lou Branson's shotgun as well as the deputy's .38, and had a second revolver tucked into the waistband of his jeans.

I sucked in a deep breath and blew it out, then thought real hard about sending another mental message to Willie. If there was ever a good time for my brother to tune to my wavelength, it was now.

"Goddamn," Puckett swore, "don't you old women ever give up?"

Old women! Does that little shit mean me?

Before I got worked up enough to do something stupid, I heard high heels clip-clip up the steps and the screen door open again. Marella Taylor, a cell phone pressed to her ear, stalked into the house. My mouth dropped open at this unexpected development.

"What are you doing in here, Wayne?" she snapped. When she saw me, she stopped, stared, and frowned, clearly trying to remember where she'd seen me before.

"Who's this? Oh, never mind…no, not you," she barked

into the phone. "There's another broad out here. I'll call you back." She listened to the person on the other end, then abruptly and sharply answered, "Fine, fine, fine!" She clicked the phone shut and stuffed it down the front of her sweater, successfully stowing it between her intimidating breasts.

"Give me that, you idiot," she said as she grabbed the .38 out of Puckett's hand and assumed a competent two-handed stance. Apparently, she knew how to handle a gun, but aiming it directly at a spot between my eyes was not the recommended procedure for confronting an ordinary old trespasser, especially an unarmed female. This case was getting very complicated.

"Grab her," Taylor ordered. "Hurry up, you stupid jerk. We have to go."

"What are we gonna do with her?"

"I don't know yet. They can't stay here. You got the key to the shed?"

"Yeah."

"Dump them in the cellar."

"Drag 'em all the way over there? By myself?"

"Come on, you asshole, get on with it."

I had a feeling these two characters didn't like each other very much, and wondered which one would end up alive and which one dead.

Puckett led the way out the door. Aware that he had the .38 pointed at the back of my head, and with high hopes he wouldn't shoot me before he locked me up, I followed him. There had to be something I could do, but I wasn't getting any brilliant ideas. As I stepped through the screen door and started to place my foot on the top concrete block, I saw Puckett stick out his foot. Before I could react, a dull *thunk* vibrated through my head and a sharp pain shot down my neck. I knew I was going to fall, but I lost consciousness before I hit the ground.

SEVENTEEN

WILLIE GLANCED AT his watch when he heard voices in the hallway, and found that thirty minutes had passed while he sat in the break room and stared out the window. Able to enter a meditative state no matter what his surroundings, he often reacted with astonishment to the images he saw as he came back to the present moment. This time proved no exception. Sylvia stood inside the old farmhouse with a gun in her hand, her face and clothes covered with dirt.

The image immediately faded.

His sister was the only person with whom he'd discussed the things he saw, and he knew Sylvia accepted these events at face value but did not consider them significant. Willie, however, knew his abilities were exceptional and therefore exploitable. He did not seek that kind of attention.

The revelations, or thoughts, whatever they were, hadn't appeared until he returned from Vietnam, so thankfully his childhood wasn't haunted by disturbing visions. These days, however, he saw something several times a week. When the thought made no sense, he happily shoved it away. Occasionally, however, the picture was clear and very upsetting. The image of Sylvia, her disheveled appearance and her air of distress, was one of those upsetting things.

Willie preferred not to share this information with Trace Parker, but he would do whatever necessary to convince the sheriff to take him back to the farm. He shoved his chair back and stood up with the intention of barging into Parker's office, if necessary, but found Parker already escorting Brian Kelso toward the lobby. Willie quickly followed. He caught up with them in time to see the sheriff shake his head as the grim-faced attorney strode toward the door.

Parker turned and mumbled under his breath, just as Willie reached his side.

"What an arrogant jerk. I'd never do business with him. And he's very successful. Go figure."

Willie ignored the sheriff's words as well as his tone. "I think we should go now," he said firmly.

"Out to the farm?"

Since Willie had already made it halfway down the hall, his answer was clear. Trace followed Willie to the car, saw they were safely belted in, and flipped on his flashers to help speed their travel through town.

Willie took a deep breath and slowly let it out.

"What's troubling you?" Trace asked with a quick glance at his passenger.

Willie shook his head.

"It's okay," Trace insisted. "It might help. If you know something—"

"No. I don't. I…sometimes I see things."

"What did you see?"

"Just…Syl…with a gun. And she was covered with dirt, as if she'd been in the middle of a dust storm. You know, white marks around her eyes and streaks across her cheeks and neck. She looked worried."

"What kind of gun, Willie?"

"What?"

"The gun. What kind of gun did she have?"

"Oh. A K-frame Smith & Wesson Model 10 with a four-inch barrel. Looked pretty old, had some scratches on it and a big nick in the grip."

Parker glanced at his passenger in surprise, but Willie didn't act as if he'd done or said anything unusual. "Were you an MP in Vietnam?"

"No, but I know guns. We were trained on everything."

"Are you sure you didn't see a Model 10, that particular Model 10 especially, only because you recently saw another one exactly like it?"

Willie thought about that. He knew precisely what Parker meant. Deputy Stoney Morris carried a .38. The sheriff probably thought Willie imagined the whole thing, that he was some kind of nervous Nelly.

Willie shook his head. "I'm not that way. Maybe I noticed Deputy Morris had a Smith & Wesson, but he never took his revolver out of its holster. I didn't see the barrel or the grip. If the scratches and nicks are on the deputy's gun, then the one I saw in Syl's hand must belong to him."

The sheriff frowned and shook his head.

Willie realized that seeing visions and sensing danger were strange concepts to most people, even those lawmen who occasionally consulted psychics to assist in crime investigations. And cops who routinely relied on intuition or gut feelings rarely acknowledged that they too used unusual powers. He also understood that he'd made Trace Parker nervous and suspicious, so he decided not to say any more on the subject unless asked.

Traffic thinned quickly as they reached the edge of town and headed toward the farm. Parker pressed down a little harder on the gas pedal. "Willie, can you bring these visions up on demand, or call them back so you can see them again?"

"No. They come when they feel like it. Sometimes I can make them go away if I concentrate on something else."

"Have you worked with the Florida police on any cases?"

"I don't want to get involved in that. The TV and the

papers get hold of it and everybody's life changes. Sheriff, do you remember when the Chicago police used a psychic to help track a kidnapped girl? It happened ten or fifteen years ago."

"I remember. The woman uncovered some clues but the kid never turned up. The psychic disappeared, and the media hounded the detective for months afterward."

"Exactly. I don't need that in my life."

The county car eased up behind a corn picker which took up most of the width of the country road. Parker flipped his siren on for one short *whoop,* then squeezed by as the farmer promptly pulled to the right. At that point, the old house was less than half a mile away. It looked as quiet as it had a few hours before. Other than the corn picker and the police car, a small cloud of dust far in the distance along the dirt road leading away from the house was the only sign of activity. As Parker pulled into the driveway, Willie was surprised to see a car, but not Syl's rental.

"Ms. Branson's car," Parker said.

"Why would she be here?"

"I'm not sure. Ms. Taylor owns the property. Maybe Ms. Branson came looking for Wayne. I think I mentioned he works both farms." Parker was quiet for a minute, then continued, "Also, there's the call Ms. Branson received while she waited for me to finish with Marella. Maybe Wayne called her."

"But why would he want her to come here? If he had a problem for Ms. Branson to solve, wouldn't it be on her own property?"

"You would think so. I don't know, Willie. Let's see if we can find her and get some answers."

The sheriff unsnapped the holster cover on his revolver as they stepped out of the car and approached the Explorer.

Parker looked into the back side window. He took a step forward to the driver's side. As Willie glanced in the back, he saw a shotgun shell on the rear floor mat. In the front, the glove compartment hung open and a few papers were strewn on the seat and floor of the passenger side.

"Something isn't right here, Willie. Don't touch anything. Especially the door handles."

The sheriff returned to his own car and opened the trunk to retrieve a couple of Kevlar vests, one of which he handed to Willie. "Better not take any chances."

"I don't understand. Why would she shoot at us?"

"I don't think she would. But I don't know why she's here, or who might be with her. And let me remind you, these vests might not do much good against a shotgun if you let a shooter get too close. Stay behind me. Don't take any chances."

Willie nodded and stepped back to let Parker move ahead.

The sheriff walked slowly into the yard with his gun drawn but held down at his side. He looked at the ground, the windows of the house, the padlock on the door of the shed, the footprints and drag marks in the dust. He stopped and called out, "Hello, anybody here?"

Willie stopped to listen. A breeze swirled through the dry weeds, trailing a riffle of sound, and then it grew quiet again. There was no answer.

Parker called out again. "Ms. Branson? Are you here?"
Nothing.

"Ms. Branson? Judge Thorn? Wayne? Is anybody here?"

Still nothing.

"I'm going to walk around the house and check the doors and windows, Willie. Stay here. Give a shout if you see or hear anything."

Willie slowly turned a full circle. For a moment he studied

the shed. "Sheriff, why would anyone lock that building? Looks like it would fall over if you gave it a hard shove."

"Storage, I guess. Tools, fertilizer, who knows? If I need to see inside, I'll try to get the key from Wayne or Ms. Taylor."

When Willie turned back, Parker had already started toward the house. Willie watched until he disappeared around the corner. Unable to stay put, he followed Parker at a distance, noting the two concrete blocks near the hole that led under the house. He saw footprints and drag marks in the dust, and leaned down to peer into the darkness, already convinced that his sister had been in the crawl space, exploring or hiding.

Parker appeared at Willie's elbow and indicated with a shrug that he'd found nothing. "Maybe your sister crawled under there," he said. "Could explain why she was covered with dirt."

"Yeah, but why would Syl go under the house? And why would she have your deputy's gun?"

"Well, if we knew the answers to those questions, we'd be a lot closer to figuring out where your sister is…and maybe where the heck everyone else has disappeared to."

"Who else disappeared?"

"I never did reach Stoney, or Ms. Branson, or Wayne Puckett. Left messages for all of them to call my office, and told the desk sergeant to let me know if he heard anything. Now we have Ms. Branson's Explorer, but no sign of her anywhere."

As Willie turned to look at the kitchen door, he spotted the blood on the concrete blocks. He had already taken a step toward the house when the sheriff stopped him.

"I see it, too, Willie. Come to the car. I'm calling for backup before we go in the house."

"But what if Syl's in there? What if she's hurt? What if she fell through the floor or something?"

"Let me call first and then we'll go in. Stay with me."

When they returned to the house, Parker signaled Willie to follow as they made a slow cautious entry through the screen door into the kitchen, through the bathroom and bedrooms, into the living room, and finally to the pad-locked parlor door.

"You can see someone has been in here," Parker said. "Footprints in the dust, and it looks like something got dragged through the door. Stand back," he ordered. "I'm going to shoot the lock off." He stepped closer to the wall and fired his gun.

A sharp *ping* and an answering *thud,* followed by a small shower of ceiling plaster, demonstrated his shooting skills.

After Parker slid the huge door open, the two men stepped into the parlor. A path tracked through the dust toward the closet. Parker walked to the closet door, opened it, and looked inside.

"It's empty," he said. "They must have dragged some-thing out of here instead of in." Parker turned and started to walk away.

"Wait!" Willie stepped into the closet and pulled out the loose linoleum covering the floor. "There's an opening into the crawl space. Dad put it in when he had new wiring installed, to make it easier for the contractors."

Willie reached down and lifted the door, then dropped it and scrambled backward with his hand clamped over his nose and mouth.

Parker stepped forward. "What is it?"

"There's another body…"

"Shit! Who is it?"

"I don't know. Not Syl. I have to get some air."

As the sheriff entered the closet, Willie tore through the house to get outside. There he stood and took deep breaths to quell his nausea and slow his heartbeat. He stared at the padlocked shed for a moment, then ran to the building and began pounding on the wall and shouting Sylvia's name.

EIGHTEEN

CONSCIOUSNESS RETURNED slowly and intermittently, like a barn swallow that swoops under a bridge, and then zooms out again to nab its prey before diving back to shelter. I don't think barn swallows suffer nausea from their swooping and zooming, but I sure was having a lot of trouble. It felt like seasickness, and that confused me because I couldn't figure out why I'd be on a boat, why I couldn't get my eyes open, why I couldn't sit up, and why my head hurt so much.

It took some time but I finally stayed awake long enough to answer some of my own whys. There were no swallows. No bridge, no boat. My head hurt because I'd been whacked with something, probably Marella's gun. My eyes were open but I still couldn't see anything, so I guessed I was in a very dark place. Or had suffered a concussion and blindness. I didn't like either of those options, so once again I tried to sit up. Then I realized my hands were fastened behind my back, and my ankles were also secured. I thrashed around a little to get a feel for the strength of the ties and had the distinct impression that duct tape held me together. Maybe that was better than rope or plastic ties or baling wire, but not much. I ran my tongue over my lips. At least my mouth wasn't taped.

Ah, another clue. I might not be seriously injured, but I suspected my location was somewhere so remote that Wayne Puckett and the delightful Marella Taylor weren't concerned with my yelling and screaming.

What about Lou Branson? Did she belong to this surly team?

A rustling sound came from nearby. I had a sinking feeling in the pit of my stomach, which easily could have been fear. Had those creeps left me helpless in a place infested by rats? Or snakes?

Those thoughts provided a powerful incentive to get free of the tape. I wriggled and rolled and tried to maneuver my butt through my arms, but it didn't help. So much for all the flexibility that's supposed to come with diligent yoga practice. Scrunching into a ball and willing my arms to stretch didn't work, either—and it hurt like hell.

All this effort didn't take place quickly or gracefully, but at least the thrashing and groaning kept rats and other monsters at bay.

After a little rest, and immediately upon hearing a click combined with some alarming *thunk* noises, I scrunched up my body with my legs tucked behind me, hoping I could pick at the tape around my ankles. It took some time to find the sticky edge conveniently located at the back between my heels, but find it I did. In a few more minutes my legs were free, and I felt a moment of exhilaration knowing I could now kick creatures as well as yell at them.

My happiness was short-lived when I realized I could rise up on my knees, but no further. My hands were useless, my feet were numb, and one of my loafers was missing. I slipped off the other shoe and sat there pounding my feet against the floor until whatever shared my space made another move, this time accompanied by a loud noise.

"Oooooh." A moan—and a human-sounding one at that.

"Who is it? Who's in here?" My words came out more like, "whoozit, whoozere," making me sound a little drunk and a lot scared.

"Oh! Son of a bitch! Ouch!"

"Ms. Branson?"

"Oooh."

It was quiet again for a couple of minutes. Then an outburst of mixed noises, including a little moaning and a lot of thrashing around, convinced me that my partner-in-captivity was human. I thought she might be suffering the same barn swallow, bridge, and seasickness sensations and decided an explanation might help.

"It gets better after a few minutes," I ventured.

Silence.

"I peeled the tape off my ankles. When you feel up to it, I can help you free your hands."

More rustling and grunting but no answer.

"It feels like we're in a cave or a room with a dirt floor," I said. "I've never been in a place so dark."

A hand clamped down on my shoulder. I let out a blood-curdling scream that would have chilled the heart of the devil himself. Every ounce of adrenaline in my body shot through my system and triggered a panic response more intense than I had ever experienced before. It should have been enough to short out all my circuits.

"Shhh, it's okay," Ms. Branson said. "I should have warned you before I touched you."

I collapsed sideways, gasping and coughing as I tried to catch my breath and recover from my systemic reaction to sheer terror. Ms. Branson fumbled with my wrists as she felt for the seams, then carefully pried the tape loose and massaged my hands to get the circulation going.

"They're like ice," she noted.

No shit!

"See if you can stand up now," she said.

I propped myself on my hands and knees while I practiced breathing in and out. It wasn't exactly normal respiration, but it seemed adequate to keep me from fainting.

With Ms. Branson holding my right arm, and with my left hand propped on my thigh, I slowly stood up and gratefully patted her hand. She let go, and somehow I miraculously remained upright. I inhaled and slowly let my breath out.

"How did you get loose? Didn't they have you taped?" I thought of Lou Branson's compact frame and couldn't imagine how she'd freed herself.

"We're not talking about the brightest man in the world. I carry everything from pruning shears to a screwdriver in these overalls. Wayne Puckett forgot about that. I worked my utility knife free. Broke two fingernails and cut my hand, but I got the job done."

"Do you know where we are?"

"I think so. My watch timer went off just before you started making all that racket. It's set for three o'clock. Which means they didn't take us very far. So I'm guessing we're in the root cellar under the old postal station."

"Postal station? Near the Taylor place?"

"On the Taylor farm. The toolshed you passed when you walked up to the house."

"Oh. Yeah. This isn't the first time I've been locked up in the shed today. I took a look into the cellar and saw a bunch of hay bales, but they hauled them away...." I stopped when I realized I was babbling.

"Wayne and Marella locked you up?"

"Wayne and Stoney Morris. She wasn't here earlier. At least, I didn't see her."

"Morris? The deputy? So he's in this, too."

"In what?" I asked. "What's going on here?"

"Clay's murder. Why else would they do this? I thought Wayne had pulled the murder off all by himself, but now it looks like the other two are also involved."

"Why did you think Wayne did it?"

"I looked for him on Thursday. He disappeared after he promised me he'd clear some brush near the road. I saw him leaving the drainage ditch in his pickup truck, following a bulldozer, and since there was a pile of stuff at the side of the Taylor field, I figured he'd planned to do the same work on both farms."

"Did you tell the sheriff?"

"Not then. After I heard about your brother finding Clay's body, I went to the sheriff's office, but then had to wait while he talked to Marella. That's when I got a call from Wayne about an injury to my horse. I drove back out here, found Wayne had disappeared again, and came after him."

"When you thought he might be a killer?"

"I had my shotgun, and I didn't expect Marella to be here. She's the one who got the drop on me. I wonder where the deputy is. That's the other thing I couldn't figure out. A patrol car is parked at my place, right in front of the barn."

"I think he's dead. I'm sure he's the one who was shot, after I hid under the house."

"Must be his blood I saw on the steps. You know, you're darned lucky I came inside. When I didn't see Wayne's truck in the drive, I almost left. I'm not sure what made me walk around the house first."

"Maybe lucky for me," I said. "But not too lucky for you. You'd be safe and sound at home if you hadn't gone inside."

"Never mind. There are two of us now, so let's see if we can get out of here. We're about the same height, but I'm stockier than you are and probably stronger, so we're going to work our way around the wall with you stepping up on my back and touching the ceiling until you find where the trapdoor is. Once we find it, we'll see if we can get out."

"Don't you think they padlocked it?"

"Wasn't padlocked when you took your peek down here, was it?"

"No. But are you sure this is the same place?"

"Try running your hand through your hair."

I put my hand up to my head to comb my fingers up through my thick curls, and felt tiny bits of something brush my cheek and hand. Could have been hay, I guessed. Maybe she was right.

"Let's try to get out of here," she said.

"Ms. Branson, even if we're in the root cellar, we'll never be able to lift up the door. There were four bags of compost piled on top of it."

"Lou. Call me Lou. Maybe they were in a hurry and didn't put the bags back. We're not going to know until we try. Come on!"

We quickly developed a pattern. Lou braced herself against the wall, and I stepped up on her back and ran my hands over the ceiling. I mumbled in the negative, stepped down, and then we moved another few steps and tried it again. When we were about half the distance down the third side, I found it.

"I'm going to lean my arms against the wall again," Lou instructed. "You stand on my back near my shoulders and push up on the door."

Made sense to me. Sort of a test maneuver. It was a little tricky to keep my balance in total darkness, but I steadied myself with one hand touching the wall and one hand lifted to find the outlines of the door. A tentative and gentle push, not surprisingly, didn't budge the heavy weight. No light crept through the cracks, so it had to be a snug fit. If those bags were on top...

I widened my stance on Lou's sturdy back, braced both hands against the door, and pushed as hard as I could. The trapdoor flew up and banged all the way open. Light streamed in and I lost my balance.

This is gonna hurt, I thought, as I flailed my arms in a vain attempt to recover.

It was my good fortune the trapdoor released to the side away from the open space and toward the cellar wall, thus breaking my downward momentum. My body was further cushioned by bouncing off Lou's strong shoulders. If I'd gone the other direction, I would have plunged straight to the floor and probably broken something important. Instead, I hit the wall with my left side and slid down backwards, butt first. Throwing her arms up to slow my descent, Lou popped me in the mouth. We both ended up on the ground.

"Ow, ouch," I muttered. Definitely an understatement. My arm scraped all the way down a surface that felt like stucco unevenly applied with a trowel. Adding to my discomfort, I landed on my tailbone—hard.

Apparently the whole thing hadn't fazed Lou a bit. She stood directly under the open trapdoor and gazed upward at the light as if God might reach down and lift us out of the cellar. I struggled to my feet and walked over to stand beside her.

"What now?" I asked. "My arms and shoulders are strong, but I'm not tall enough to pull myself through the door by standing on your back. Would you be able to lift me up on your shoulders?"

Lou gave me a look that clearly said she could do anything she needed to do to get us out of there. She sized me up, judging my weight and build, then got down on her hands and knees with her head near the wall directly under the trapdoor.

"First you'll need to sit with your legs hanging down between me and the wall," she said. "I'll use the wall for support, to help me get up. Then you do the same, so that you're standing on my shoulders. I'll turn very slowly until you're centered under the opening. Then it's up to you. Once you're up there, you'll have to find a way out. And get some help."

I think it would have worked, and was certainly ready to give it my best shot. But before I could straddle Lou's shoulders, I heard a loud banging. The noise came from outside the shed.

The racket continued and moved close to us. Then I heard a shout.

"Syl? Syl, are you in there?" More banging. "Ms. Branson?"

"Willie?" It came out as a surprised whisper, certainly not loud enough for Willie to hear me. *"Willie?" Much better.*

"Syl, are you okay?"

"We're fine. Just get us out of here."

In seconds we heard an enormous crash accompanied by the sound of splintering wood, the slam of the door hitting the wall, and the loud tromping of booted feet rushing into the shed.

Soon we stared up at Willie and Trace Parker.

"What the heck are you doing down there?"

Willie does have a sense of humor, I thought.

"Trying to figure out how to get up there," I replied. "Do you have any ideas?"

Trace just stood and shook his head, like a bobble-head doll in a sheriff's uniform.

NINETEEN

"WHAT WE NEED is a ladder," I said.

I thought it sounded like an intelligent suggestion, but Trace looked down at me like I was nuts. He turned and walked away, still shaking his head. Willie sat on the floor with his feet dangling into the cellar. He watched me without saying a word.

"What's wrong?" I demanded.

Lou tapped me on the shoulder, but I brushed her hand away.

"Willie, is Trace going to get a ladder?" By now, no one could miss the edge in my voice.

"There isn't one up here." Willie shrugged his shoulders as if there was absolutely nothing he could do.

"Sylvia." Lou tugged at my elbow.

I turned around, planning to unload some of my irritation on her. Before I could say anything, I looked in the direction she pointed, toward the floor by the fourth wall of the cellar. The wall we hadn't explored in our search for the trapdoor. The wall we hadn't even looked at as we tried to figure out how to climb up into the shed.

That, of course, was where a long, sturdy-looking wooden ladder had been abandoned by an overconfident Wayne Puckett.

If Lou and I had worked our way around the cellar in a counterclockwise direction, rather than clockwise, we would have stumbled over the ladder before we found the door, thereby saving ourselves a lot of time and a couple of injuries. I hugged my scraped arm to my chest as I remembered my painful slide down the wall.

Without another word, we grabbed the ladder and shifted it into place. I carefully climbed up and waited until Lou joined me. Willie watched us without comment.

"It was dark down there, Willie. We barely managed to get the trapdoor open before you showed up."

"Syl, I didn't say a thing."

Lou ignored us and strode out of the shed. I looked around the room, focusing on what had happened that afternoon, and wondering what Marella Taylor, Wayne Puckett, and the probably-dead Stoney Morris had been up to, why Clay had died, and which one of those characters had killed him. Other than the hay bales that had been removed and the displaced compost bags, nothing in the shed looked any different than it had earlier.

Willie finally pulled his legs out of the opening in the floor and rose to his feet. As he brushed bits of hay off the seat of his pants, we both heard something small and solid bounce on the floor. I spotted it first and pointed toward a small, irregularly shaped…rock? Willie leaned down to pick it up but then stopped without touching it.

"What is it, Willie?"

"It looks like a piece of bone."

"Oh." I backed up a step. "Okay. We better tell Trace to send someone in here with an evidence bag."

With a great sense of relief, I walked out of the toolshed and took some deep breaths of fresh air that didn't smell like grease, oil, and kerosene-soaked wood.

Approaching sirens caught Trace's attention, and he hurried off toward the driveway before any of us had a chance to corner him and ask questions. We leaned against the shed and waited while he directed his deputies to mark off the house with crime scene tape and examine the property for evidence. Another twenty minutes passed before a black van rolled to a screeching halt in the drive. A man, probably in his mid- to late-sixties, his wispy white hair sticking out in all directions, climbed out of the driver's seat and stomped up to the house. Pulling on a pair of white latex gloves, he yelled for the sheriff. His blue jumpsuit bore a yellow stenciled Lincoln County logo on the back.

"I don't have all day, Parker. Where the hell are you?" Trace walked out of the house and signaled us to join him.

The grumpy visitor turned and looked me up and down. "Is this the judge?"

"Judge Thorn, this is Doc Mason, our county medical examiner. Doc, Judge Sylvia Thorn. And this is her brother, Willie. Their dad owned this farm when they were kids. Willie found Clay's body, and when he tried to tell Stoney what he'd seen, he was written up as a vagrant and dumped off at the county hospital."

"Why the hell did Stoney do that?"

"I don't know. I suspended him, but…well…"

As Willie and I shook hands with Doc Mason, Willie interrupted Trace to mention the bit of bone we'd found in the shed. Trace and the medical examiner exchanged a glance as Doc Mason pulled a couple of small, clear plastic bags out of his pocket.

"Is that significant?" I said.

"Remember the bits of glass we found by Clay's body?" asked Trace.

I saw Willie's nod out of the corner of my eye.

"Shattered test tubes," Mason said, "mixed with dirt and other particles. Taylor had apparently taken soil samples, probably in the vicinity of the drainage ditch. We scooped up the glass and everything around it and bagged it for analysis. The visual and microscopic exams indicate bits of bone in the samples. Hopefully, the lab in Springfield can give us more detailed results. Identify the particles as well as their age. Collect other clues from the soil. And maybe help us figure out what Clay Taylor hoped to find."

"Did the lab say how long it would take?"

"They won't make a firm commitment on the final report, but we'll get preliminary results by the end of next week."

I was disappointed. I'd hoped Clay's murder would be solved before we returned to Florida, but I couldn't delay my return, not even if Willie—or both of us—might have to come back later as witnesses. For now, I had a courtroom and a full docket of cases waiting, and there was the new storm on its way to the Caribbean. We had a lot to do at home.

Suddenly I felt exhausted. My afternoon had been fueled by periodic bursts of adrenaline, and now that they had been rendered unnecessary, I felt drained. I walked over and sat down on a cement block. Doc Mason returned from the shed with his evidence, dropped it into his black bag, and proceeded toward the house. I thought about the lock on the sliding door into the parlor and wondered if it had been smashed in or carefully pried free, but didn't care enough to go see for myself.

No way would I go anywhere near that body!

After Trace followed the medical examiner into the house, Willie and Lou came over and sat beside me, on the ground. We were silent for a few minutes while I thought about my adventure with Lou in the root cellar. But questions popped into my reverie like the insistent thoughts that intrude on my occasional attempts at meditation.

"Lou, I read in the newspaper that you and Clay disagreed about taking some land out of agricultural production and converting it to prairie. Was the article referring to this farm?"

"Yep. It runs along the drainage ditch, out to the road on the east, and south to my property line. Includes all these buildings, of course."

"But this farm belongs to Mrs. Taylor, doesn't it?"

"Oh, yeah. She fought him tooth and nail."

"Because the landowners around here, you and Marella Taylor for instance, wanted the land available for residential subdivisions?"

"The newspaper got it wrong, Sylvia. Or should I call you Judge Thorn?"

"Sylvia's fine. How'd the newspaper get it wrong?"

"Marella wanted to develop her property for commercial use. I heard rumors that she was prepared to sell the whole farm to a fertilizer company, so I planned to fight that battle, as well. What kind of idiot wants to take good farmland and cover it with a factory and a big parking lot, or streets and houses, bring in all the traffic, kids tromping all over the place? Crazy idea. Irresponsible. Probably against the law.

"My spread has been in my family since the early eighteen hundreds, so I have no intention of allowing anything to interfere with how I use it. I'm paying Brian Kelso a lot of money to pull the facts together. He's a little twerp, but he does know the law."

"So, if you're opposed to commercial or residential development, why would you object to a natural area? Prairie grass and wildflowers?"

"Almost the same reasons. Takes good farmland and makes it useless to farmers. First they restore the prairie grass and the flowers and attract pesky wildlife like Canadian geese, and then they decide they have to let the public in to enjoy the wonders of nature, so they add a big parking area, some public restrooms. Somebody else comes up with the bright idea of adding rustic campsites. Then the campers decide they need electric hookups, modern restrooms, and showers and laundry facilities.

"To protect the vegetation, naturalists demand hiking trails that run right up next to my fields or pastures, so the next thing you know I have to spend a fortune putting up bigger and stronger fences. Then I have to increase my insurance to cover the fools who get hurt when they sneak in to make crop circles in my cornfield or when they taunt my Angus bull who's meaner than hell and hates kids even worse than he hates fools."

"I guess you have a point."

"You're damned right I have a point. But I couldn't get Clay to see it. He's definitely…was definitely the most bullheaded man I've ever known. I'd given up talking to him and counted on Kelso to fix the problem."

"Fix the problem," I repeated.

"Oh, don't get any funny ideas about Kelso. He's a pain in the rear end, but he's a stickler for the law and wouldn't jaywalk if his life depended on it. He's a barracuda in the courtroom, but he's not likely to do anything that would jeopardize his career or his future. The little worm plans to run for office someday, so he'll keep his reputation squeaky clean. No one will ever find anything to gossip about, and he sure as hell wouldn't kill anybody."

"Narrows the options, doesn't it? Especially knowing Wayne and Marella were responsible for shoving the two of us into the cellar. What I can't figure out, though, is why they killed Morris, assuming that's his body in there. He locked me up in the toolshed in the first place. He must have been part of all this."

Lou shrugged. "Maybe he tried a little blackmail."

Willie had listened quietly up to that point, but the mention of Morris piqued his interest. "What about Stoney?" Willie asked. "How long did he work for the sheriff's office? How'd he get a job in law enforcement in the first place?"

"Stoney always seemed harmless," Lou said. "When Parker was elected, he kept all the deputies on the payroll and tried to upgrade systems and procedures as he went along. All his improvements were well-publicized. He set up a rotation program for deputies to take refresher courses. He reviewed all personnel records. I guess Morris came out of it okay. If the sheriff ever suspected one of his deputies was up to something illegal, he sure never let it get into the newspapers. And unless something really bad happens, those guys don't get fired. They get retired."

Lou came back with questions of her own. "Why do you suppose Wayne and Marella didn't kill us? Why would they just lock us up?"

"I don't know. Unless they expected us to die down in that hole."

"Probably had to figure out some way to dispose of the bodies," said Willie. "I couldn't understand why they didn't kill both of you, leave you in the house, and then burn it down. That would take care of the deputy's body, too. Maybe it's what they planned to do. Probably had to go get gasoline and matches."

That was a sobering thought. Lou and I gave Willie dirty looks to discourage any further speculation along those lines. I'd run out of questions for the moment. We sat quietly and waited for Trace and the medical examiner to bring the corpse out. When we finally heard their voices, we stood up and stepped back from the house so we wouldn't be in the way.

Trace and Doc Mason came out first. They were

followed by two deputies who effortlessly carried the stretcher on which the bagged bulky figure was to make its trip to the morgue. The deputies swept past us, headed for the medical examiner's van in the driveway, but Doc Mason stopped beside the sheriff.

"Is it Stoney Morris?" I asked.

"Yes," Trace answered, then shook his head as if he still didn't believe it.

"Anything else on the body? Or in the parlor?"

"The only things Stoney had on him besides his clothes were his wallet and badge and an empty holster. But I guess you know about the empty holster."

Trace raised his eyebrows and waited for me to answer. I stood there like an idiot for a minute, wondering how on earth he could have known I took Stoney's gun. I nodded yes in answer to his question. He glanced over at Willie and they exchanged a look that left me even more confused.

Unless… I looked at Willie. He shrugged his shoulders and turned his attention back to the sheriff.

"The parlor had been emptied very recently," Trace continued. "There were scuff marks across the floor. The only things we found in the room were one small chunk of metal with some chip marks on it, and a piece of glass…well, more like a piece of a flowerpot. We've bagged both samples for the lab."

"Could we see them?" Willie said.

"Sure."

Doc Mason pulled the two specimens from his bag and handed them to Trace, then stood and watched us study the items. Something picked at my memory but didn't turn into a complete thought. Willie perked up and leaned forward for a closer look, but Lou Branson shrugged and stepped back.

"Sheriff, am I free to go?" she asked. "I need to head back to my place and check on my horse."

"Sure, Ms. Branson. I know where to find you if I need anything."

"By the way, in case you run across Wayne or Marella, one of them has my shotgun. Belonged to my father. I'd like to have it back."

"We'll keep it in mind. But you know…if one of them uses it while committing a crime…."

Lou sighed. "I know."

She turned to me and offered her hand. "Judge Thorn… Sylvia…I can't say this experience has been a pleasure. If you get back up this way again, perhaps we can try something a little different. Maybe clean the stables, or repair a fence."

I shook her hand and responded with a serious nod. "Or you could come down to Florida," I suggested, "and we could spray for cockroaches or clean tar balls off the beach."

"Definitely sounds like we could be friends. So long, Willie, Sheriff, Doc."

She nodded toward the three men and walked toward her Explorer. A tiny frown wrinkled Trace's forehead as he watched her start her car and back out of the driveway. I had the distinct impression he still had questions for Lou Branson, but it looked as if Willie and I were going to miss out on the interview.

Doc Mason said, "I'm outta here, too, Sheriff. As soon as we get anything useful from the body or any of the evidence we've picked up, I'll be in touch. Nice to meet you folks."

We watched as Mason and the deputies loaded the stretcher into the van, secured the doors, climbed into their vehicles, and left.

The one car remaining in the driveway belonged to Sheriff Trace Parker.

"What now, Trace? I guess finding Wayne Puckett and Marella Taylor is pretty high on your priority list. And there has to be at least one other man. While I was in the crawl space of the house, Wayne came back with a truck and a driver, and they pulled all the hay out of the cellar. They left together, and as far as I know the other man never came back. When Wayne returned, he came with Marella, or at least they arrived at the same time. They must have been in touch with each other."

"That's new information, Sylvia. What else happened before Willie and I arrived?"

"That's the biggest thing, besides Morris getting shot, and Wayne and Marella teaming up against Lou and me. Why did Wayne bring a truck back here to get the hay when he knew he'd stashed a dead body under the house? He must have thought I was gone. And what could be so important about those bales of hay? Why store them underground? Where would they take them?"

"I need to call this in and get it added to the APBs I already have out on Puckett and Taylor. I don't suppose you have a license number for the truck? I guess not," he said, as he saw the expression on my dirty face.

Trace walked out to his car and climbed in. He spent a good five minutes on his radio before returning. "They don't have anything on Wayne or Marella yet, but they did find your vehicle, Judge Thorn. It was parked in the lot behind the old church on Bondville Road, sitting square behind Clay's car. They couldn't find any damage, and the keys were in the ignition. They were going to impound it and have it towed back to town, but I don't think that's necessary. They checked it over and looked in the trunk. It looks clean."

"We can have it now?"

"Sure. I asked one of the deputies to drive it back here

for you. Shouldn't be more than twenty or thirty minutes. I can wait here with you—"

"No. You don't need to do that. It's unlikely anyone will return now. They've had time to drive halfway to Chicago."

"I'll leave my personal cell phone with you in case my deputy gets delayed or something else happens. You can bring it to the office before you go to your hotel. You'll have to provide a full statement when you come in, everything you saw and heard before Willie and I arrived."

"Thanks, Sheriff. We'll see you later then."

"My pleasure, Judge Thorn."

Everything nice and formal. Rats.

TWENTY

TRACE TOOK HIS time leaving, which may have been intentional. I don't think he was comfortable leaving Willie and me on our own. If Marella or Wayne did return, as foolish as it might be, they would easily overwhelm us with all those weapons. In addition to what they carried originally, they were now in possession of Stoney's .38 and Lou's shotgun.

I told Trace what little more I could remember about the driver who helped Wayne Puckett while I hid in the cobwebs and dirt of the crawl space. I also suggested he tell the medical examiner I'd whacked the deputy with a posthole digger when I escaped the shed. It might save them some work trying to figure out how he got those particular cuts and bruises.

A cloud of dust appeared in the distance on the dirt road leading away from the Taylor farm. It sped closer until it became two separate clouds, and they became two cars, the one in front my rental, the second a department vehicle. I glanced at my watch and noted only ten minutes had passed since Trace told us they'd found the car. The deputies had not wasted any time.

Trace went out to meet the two officers and look over the outside and inside of the rental car. He pointed toward the trunk as he talked to the two men, apparently confirming they'd examined the car thoroughly and found nothing useful for their investigation. Then he walked over to meet Willie and me as we came through the gate.

"Keys are in the car. Looks like you have plenty of gas. The officers checked under the hood and under the car to make sure nothing had been tampered with. Even so, drive carefully and be alert to anything that doesn't feel or sound right."

"You think they might have sabotaged the car in some way?"

"No. Just an extra precaution. I know Mack isn't concerned or he wouldn't have driven the car back here, and he certainly wouldn't let me turn it over to you. It's late. You two need to eat and get some sleep. Tomorrow morning is soon enough to stop by my office and give your statements."

"Oh, Trace… Sheriff…your phone. Here…."

"No, keep it until morning. You never know."

Never know what? If he was worried, why didn't he follow us back to town? Or let the deputy drive my rental while Willie and I rode with him? Was this another distancing maneuver?

I opened the gate and looked over my shoulder to make sure Willie followed, but turned back in time to see Trace jump into his car, back out in a rush, and follow the deputies toward town. Both vehicles had their lights flashing. I turned to Willie to comment on the officers' hurried departure, but my brother had wandered off toward a few bits of hay sprinkled across the driveway. From my hiding place under the house, I'd thought the flatbed was probably driven over the fence to get close to the shed. Now I realized the fence remained intact, so maybe the truck had been pulled close to the fence behind the shed and the bales hauled around the far side or carried through the gate. I wondered if they'd used some kind of trolley or two-wheeler, or if they'd lugged them out by hand. There weren't that many bales in the cellar—maybe stacked three high, but certainly not more than four. If there were only twelve, it wouldn't have taken long to load the truck, even if the bales were toted out one at a time.

Willie slowly patrolled the area, back and forth, occasionally using the toe of his boot to move debris aside. Finally, he squatted down and studied something I couldn't see from where I stood. Curious, I walked over to stand behind him and peer over his shoulder.

"What is it, Willie?"

"Not sure. Take a look and see what you think."

I stooped over, propped my hands on my knees, and studied the ground around Willie's feet.

"It's not rocks," I said. "Looks more like the stuff the medical examiner found in the house. Do you have something we can pick it up with?"

Willie nodded and pulled a white handkerchief out of his hip pocket. He unfolded it and carefully picked up the largest piece, then flipped the handkerchief open so the item fell into his palm and the center of the cloth.

"I know what it is," I said with surprise. "I thought the smaller piece in the plastic evidence bag looked familiar."

"Me, too. We saw plenty of these when we were kids, didn't we? How many arrowheads and chunks of pottery did we find over the years?"

"Plenty. Do you suppose that's what this is all about? Indian artifacts?"

"I don't know, Syl. Seems a little far-fetched to think there'd be enough money in these little pieces to provide a motive for murder."

"Maybe not all the pieces are so small. Maybe each one of those bales is a shell. Could be whole pots, arrowheads, tools—"

"Still, how much money would a museum or collector pay? These things aren't that rare."

"Maybe not, but there has to be some kind of connection. Otherwise, the stuff wouldn't be hidden in the root cellar and Wayne Puckett wouldn't take the risk of moving it out of here in such a hurry. He didn't know where I'd gone or what I might see."

Willie wrapped the arrowhead chunk in his handkerchief and stuffed it into his side pocket. "We'll give this to the sheriff tomorrow. Look, Syl, it's getting dark. Even if there is more evidence here, I'm not sure we'd see it. Let's go back to town, get some dinner, and turn in early. I've had enough adventure for today."

"We could come back out here tomorrow. If we don't fly home until Monday, we can meet with Trace early and then have the rest of the day to explore around the drainage ditch and the field that runs up to Lou Branson's property."

"Sounds good to me. As long as we don't run into Mrs. Taylor or that hired man."

Of course, that assumed nothing, or no one, diverted our attention from the plan—a glimpse of something interesting, for instance, as we left the farm and headed the car toward town. That "something," seen out of the corner of my eye, consisted of a few wisps of hay strewn across the road. As I drove on slowly, I scanned the way ahead and what I could see of the grassy patch along the fencerows. Willie glanced at me curiously, but didn't say anything until I paused at the first intersection and gazed straight ahead at the area lit by the car's headlights. I switched briefly to my brights, but still couldn't tell if the truck had gone in that direction.

"What are you looking for, Syl?"

"I think the driver might have spilled some of his cargo. Wondered if we could see more, so we'd know which direction he went."

Willie looked out his side window. "Too dark to see this

way. Turn left so the headlights light up the road. If we don't see anything, you can back around and shine the lights in the other direction."

Edging the car along a few feet to the left revealed nothing. I turned around and drove less than a car length before spotting more hay at the side of the road. "Bales weren't very tight," I said.

Willie nodded. "Probably not bound with baling wire. They could've cut the original wires, hollowed out the bales and filled them, then wrapped them back up with heavy twine."

"If that's the case, Willie, there could be a trail here to follow. But if we find where the truck is, we might also find Wayne Puckett and Marella Taylor."

"Could be. But it's getting dark and we need to keep the lights on. If they're paying attention, they'll be suspicious if they see a car creeping along the road. They'll know right where we are."

"Which wouldn't matter as long as we don't drive right up to their front door. All we have to do is find out where the truck went, and then we call the sheriff and let him handle it."

"We could call him now."

"He won't be there yet. The way they took off with their lights flashing probably means they're out on another call. If it gets windy, the hay'll blow all over the countryside. It'll be impossible to follow the trail. I think we should do it now while we have the chance."

Willie shrugged and gave up, as I knew he would. He might worry about me getting into trouble, but he never hesitated to place himself in danger. Some of his volunteer work put him in the middle of rough neighborhoods from Miami to Delray Beach, in homeless centers where tensions simmered just below the surface, ready to erupt at the least provocation, and Willie waded into the middle of these situations without flinching.

"Here we go, then." I kept the car at creeping speed as we both scanned as much of the road and roadsides as we could see. Occasionally, Willie pointed out the front windshield when he saw something that confirmed we were on the right track. I did the same. We stopped at Route 10, only a mile from where Willie had first met Stoney Morris.

"Do you see anything?" I asked, peering through the windshield. "I don't know if we should cross the highway or turn."

"Just a hunch, Syl, but I think we should turn right."

"There may be more traffic on the main road. I don't want somebody to roar up behind us while we're not paying attention. Should I put on the flashers?"

"Might as well. Flashers could also convince anyone who's watching that we're having car trouble instead of snooping around."

Less than a quarter mile along the highway, we spotted more hay swept to the side and scattered about the area as though one of the bales had fallen off the truck. A few feet beyond the debris lay the entrance into a long driveway that led to a large two-story farmhouse, a red barn, a few wooden sheds, and a couple of metal outbuildings. A blue mailbox on a wooden post stood at the edge of the drive, just far enough off the highway to give the mailman a safe place to stop. The name on the mailbox read "L. Branson." Another small pile of hay had spilled about thirty feet into the driveway.

I drove past the mailbox and scanned the road for more debris, but saw nothing.

"What now?" I muttered.

"The pull-off near the drainage ditch is another quarter

mile or so. Let's turn in there and call the sheriff. Turn off the lights first."

As I expected, Trace hadn't returned to his office. I left a message for him to return the call to his own cell phone, then dropped the phone into one of the cup holders in the carousel between the driver and passenger seats.

"I think we should wait awhile and see if he calls back," Willie said. "We can see the farm and the driveway from here, so we'll know if anyone comes in or goes out."

"And if Trace doesn't call back?"

"I don't know." Willie pressed a button on the side of his watch and the face lit up in a pale green glow, which reflected off his eyes. "It's six-thirty. Let's give him thirty minutes. If we haven't heard from him by then, we'll call and give the information to the desk officer."

The sudden sharp rap of metal against metal sounded all through the car.

I jumped and jerked my head around to look out the side window. My gaze lit on the gun first. Then the grimy hand attached to the gun. Finally, the scrawny face of an outraged Wayne Puckett. He motioned for me to roll down the window, which I could not do.

"Power windows," I shouted.

Puckett grabbed the door and tried to open it. "Unlock the damned door," he yelled back.

"Shit. Willie, is there any chance I can get this car out of here before he shoots both of us?"

"No," Willie said. "Unlock the doors."

I hit the button.

The driver's door jerked open. Puckett leaned over and stuck his head inside, close enough that I could smell the rank body odor of a man who hadn't bathed since God knows when. He held his gun so the barrel ended about two inches from my nose. I resisted the temptation to swat it away from my face, while I concentrated on looking innocent and unconcerned. Hard to do when sweat is popping out on your forehead and your hands are shaking violently.

"What the hell are you doing out here?"

"Something's wrong with our car. We were going to Ms. Branson's to call for a tow truck, but I missed the driveway, so I pulled in here to turn around, but then the engine cut out so we thought we'd wait a few minutes to see if it would start again. If we couldn't get it started, we were going to walk to the house."

I was babbling. Maybe a different approach would be better.

"And what the hell are you doing here?" I said. "Why did you and that crazy witch hit me on the head? The sheriff wants to talk to you!"

I said this real fast and totally on the fly, but before I could pat myself on the back, the shrill ring of Trace Parker's cell phone made me jump again. Maybe stupid panic reactions to unexpected noises are contagious. Puckett reared up and hit his head hard against the top of the door frame. At the same time, the hand holding the revolver dropped. One solid hit with my elbow jammed his arm against the side of the car, and the gun fell to the ground. Puckett yelped and dropped to his knees. He scrambled back and forth in the dark, searching for his gun. The phone continued to ring while I frantically struggled to free myself from the seat belt.

I finally released the damned thing and burst out of the car, ready to jump on Puckett and fight for the gun, but Willie beat me to it. Just as Puckett spotted the weapon in front of the left rear tire, Willie pulled it out with his foot and kicked it so hard it sailed into the drainage ditch. Puckett jumped to his feet and ran after it.

"Get back in the car, Syl. We need to get out of here."

Sounded good to me. Besides, Trace's stupid cell phone kept on ringing. Why the hell didn't he have voice mail?

Willie answered the call while I started the car and backed out onto the highway. I aimed toward town, flipped on the headlights, and pushed my foot down on the accelerator. At the same time, I kept one eye on my rearview mirror, just in case Puckett came up out of the ditch and started shooting. I saw nothing, however, as I sped past Lou Branson's driveway with every intention of getting us back to Sangamon City as fast as possible.

TWENTY-ONE

WILLIE WAVED HIS ARM and pointed to the left. "Turn, turn," he ordered.

I turned left at the next intersection, which also happened to be the road from Route 10 back to the Taylor farm. Willie was still listening to someone on the cell phone, so I slowed the car and checked in all directions to reassure myself that no one followed. The moon wasn't bright enough yet to provide comfortable visibility, so anyone could sneak up on us, just as Wayne Puckett had. I took my foot off the accelerator and switched off the headlights. We coasted to a stop in a world so dark we could have been cruising through outer space. I took my foot off the brake but left the car in Drive, just in case we needed to take off in a hurry.

"Okay…okay…but listen…wait…when?" Willie seemed to be frustrated with the caller. "Nuts! He delivered a message from the sheriff and now he's transferred me to voice mail."

I guess flexibility and initiative weren't required for county administrative personnel.

"Sheriff, this is Willie. I'm still out in the country with Syl. We followed a trail of hay up to Route 10. Looks like the truck went into Ms. Branson's farm. When we pulled off the road at the drainage ditch, we were ambushed by Wayne Puckett who waved a gun at us, but we got away. You need to send some cars out here to the farm and see what's going on. Ms. Branson could be in trouble."

That was a lot of words for Willie. He fiddled with the phone for a couple of seconds. "I can't see anything," he said. "I need to shut off the ringer. Oh, hell, I'll turn the whole thing off."

Oh, hell? Willie never says hell.

"Willie, relax." I reached out and put my hand on his shoulder. "Are you okay?"

"I'm fine. I can't stand these stupid contraptions with their little buttons. There's no way you can use one of these in the dark." He tossed the phone into the carousel. "Forget it. It's off. Let's go."

"Are we going to the Branson place?"

"You bet we are. The law is busy chasing down a hit-and-run driver. By the time the sheriff picks up the message and sends someone out here, these creeps and their evidence could be gone."

"We can't just drive up to the house," I said. "What if we cut through the Taylor field? Wasn't there an access road running along the ditch? When we get to Lou Branson's fence, we can leave the car and hike to the outbuildings."

"What if we run into Puckett again?"

"I'll get the tire iron out of the trunk. I feel like putting a big dent in Wayne Puckett's knuckles. Or his head."

"I worry about you, Syl. People are supposed to mellow as they get older."

"Sorry. Hadn't heard that."

Willie looked back toward the Branson buildings, then along the roads and across the fields. I put my foot on the accelerator and slowly moved forward. This would require every bit of my attention, I thought. It was way too dark to go fast, and the drainage ditch was nearly two miles away. Before long the moon would be high enough and bright enough to reflect off our car. Creeping along the road without headlights would look pretty suspicious.

"Willie, maybe this isn't such a good idea. It'll take too long. Isn't there a way into the Branson fields from this side?"

"Maybe. I was busy looking for hay when we drove this direction so I didn't notice, but it's logical there would be. Look left, and hope we've got enough moonlight to see it."

I kept glancing left, until I saw a hard-packed dirt lane. It had been built over a metal drainpipe which kept rain water flowing through the trench and away from the road. I turned the car into the field and stopped. "We'd better walk from here. It's not very far."

"Probably a quarter mile to the highway. More from there to the Branson place. We'll walk less than a mile, I think. No problem. Better grab the tire iron."

Apparently, Willie didn't intend to wield the weapon. I removed the tire iron from the trunk after a brief struggle with a tightly screwed wing nut, while I tried to ignore Willie's demands for me to hurry. Together, we set out across the field toward the lights of the Branson farm. It was rough going. The field had been harvested and rows of short, stiff stubble stretched into the distance. We needed to travel west and south. Even though the rising moon was now an advantage rather than a disadvantage, what would have been a twenty-minute walk on a city sidewalk took us more than thirty-five.

There was no sign of activity as we approached. An outside fixture on a pole by the barn cast a cone of light toward the house. We came up behind a large metal shed and followed along its east side to the front, which faced the back of the barn. I rounded the corner and stood in the shadows, squinting as I tried to see what lay ahead. I edged forward with shuffling steps, the tire iron thrust out in front of me as I waved it back and forth like a cane. Almost immediately, the iron clanged against metal. At the same time, my chest collided with the corner of the truck's wooden bed.

"Ouch. Shit." I spat the words out between clenched teeth but managed to do it quietly.

Willie heard me, of course. He didn't say anything, but I could imagine his scowl.

"I ran into something," I muttered.

"Are you okay?" Not waiting for an answer, he brushed by me and extended his arms.

My eyes were adjusting to the darkness, so I could now see an expanse of packed gravel between the two buildings, spacious enough for heavy farm equipment. Plenty wide enough to park a flatbed truck and still leave room for other machinery to get through. The truck sat even with, and very close to, the west end of the huge shed. Since it sat in the shadows, it was impossible to see from the highway, or from the Branson driveway, or from the pull-off by the drainage ditch.

Willie stood at the right rear corner of the truck. His hands gripped the wooden side slats. He edged toward the front end with his left hand moving along the boards and his right hand feeling the space between the bed's floor and the side rails. From where I stood, I could see the lighter color of the load on the truck but still couldn't tell whether we'd found the hay bales. When Willie reached the load, however, I knew. As he ran his hand back and forth across the cargo, he made a scratchy uneven sound that eliminated all doubt.

I carefully made my way to his side. "Now what?" I asked. "Shouldn't we check to see if Lou's okay? I could sneak up and look in a window while you pry one of the bales open."

"You won't do anything else? Just look in a window and then come back?"

"Of course."

"You'll be very quiet? And very careful? If you see anyone outside, you won't go any closer?"

"Absolutely."

I heard a little explosion of breath from Willie that strongly suggested skepticism, but I knew he wanted to break into one of those bales, and he also wanted to get away from the Branson farm as soon as possible.

"This won't take long," he whispered. "If you're not back by the time I finish, I'm coming after you."

"Fine."

"Hurry."

Sure. Hurry, but don't fall, don't make any noise, don't let anyone see you, don't get caught, don't, don't, don't.

Meanwhile, I thought ahead to an imaginary run-in with Puckett, and how I'd crack him so hard he'd never stick a gun in my face again. I kept my right hand on the truck as I walked to the back and then across the rear. After that, I was on my own.

With my arms stretched out in front at chest level, the tire iron grasped firmly in my right hand, I moved slowly but steadily toward the barn. From there, I had better light from the moon as I trotted toward the front of the building and stopped to peer around the corner.

Now I had a problem. The barnyard was well lit, as was the yard between a white picket fence and the back porch. If I wanted to peek in the windows, I had to cross this lighted area and risk being seen, or I had to go all the way around the barn to the west end and work my way from chicken house to garage to toolshed, until I reached the front of the house which faced the highway. The least little noise would alarm the chickens. I might as well stand in the middle of the yard and bang my tire iron on somebody's car.

The porch door opened and Wayne Puckett graciously solved my problem. I froze and shrunk back against the side of the barn. Puckett slammed the door and ran down the steps, his pistol held out in front of him. If he headed toward the truck, and if Willie didn't hear him, then Willie could be in trouble. While I tried to decide whether I should chase Puckett down with the tire iron, or just create a big diversion, the little jerk started yelling at the top of his lungs.

"Come on out, you old bitch. I know you're here. If you don't come out, I'll search every goddamned building on the farm."

Is he talking to me?

"By God, I'll shoot that horse of yours if you don't come out here right now."

Guess not.

At least I no longer had to worry about him taking Willie by surprise. The chickens squawked in terror and the horse whinnied nervously as though it understood every word of Puckett's threat.

He continued to storm toward the front of the barn. I waited in the shadows, hoping he'd go inside to search the downstairs and haymow before moving on to the other buildings. I planned to sneak back to the truck and join Willie while Puckett was occupied, so the second he went inside, I turned around—and ran smack into my brother, nearly knocking him down.

Motioning Willie back, I whispered, "Go, go."

He led the way past the barn, toward the truck, and on around the back of the shed. There he stopped short and I nearly bowled him over again.

"What about Ms. Branson?" he asked. "What if he finds her? Will he kill her? We can't just leave her here."

"I know. We'll have to trap him, somehow. If you go around one way and I come up behind him…"

The discussion and the need for drastic action ended when the truck's engine roared to life, around the corner from where Willie and I stood. We both ducked back to the shelter of the outside wall and crouched down as the truck's driver ground the gears and drove away. The truck rounded the west end of the shed. Wayne Puckett sat in the driver's seat, his face clearly visible as he struck a match on the steering wheel and lit his cigarette. He drove away in the direction of the field road which led along the drainage ditch toward the Taylor farm, and he showed no sign of knowing that Willie and I were watching.

"Let's go look for Ms. Branson," Willie whispered. "Stay against the wall but get around the corner fast."

"Okay. Where should we go first?"

"To the barn. See if the horse is there." Willie was right on. As soon as we rounded the corner, we saw Lou coming out of the barn with a small rifle held at her side. She jumped and jerked the gun up when she saw us, then dropped it down again as soon as she realized who we were.

"Are you okay?" I asked.

"Yeah. Is Wayne gone?" She looked around as though she expected him to reappear at any moment.

"He drove the truck away, toward the northwest. Where did he go?"

"I think he'll dump the hay and get rid of the truck. I have to get inside and call the cops." She looked from me to Willie and back at me. "What are you two doing here?"

"We saw the trail of hay from the Taylor place," I said. "Got worried you might be in danger."

"Where's your car?"

"Back on the north-south road on the east side of your farm. We walked across the field."

"You want me to drive you there? It'll only take a minute to make this call."

I looked at Willie. He shrugged. "We can walk back," he said. "But what about you? What if Puckett shows up again?"

"He won't come back. When he yelled those threats, he

was bluffing. He knew I'd stick close to my horse and give him time to get away. I think he has his pickup stashed somewhere else, maybe where he plans to leave the truck. The deputy's car is gone, too."

"Then Marella brought him here?" I asked.

"Yeah. She cruised in like she didn't have a worry in the world, dumped Wayne at his trailer, and drove away. Wasn't more than thirty minutes ago. As soon as I saw her leave, I grabbed my rifle and ran to the barn. I hid behind the straw at the front of the haymow and waited to pick Wayne off if he came inside. I didn't come down until I heard the truck leave."

She backed away as she talked, her urgent desire to call the authorities beginning to show. It was the right thing to do, of course. Even though Willie had left a message for the sheriff, a pressing call from Lou Branson might speed up the process. We waved her on her way, then retraced our own steps from the buildings to the field. Puckett and his truck were visible only as tiny lights in the distance. We felt quite safe moving across the open space to get to our car.

The walk progressed more quickly now that we knew how to adjust our strides to navigate the rows of stubble. We crossed the field in twenty-five minutes without falling or turning an ankle on the rough ground. I'd watched for car headlights but saw none, so it was an unpleasant surprise to find Marella Taylor's car pulled sideways behind ours. Marella leaned against our hood with a .38 pointed at my chest. I pulled the tire iron in close to my side.

I was getting awfully tired of people pointing guns at me. "Crap, crap, crap," I muttered.

"Ditto," said Willie.

"My, my, what have we here?" Marella said. "Been out for an evening stroll?"

It didn't sound like a friendly query. My mind whirled

with questions of my own. If this woman wanted to kill us, wouldn't she have shot us from her car and then kept on going? Maybe she'll call the sheriff and report us for trespassing. Stupid thought. She was already in trouble up to her eyeballs because of her presence at the farm with Puckett. Let's see. Assault with a deadly weapon, unlawful imprisonment…I knew I could think of more if I had the time.

Marella kept her gun pointed at me while she walked to her car and opened the trunk. She waved us over, slowly backing away as we took a couple of tentative steps forward. "Get in there," she ordered, pointing.

"Both of us?" I peeked into the BMW's trunk and tried to imagine both Willie and me scrunched into that space. Unh-unh. This wasn't going to work. No way would I would climb in there.

Willie must have reached the same conclusion, because he bumped my shoulder hard as he leaped past and ran at Marella in a zigzagging motion. She waved the gun back and forth in an effort to track him, while I, unable to regain my balance, stumbled and fell on my ass. I somehow managed to keep my grip on the iron as I hit the ground. When I heard Marella fire her gun, I jumped to my feet and ran around the front of the BMW. Willie still moved erratically in her direction, and now I placed myself in position to close on her from behind.

When Marella was less than three feet from me, she abruptly flew out of my reach, sailing past with Willie's arms wrapped around her knees. She landed on her back, and the breath *whoosh*ed out of her lungs a split second before her head cracked against the ground. The gun flew out of her hand and dropped at my feet. I reached down and picked it up, then peered closely at it in the moonlight.

It was the same .38 I'd borrowed from Stoney Morris earlier.

"Nice tackle, Willie."

"Didn't want to get in the trunk." He struggled to his feet, then took hold of Marella's ankles and pulled her closer to her car.

"Stop, Willie. She'll have gravel burns all over her arms."

"Okay. Help me lift her," he said.

"You're going to put her in the trunk?" My turn to raise my eyebrows. She must have really made Willie mad.

"No, 'we' are going to put her in the trunk. 'We' need her keys before we put her there. Did she drop them? Check her pockets." Willie talked fast, clipping his words.

I calmed my own movements and slowed my breathing as I searched for the car keys, hoping Willie would tune in to the change and relax. "Here we go," I chirped. "I'm putting them in my pocket. Wait a minute. Let me check to make sure she's okay." I put my hand on Marella's chest, then checked her pulse. Using both hands, I felt the back of her head and arms to make sure she wasn't bleeding. She seemed fine, if you didn't count being out cold.

"I think she'll be okay," I said, "but we can't leave her here. She might have a concussion. We have to take her to a hospital."

Willie didn't say anything, but I could practically hear his internal debate. Finally, he sighed and shrugged his shoulders. "In the backseat?"

"Yes," I said, grateful for his change of heart. "Make sure you don't hit her head again." After placing Stoney's gun in the trunk of the BMW, I directed Willie to lift Marella's shoulders while I held her knees. We carefully scooted her limp body across the seat.

"Can we get out without moving her car?" Willie asked.

"I don't think so. I'll pull hers forward. We'll take the

keys with us and give them to Trace. You better turn his phone back on. We need to place a 9-1-1 call on the record, and we can get directions to the nearest trauma center."

On my way to the driver's side of Marella's car, I saw the headlights of two fast-moving vehicles on the road from the Taylor farm.

Wayne Puckett had gone west, I thought. Who would be traveling east? Would they turn south toward us at the intersection?

"Willie. Hurry. Cars coming."

I jumped into the BMW and started the ignition. The damned daytime headlights came on all by themselves, and before I'd finished moving the car forward, the driving lights popped on. I slammed the car into Park and turned it off to kill the lights. I jumped out and raced toward my rental car as I pulled its keys out of my pocket. Willie beat me to the car, climbed in the passenger seat, and threw the driver's door open. I tossed Marella's keys into his lap with my left hand while I jammed the rental's key in the ignition with my right.

The car started, slammed into Reverse, screeched out to the road, popped into Drive, and accelerated rapidly toward Route 10. I think I might have contributed to all the car action, but it happened so fast and so automatically I can't remember any conscious thought involved. As I sped toward the highway, I glanced in the rearview mirror and saw the two sets of headlights had indeed turned south and now raced to close the distance between us.

The stop sign at Route 10 didn't faze me. I quickly looked both ways to make sure there was no oncoming traffic, barely slowing as I swerved onto the highway. One more look back confirmed both vehicles were stopped by Marella Taylor's car.

Thank you, thank you, and thank you. "You okay, Willie?"

"Yeah. But…"

"What?"

"Syl, you don't have your seat belt fastened."

Yeah, Willie was okay.

This time we actually made it back to town without being ambushed, followed, or tempted to do any more sleuthing on our own.

We followed the 9-1-1 directions and made our way to Sangamon Hospital. Marella complained of a headache when she came to, just as we pulled up to the emergency room doors. She had plenty of time to come up with a good story for the city policemen who met us at the door, and I didn't want to take a chance on what she might say. We referred the officers to the sheriff's department and made a fast exit.

TWENTY-TWO

As much as I wanted to stop for food, I wanted even more to huddle in the safety of Trace Parker's office until the county had all the bad guys and girls tucked behind bars. I even looked forward to visiting the vending machines. Hopefully, one of them would dispense martinis.

"There are sandwiches, soups…" Willie was at it again.

"I know, but I hoped…"

"I know."

"Willie…"

"Do you think…" We spoke at the same time then stopped and waited. I let Willie start.

"Do you think Ms. Branson is as innocent in all this as she claims to be?"

I thought about it for a minute. "Why do you ask?"

"Because she ended up down in the cellar with you, but she never mentioned getting hit on the head, and I didn't see anything to prove she'd been trussed up with duct tape, even though she told you she was."

I thought a little more about Lou Branson. If her farm had been in her family for as many years as she said, why had Willie and I never run into her? We'd been neighbors, and she had to be about Willie's age. "Did you know her? Did she go to school with you?"

"I knew who she was. Kinda snooty, sometimes. Even now, it's like she has two separate personalities. One, the fine lady from an old family, and the other, the down-to-earth farmer in overalls and boots. Makes you wonder."

I nodded. "Did you hear Lou tell me about the land-use controversy? She opposes all types of development, and she said she'd heard a rumor Marella wanted to sell to a company that intended to build a fertilizer plant. If those plans are in the works, if zoning variances are required, maybe this is about bribes. Didn't someone say Marella's father dealt in some shady business in Chicago?"

"Yes. But maybe Ms. Branson doled out the bribes. Or the lawyer."

Since I knew Willie thought Marella Taylor was the most likely suspect, I couldn't understand why he kept returning to Lou and her lawyer. "Regardless," I insisted, "everything gets us back to the land-use conflict. Over two hundred acres of farmland. Didn't seem like such a gold mine when we were kids."

This time he nodded.

"Okay, let me see if I understand this," I continued. "Clay wanted the county land development board to establish a nature preserve on his wife's land, specifically a prairie grass preserve, presumably because the soil is perfectly suited to cultivation of native grasses. That's why the stands you saw had been planted along the ditch…as part of Clay's testing. Marella found out about it and knew the little deal between her and her father was about to go down the drain. If Clay succeeded, her land would be reclassified and purchased by the board. Someone pulled up the grass when they dumped the body by the ditch because he or she didn't want to call attention to the test plot."

I thought for a minute. "But there's too much missing, Willie. What about the business with the bales? There'd be no reason to hide clumps of prairie grass inside bales of hay."

"Oh. I forgot to tell you." He unfastened his seat belt, reached into his pocket, pulled out his crumpled handkerchief, and gently folded back the edges.

I glanced at his hand but it was too dark to see. "What is it?"

"A sample of what they're hiding in the bales."

"Which is?"

"Indian artifacts. Kickapoo, as a matter of fact."

"Willie—"

"Okay. Besides the chunk we found earlier, I now have a whole perfect arrowhead. Not actually distinguishable as Kickapoo, but an excellent specimen. This other thing is a piece from a broken seed pot painted with religious symbols. I took one of the small sections, but it'll fit back into the whole like a piece of a jigsaw puzzle. One of the recognizable drawings on the pot is a prayer stick like the ones created by Kenekuk, the Kickapoo Prophet."

"I've never heard of Kenekuk. Was he a chief?"

"A chief who created a new religion. He took beliefs about the Great Spirit and mixed them with teachings from the Christian bible. His message to his people included peace, harmony, and co-existence with the white man. It worked for a while, bought them a little time, but eventually his tribe moved out of Illinois and across the Mississippi River, just like the rest of the Kickapoo."

Willie can be extremely voluble when he gets a chance to talk about one of his special interests.

"They lived in this area?" I asked. Well, of course they did, why else would there be a Kickapoo State Park east of Sangamon City, close to the Indiana state line?

"Wisconsin, Indiana, Illinois…there's a site by Leroy where the Kickapoo held a powwow at least once. And here's the other thing. There's an ongoing dispute in several parts of the country—Native American tribes versus landowners. There are still lawsuits pending."

"The tribes want their land back. I heard about that."

"The land or compensation. Sometimes they're satisfied if they get a piece of property, plus whatever zoning variances are required, to build a casino. That's what they want in the Denver area. I don't know if the Kickapoo are involved in any of these suits, but I do know they didn't get fair treatment back in the eighteen hundreds."

"But, Willie, they shouldn't have a claim against local landowners. These aren't the people who forced the Indians off their land. Their claims should be filed against agencies of the federal government."

"I agree. But they've been unsuccessful over the years in collecting their monies from the feds. But that isn't relevant in the case of our two hundred acres. What does matter is the size of the find. Might be enough to get the land protected from any kind of development, including a nature preserve. Everything will stop and a truckload of archaeologists will appear faster than you can say 'Indiana Jones.' If the dig turns up human bones, as in Indian burial mounds, this land will be designated sacred ground. No ones digs, no one builds, no one plants."

"Ah. So the samples Clay had in the test tubes?"

"Contained artifact fragments, or possibly bone."

"That would have alarmed Lou as much as it would Marella and her father. Do you suppose she found out about it? Maybe she went out with the idea of yanking up clumps of prairie grass and found some arrowheads, saw Clay taking samples by the ditch and…oh, surely not. I can imagine her pulling up the grass, even hiding knowledge of an archaeological discovery, but I don't believe for a minute she would kill someone…"

The image of Lou toting her shotgun and her two

separate threats to shoot Wayne Puckett stopped me from defending her any further. I really didn't know what Lou Branson might do to protect her land, or to safeguard plans for future development.

"Willie, we could be in a lot of trouble here, even after we go back home. Lou Branson, Marella Taylor, Wayne Puckett—we don't know what any of them might have done, or how far they'll go to protect themselves."

"You're right. We know very little. Both Ms. Branson and Mrs. Taylor could pin the murders on Wayne Puckett, especially if he leaves town. They can also blame him and his unknown accomplice for the theft and concealment of the artifacts."

"Plus, Marella was within her legal rights to confront Lou and me for trespassing on her property. She can claim she didn't know anything about us getting tossed in the root cellar because she'd already left the farm before Wayne whacked me on the head. If I were to say anything different, then she could blame my head injury and say my memory was impaired. Trace is going to have a rough time getting anybody but Wayne Puckett behind bars, and that's only going to happen if he finds Puckett alive."

"I don't think Mrs. Taylor will waste her time on us. It's our word against hers, so all she has to do is come up with a logical explanation for her behavior. Puckett will disappear, either on his own or with help. And Ms. Branson—"

"Has a lawyer who's 'a barracuda in the courtroom' with a 'squeaky clean reputation.' Brian Kelso is probably all the protection she needs, unless someone actually saw her do something to Clay."

"Exactly."

Even though I'd been assured by Willie that he and I were in no physical danger, I still rejoiced when we pulled into the parking lot of the county building. I thought that once we made and signed our statements, there was little more we could do to threaten the people involved in the case. Hopefully, we would be out of town or back home before anything else happened. I didn't particularly want to see the old farm dug up for a fertilizer plant, or a parking lot, or even an archaeological dig. I'd rather remember it the way it used to be…home.

We sat in the lobby for over an hour before a weary Trace Parker showed up. As soon as he found out we planned to head for the airport the next morning and wait standby for the first available flight, he was all business.

Ah, yes, keep your distance, Trace. Don't take any risks.

We signed our statements, discussed the unlikely possibility we would be subpoenaed as witnesses for someone's prosecution, and started to leave Trace's office. At the last second, I turned back, flashed my nicest smile, and winked. "Bye, Trace." I waggled my fingers at him and walked out the door—and collided with a deputy who hurriedly apologized, then squeezed past us and rushed into Trace's office.

"Sheriff, you better come out here. There's a bunch of people in the lobby and they don't seem to be getting along too well. Mrs. Taylor's father is one of them."

Trace groaned and pushed himself out of his chair. He made eye contact with me as he hurried by. "Wait here," he ordered.

Great! My grand exit spoiled. I glanced at my watch. Nearly midnight. If Willie and I didn't return to the motel and get some sleep, we'd never be able to catch an early flight out of Indianapolis. It took at least two hours to drive, and the rental car had to be returned. I leaned against the wall and closed my eyes. *Food. Exactly what I need.*

When Trace ordered me to "wait here," I thought he

meant stay in the building, or the immediate area. He certainly wouldn't care if I bought a sandwich and a bottle of water. *Wimpy,* I told myself. To tell the truth, I didn't give a rat's ass if he cared or not. I charged down the hall and into the break room, pulling dollar bills out of my pocket as I ran. Willie could come along if he wanted. I needed food.

The choices were egg salad, egg salad, and egg salad, something I liked only marginally better than calamari or raw oysters. I won't claim the sandwich tasted heavenly, but it was better than nothing. I bought a bottle of water to wash it all down, then started perusing the contents of the other vending machines as I tried to decide whether I'd prefer salt or sugar. Sugar won. Miniature peanut butter balls dipped in chocolate. Now I was happy.

When I'd advanced far enough along in my feeding frenzy to check on Willie, I saw he had a cup of chicken noodle soup and an oatmeal raisin cookie. I rolled my eyes and peeled the red foil wrapper from another ball, popped it in my mouth, savored the chocolate as it melted on my tongue, and sighed at the explosion of nutty flavor from the candy's center.

In a few minutes Trace stuck his head in the door. "All clear. You two can leave now." He turned to walk away, the big jerk, without saying anything about the commotion in the lobby.

"Wait, Trace. Did Marella's father really come here? What happened?"

"He came in to report his daughter missing. Says they found her car out in the country with the trunk lid and the driver's door open, a gun in the trunk. There were no keys and no sign of Marella."

"Oops." Willie dug down in the pocket of his jeans and pulled out the car keys. He handed them to Trace. "Syl's fingerprints will be all over Marella's car. Mine, too."

"I know. Mr. Vortinto didn't pursue the issue after I told him you'd taken Marella to the hospital. If they're worried about you as witnesses, they can always claim you were trespassing and Marella confronted you. Charging you with assault would only open up a can of worms since she had a gun and appeared to be dangerous. I suspect we won't see or hear anything more from either one of them.

"Ms. Branson came in, as well. She says Wayne threatened to kill her, but then he took off across the fields with a flatbed truck. She wants to file charges against him for using her property to hide a stolen truck, or death threats, or whatever might stick. She claims she doesn't know what he's up to, but thinks he might have murdered Taylor and my deputy. We already have an APB out on Wayne."

Trace pointed down the hall toward the lobby, effectively cutting off my questions about Marella's father and the fact his name was Vortinto, a well-known Jersey family with some very unsavory connections.

"You two get out of here," Trace said. "You've done all you can do. Have a safe trip home. With any luck, the next time I see you, I'll be on my annual Florida vacation. Do you like deep-sea fishing, Syl?"

Wow. Look at that warm smile, I thought. "I haven't been fishing in years," I said. "It would be great, Trace. I'll look forward to seeing you."

TWENTY-THREE

AFTER THE COOL, dry Illinois weather, the humidity of South Florida in September felt like a slap in the face with a hot, wet towel. It always seemed harder to breathe in the thick, heavy air after a trip to northern states. In January and February I would be grateful I wasn't traipsing through the dirty-slush aftermath of a Midwestern snowstorm, or bundling up against wind chills that penetrated to the bone. But right now I longed for a fall breeze perfumed with a hint of burning leaves, a glass of raw apple cider, and Chief Illiniwek bursting past the band to the enthusiastic applause of U of I football fans.

Willie and I had picked up an early flight to Fort Lauderdale. Since my car sat at the airport in West Palm Beach, we wasted a couple of hours shuttling from Fort Lauderdale to West Palm and then backtracking to Boca Raton. I dropped Willie off at his apartment after he declined my offer to take him grocery shopping. I think he was tired of the constant company and looked forward to some peace and quiet. There were plenty of restaurants as well as a large market within walking distance of his place, so there was no danger he'd starve.

An evening of solitude sounded good to me, as well. My condo is in a gated community on a system of canals and waterways feeding into the Atlantic Ocean, allowing convenient access for the residents who own sailboats. Private patios and balconies face the canal, but it's impossible to enjoy this beautiful outdoor paradise, especially at dusk, unless you slather yourself with the smelly gunk that repels no-see-ums and mosquitoes.

A mile farther south, in an even more secluded and guarded complex, the multimillion-dollar homes are palatial, and residents tie their yachts to docks a few hundred feet from their back doors. The rich folks do have their problems, however. They still have to fight bugs, which have no conscience about attacking the rich and the famous. And the super-privileged must be cautious about approaching their neighbors. The new guy on the block could easily be a football hero, a notorious rock star, a nice genius who made a fortune in dot.coms, a successful drug dealer, or an embezzler.

Most of the year it's too hot to leave the windows open. The sun is the enemy, air-conditioning the friend. As a result, life in South Florida can be claustrophobic—a little like living in a cave. Whenever possible, I take the fifteen-minute walk to the beach and wander along the surf. Ocean breezes keep the bugs away and offer the illusion of moderate temperatures. There are some minor inconveniences: little balls of tar squishing up between your toes; jellyfish or men-of-war abandoned on the sand by the incoming tide; and used hypodermic needles and broken beer bottles. It pays to be alert, to slip your shoes back on at the first signs of dusk. And you probably shouldn't be out alone on the beach at dusk, anyway. Even in Boca.

It was good to be home in spite of the fact that Palm Beach County sat in the center of the next hurricane's most likely path. I still had a few days before I'd have to deal with it. The worst things I faced immediately included an overcrowded docket, a slew of motions presented by bored lawyers, and several chronic lawbreakers who always got caught, sent to jail, paroled, caught again, etc.,

etc., etc. No spider-infested crawl spaces, no guns pointed at my nose, no dead bodies. It felt good to escape the nightmare.

I deliberated a long two minutes on whether I should start up my computer and try to access the new database, just for practice. Then I rejected the idea as obsessive. A little relaxation was in order. One glass of Riesling, a slice of cheddar cheese, one chocolate truffle, a new China Bayles mystery, and a long soak in a tub full of lavender-scented bubbles. Heavenly.

I did wonder, however, what had happened in Illinois after Willie and I returned to Florida. My curiosity finally forced me to phone Trace on Tuesday morning and ask him.

"I was about to call you," he said.

"Why? Did something happen?"

"Little bit. We located the flatbed, abandoned behind the Bondville church. Same place we found your rental car earlier. When we traced the plates, we found the truck on the stolen vehicle list. No surprise there. The bales were gone, as expected. Eventually, we discovered loose hay on the ground around a gravel pit a mile north of the church, close to the interstate."

"Did you drag the pit?"

"It's too deep. If the bales are on the bottom, they may be lost forever. We'll know more about that in a few days."

"Did you find Wayne Puckett?"

"Not exactly. We did find his pickup truck, parked behind his trailer. There was blood on two of the things he'd left in the back of the truck—a spade and a tarpaulin. Doc Mason has gone to work on them, but hasn't called me with any results yet."

"So the blood could be Clay's."

"Or Wayne's. Or Stoney's, for that matter."

"But Stoney was shot."

"After receiving a hard blow to the back of his skull, totally separate from the little whack you gave him with the posthole digger. We think he hit his head on one of the cement blocks at the farmhouse, but Doc hasn't had the spade long enough to rule it out completely."

"But you haven't found Puckett, right?"

"Not yet. If the blood samples don't match up with Clay or Stoney, they might belong to Wayne. The hospital has good records on him because he had surgery on his knee a couple of years ago, so we'll be able to establish whether Wayne is a possible match. At that point, we may be looking for another body instead of a fugitive. Unless we find him, we may never know for sure if Wayne's dead or alive, or exactly what part he played in all this."

"So it could end up being one big unsolved crime. Seems a shame."

"Well, there's more. We got a search warrant for Wayne's trailer. He had a collection of arrowheads in a big box, mixed in with wires, fishhooks, all kinds of junk. At the bottom of the box were a couple of pages torn out of a plat book with a big X in four spots and some scribbled notes. One X is marked 'bones.' The interesting part is the location. Every single X is on Branson property."

"What did she say?"

"She doesn't know yet. I asked her to come in as soon as she could, but she told me she'd let me know after she'd talked to Kelso. He won't let her say anything unless he can come with her. As long as we don't find Wayne alive, and as long as Marella is missing, there's no one to prove Ms. Branson knew about the artifacts."

"Wait! Did you say Marella's missing?"

"Oh, yeah. Forgot to mention that. She disappeared from the hospital the same night you dropped her off. Within an hour of the time her father left my office."

"And you haven't seen either of them again?"

"Not a glimpse. Haven't been able to track Vortinto down by phone, either."

"Trace, if the artifacts are on the Branson place, Clay's murder makes no sense. His body was found on Marella's farm and the soil samples—"

"The archaeologists will take new samples from both farms and probably other locations, as well. There were probably Indian settlements all around the Sangamon. Most of the ditches were originally feeder creeks, dredged out and deepened when landowners put in drainage tile. Every farm bordering the ditch will be vulnerable now. The university will have a field day trying to stop land sales, disrupt plowing schedules, and set up digs. But at least it'll be out in the open. We shouldn't find any more bodies."

Except for Wayne's! "Trace, do you think Wayne killed Clay?"

"I think it's possible. The spade and tarp are in Wayne's pickup, so if the blood turns out to be Clay's, then I'd peg Wayne as the killer."

"You think he did it on his own? Or was he helping Marella?"

"Maybe Wayne thought he could do Marella or her father a favor. The Taylors did a lot of screaming and yelling, sometimes not so private. If Wayne knew the situation, he may have tried to get on Vortinto's good side without realizing how much publicity and trouble he'd cause. As for Marella, I doubt she's capable of murder."

"Not even ordering a murder?"

"I don't think so."

"But her father won't get his hands on the farm now, will he?"

"Not in our lifetime, Judge Thorn. Listen, gotta go. I'll be back in touch as soon as I know something worth telling."

There was that Judge Thorn again. This time I would wait for *Sheriff Parker* to call me.

To my surprise, one week later, after a long night spent in a Red Cross hurricane shelter, helping Willie serve snacks and run population counts to the ham radio operators, Trace did call.

My clerk handed me a stack of phone messages with Trace's request to return his call on top. The second message reminded me that I'd missed an acupuncture appointment with Tequila…did I want to reschedule or just get together for lunch? I called Trace first.

"A couple of interesting developments, Judge Thorn."

"Trace, could you please call me Sylvia? I always feel like I should wear my robes and sit up straight with a grim expression on my face when someone addresses me as Judge Thorn."

He chuckled. "Absolutely, Sylvia."

"So what's new?"

"I think we know the rest of the story now. According to Clay's accountant, Clay and his wife had a verbal agreement to donate the farm to the county development board as a nature preserve, but Clay complained that Marella reneged on the deal because her father wanted to purchase the property. Vortinto put out a story about the fertilizer plant, promised jobs and other economic benefits.

"However, the land-use variance application says the plan is to build a fertilizer storage warehouse. One of the reporters at the *Illinois Gazette* did some digging and found a couple of interesting stories. The feds are investigating a network of rural feed, grain, and other warehouses used to store and distribute illegal goods, including unstamped cigarettes, forged antiques, and, of course, drugs."

"So they think Marella's father wanted to expand his network of locations downstate, like transport depots."

"Right."

"Surely Lou Branson isn't involved with the Vortinto family."

"She and her lawyer are supposed to come in tomorrow, so I don't have a statement from her yet. But she originally thought her fight was against the Taylor plan for the nature preserve. When she found out about the commercial development, she joined the battle, at least until she discovered the Vortinto connection. I'm guessing she had second thoughts about tangling with someone that powerful."

"Good guess," I said.

"But then the artifacts turned up, and if she knew about them, she could have enlisted Wayne's help to hide the find. By the way, Brian Kelso declared he has a conflict of interest. He won't be representing Ms. Branson after this week."

"Who's the other client?"

"The Tribes of the Sangamon, a Native-American political action group. I don't know what the conflict is. Maybe Kelso knows about the artifacts, or maybe the PAC does. I'm sure we'll find out soon enough."

"So Lou has to find a new lawyer," I said. "And as of now, you don't have enough evidence to bring charges against anyone. Which means Willie and I won't be needed to testify, at least not in the foreseeable future."

"Correct."

I was relieved, but then there was this tiny twinge of regret. Who knew if or when Trace would really take a vacation to Florida?

"Sylvia, I'm being paged. I have to go. But if anything else happens, I'll call you."

When that man decides to get off the phone, he gets off in a hurry. An easy way to escape a conversation? I shook my head and focused on the information I'd received.

So much for my sleuthing abilities. I'd come to believe Willie's theory that Marella Taylor had a boyfriend and wanted to get out of her marriage without jeopardizing her financial position. But if her powerful father actually ran the show, then he probably arranged for Marella to marry Clay in the first place. Her assignment was to sabotage the plans for a nature preserve, thereby paving the way for commercial development. Once she'd wrapped up the deal, she could get a nice, tidy divorce.

I wondered what Illinois law said about divvying up the proceeds of a land sale in a divorce settlement. If no prenuptial agreement existed, then Marella might have thought murder a more efficient solution. And there we were, back to Willie's theory.

Regardless, it was unlikely we'd ever see Marella again. If her father wanted to keep her alive, then he'd whisk her away to safety. A new hair color, a new identity, a villa in Italy—a piece of cake. I wondered how ownership of the two hundred acres would be transferred from Marella to her father. Forged quitclaim deed, maybe? It would be a while before this story played out to the end.

I called my brother that evening to tell him about Trace's call and to see if he needed anything. Willie sounded fine and quite content to be home. I hoped his wanderlust was satisfied for the time being.

Willie, however, had something totally different on his mind. "Who's your new neighbor?"

"What new neighbor?" I couldn't imagine what he

meant. Willie hadn't been to my condo since we returned to Florida, nor had I discussed anything about my neighbors with him. To the best of my knowledge, no one had moved in or out of the other three units on my floor, not while we were gone and not since we'd returned.

"A woman moved into 4B," he said.

"But 4B belonged to Mrs. Dawson. What happened to her?"

"I don't know."

"Willie…"

"When you find out, will you tell me?"

"Yes, of course."

I wasn't sure why Willie would be so interested, unless he needed reassurance that his imagination wasn't working overtime. But I'd find out. Odds were, I had a new neighbor and there would be a good reason why Willie knew about her.

Despite my curiosity, I decided not to rush next door to investigate. In South Florida it wasn't normal, or smart, to intrude on the privacy of your neighbors, or to invite total strangers into your life. Once the door to intimacy was opened, it could be extremely difficult to close. I would wait, eventually running into the new resident in the hallway or at the mailbox. Whereupon, I could decide on the spot whether to strike up a conversation.

Meanwhile, there were a couple of case files to review before I went to bed, as well as a computer database to check out. I'd procrastinated long enough. After powering up the desktop and connecting to the Internet, I accessed the new system on the first try. I decided to check out the program by running a few inquiries.

One query in particular. I typed in *Parker, Trace* and entered data in the city, county, and state fields to narrow the search. In fifteen seconds, the program returned a list of topics under the heading of *Parker, Trace: Sheriff of Lincoln County, Illinois.*

I perused the list, then clicked on *Personal Records.*

A full page of information on Trace—everything from his weight to his marital status. I stared at the last entry for a long time. *Marital Status: Divorced.* Trace told us his wife died. Yet this national database was supposed to be extremely accurate—lawmakers and enforcement officers had insisted on it.

Made me wonder.

Returning to the list of topics, I clicked on employment history. I scanned the dates, searching for his time with the City of Chicago. He had worked there from 1972 to 1976, just as he'd said. But a notation at the end of the entry caught my attention, and I read it several times. *Reason for leaving: Officer subject of IAD investigation re association with known criminals. Charges filed but dropped when officer resigned.*

I was stunned.

Had no one in Sangamon City investigated Trace's history when they hired him as the city's liaison with the police department? Or had they only contacted more recent employers? I returned my attention to the other entries and looked through the sparse information on the two private security companies: company name, human resources contact, date hired, date left, and nothing else. I jotted down the names of the two firms. Maybe I'd learn more if I tried an Internet search.

I returned to the first query screen and entered a new name: *Branson, Louise.* After typing in the county and state, I clicked the submit button. *No Data Found.* If Lou Branson did not have a criminal record, was not currently facing charges, and did not work for law enforcement, then her private business did not belong in this database.

Convinced I knew how to access and use the system, I decided to postpone any further experiments, as well as any more digging into Trace Parker's past.

I shut down the computer, fixed myself a cup of tea, and settled down in my favorite chair to review case files.

TWENTY-FOUR

TIME PASSED, AND MY courtroom took over again as the priority time-consumer of my life. I lost interest in my next-door neighbor, along with my curiosity about progress in solving Clay Taylor's murder. Since I had questions about the honesty and integrity of my old boyfriend, the sheriff, I chose to put the man out of my mind. Social and charity events, which dominated the fall and winter calendar, often shanghaied what little leisure time I had. Still, I made plenty of time for my family when I could get them to slow down long enough to see me.

Upon their return from Key West, my parents had agreed to join Willie and me for stone crab claws at Jelly's Pier. Two days later they took off on a bus tour to Branson, Missouri. I envied their shared interests, their good-natured friendship, and their durability. That's the kind of life I wanted for myself, but I wasn't doing the right things to get there.

Willie had finalized the deal to sell his public accounting business, so he had more time than ever to volunteer at the homeless shelter in Delray Beach. He took the bus back and forth in spite of my offers to provide transportation, so we hadn't talked recently about the murder case, or whether I really had a new neighbor.

As a result, that was the last thing on my mind when I opened my door a month later and nearly collided with a gray-haired woman whose bruised and battered face made me suck in my breath, astonished and horrified. A tall, beefy man tugged at her elbow as she instinctively turned toward my gasp. She quickly looked away and let her escort hurry her toward the door of the next unit.

I stood in my own entrance for a moment and thought about what I'd just seen. Nearly identical lines around both eyes and at the jaw line, a symmetrical but hideously swollen and discolored nose, no noticeable marks on the woman's bare arms, no difficulty walking. I'd guessed wrong when my first impression told me she was the victim of domestic violence. It appeared my new neighbor had subjected herself to a surgical solution to aging. The face-lift "blues" isn't an unusual sight in South Florida, which is one of the plastic surgery capitals of the world, although many women prefer to hide out until the bruising fades.

I shrugged off the encounter, closed and locked my door, and headed down to my car.

From that point on, I began to notice little things. I caught glimpses of movement or vague shadows out of the corner of my eye when I approached my car or walked out onto my balcony. Twice I thought I saw my neighbor's big friend near the restaurant where I routinely eat lunch when court is in session.

Then one day, as I drove home, I realized the black Mercedes which followed me through the security gate had been behind me from the moment I left the courthouse parking garage. I stayed inside my vehicle with my doors locked while the big man climbed out of his sedan and walked unnecessarily close to my car before strolling on toward the elevator. He turned and watched me for a few seconds before facing away and pressing the call button. Finally, he stepped inside, turned and gave me one more unfriendly glance, then stared into space until the door slid shut.

There was something wrong here. Something scary.

But nothing illegal, as far as I knew. Nothing overtly threatening. Nothing I could report to the police, or to the condo security guards, without sounding foolish. I restarted my car and drove to Willie's apartment.

My brother started talking to me as he opened the door, apparently not surprised to have me show up without phoning first, which is my usual practice. "I tried to call you," he said.

"Sorry." I hadn't contacted Willie because I didn't want to go back to my condo knowing the big guy might be lurking in the hallway, and I still refused to be in constant touch with the world via the cellular umbilical cord, even after my unpleasant experiences in Illinois. The only other time I regretted that little oddity occurred last year when I had a flat tire on Alligator Alley and had to hike over two miles to get to a phone.

"I'm glad you're home, Willie. I just had the strangest experience."

"It scared you."

"Yes, I think it did."

"I felt it. That's why I tried to call. What happened?"

Willie gives me the creeps sometimes. Not the menacing kind of creeps I got from the big guy, but the chilly kind of creeps. There are things out there we don't understand but might have great significance if we could only figure them out. I shivered and gave Willie my look that told him to cool it.

He shrugged and pointed toward the kitchen. "Want some tea? Chamomile?"

I wrinkled my nose, but nodded. "Tea would be good."

A bar formed a half wall between the kitchen area and the living room, allowing me to sit on one of the stools and watch Willie at work as he heated mugs of water in his microwave and dropped a tea bag into each one. He leaned against the refrigerator and looked at me expectantly while we waited for the tea to steep.

Starting with my near collision with the woman and her friend in the hallway outside my door, and including the big-guy sightings away from the condo, I described the growing sense that someone watched my balcony and my car. I told Willie everything I could remember, ending with the blatant and menacing encounter that had just occurred.

"You've never seen this guy before? Or the woman?"

"I'm sure I've never seen the man before. The woman… I don't know. I only glimpsed her battered face. What some females will go through just to get rid of wrinkles and droopy eyelids! I don't think I know her, but even if I did, why would her buddy be interested in me?"

Why indeed? If one considered the number of people who'd made appearances in my courtroom with unhappy consequences, it would give one a vague idea of the number of people who might feel compelled to worm their way into my life and make my existence uncomfortable, if not totally miserable.

Would I have to move?

This was not the first time I'd had second thoughts about my choice of careers. I've flirted with the idea of changing my life, selecting an alternative occupation, moving to another state. A simple existence, a peaceful environment, lots of leisure time.

"A bookstore!" Willie shouted.

"What?"

"You could open a bookstore. A mystery bookstore."

I gave Willie the look again.

"Or write a book," he added. "One of those legal thrillers. Or something really excellent, like *To Kill a Mockingbird.*"

"Stop it, Willie."

He busied himself removing the tea bags from our mugs, but I could see he had a smug little smirk on his face. My brother had advised me against going to law school in the first place, so whenever I dared complain, he felt free to remind me that he'd told me so.

I deftly changed the subject by asking Willie about the homeless shelter. The main topic of conversation for the next twenty minutes was Benny, a ten-year-old African-American whose family suffered from chronic unemployment. Benny's father was in jail, his mother often drank herself into a stupor, and his older brother belonged to a gang known for drug-dealing. The child had inherited strong, intelligent, and healthy genes in spite of his parents and his living conditions. Knowing the boy could have a real future, Willie busted his butt to make sure this kid got an education and the chance for a decent life. I finished my tea as Willie wound down and stared moodily into his empty cup.

"That's all I can do," he concluded. Then he smiled at me. "So, what about you? What are you going to do?"

"I need to return to my condo instead of hanging around here like a scared rabbit. I'll call you when I get inside. Tomorrow is Saturday. I'll give Security a call and see if they have any suggestions."

"Do you want me to go with you? I could stay overnight."

"No, that's not necessary. I'm sure I overreacted. But if I don't call you within the next thirty minutes, you can phone Security and have them check on me."

Twenty minutes later I stood inside my condo with the doors locked, alarm codes activated, and the safe-arrival call made. I'd seen no one lurking near my parking space, the elevator, or the hallway. I felt a little silly, but not silly enough to leave my apartment that evening. Also, not silly enough to stick my nose in a murder mystery or watch a scary movie.

While I waited for the computer to boot up, I toasted an English muffin, slathered it with crunchy peanut butter, and made a cup of Earl Grey tea. Careful not to drip anything onto the keyboard, I connected to the Internet and brought up my favorite search engine. After consulting the notes I'd made from Trace's employment record, I entered the name of the first security firm. When that yielded no results, I tried the second company. Again, no results.

After entering other possible spellings for each of the employers, and then doing a search on security firms in Michigan, I gave up. The absence of information on these two companies didn't make sense. These days, it was difficult to do business if you didn't have a presence on the Web, including a detailed description of the company, pictures, job openings, and a contact link. There had to be other ways to track down the information, but I didn't know where to start.

For the time being, I planned to put the whole thing out of my mind and do something constructive. I shut down the computer and began to work.

It was after midnight when I finally finished. I stepped back to admire my newly lined kitchen shelves and the tidy arrangement of foods and spices inside. I shoved the nearly filled wastebasket inside the pantry, and went to bed.

TWENTY-FIVE

SATURDAY MORNING WAS my errand-running, grocery-shopping, bathroom-cleaning time. I mulled over the whole neighbor problem as I accomplished what needed to be done, saving the visit to Security for afternoon. It was two-fifteen on a gloriously beautiful and mild October day by the time I finally drove over to the main office of the condo complex. A "Will Return By" sign hung on the door with a picture of a clock face showing four o'clock. Apparently a skeleton crew manned the complex on weekends. Or there was a crisis somewhere. I found it odd that a security office would be left unattended at any time and resolved to question the practice when I returned promptly at four.

Afternoons were normally hot and muggy and dominated by short but fierce thunderstorms right on through to the end of hurricane season. This day proved to be an exception. I opened my doors and windows to let the breezes clear out the stale air, then dusted off my balcony furniture, poured a tall glass of iced tea, and stretched out on the chaise longue with the latest Sue Grafton paperback. Reading mystery novels may not be my only addiction, but it's certainly my favorite, ranking right up there with mocha truffles and martinis on the list of things that make me feel better.

That indulgence didn't last long. A female voice, rambling on and on, gradually edged its way past my concentration and became one of those petty annoyances, like a persistent mosquito buzzing around your ear or a child whining up and down every aisle in the grocery store. The woman's voice became louder and increasingly agitated. My attention abruptly abandoned, I tuned in to the voice that I now realized came from the balcony of the neighboring condominium. I could hear the speaker clearly in spite of the privacy wall between us, so I dropped the book to my lap and focused on the one-sided conversation. If my neighbor wanted privacy, she'd certainly picked the wrong time and place to get it.

"How long do I have to stay here?" she asked.

Little kids aren't the only ones with whiny voices. I could imagine the pouty expression that would accompany her question.

"Damn it, you bastard, you promised to take care of everything!"

Whoops! One quick change of tone and we'd moved from petulant little girl to bitchy shrew. And the shrew's voice sounded very familiar. Where had I heard that shrill note before? I tried to remember. The day I saw my new neighbor and her big friend in the hallway there had been no conversation. This was the first time I'd opened my windows or sat on the balcony since Willie and I had returned from Illinois. Maybe I'd met the woman at some social event, but didn't recognize her because of the stitches and bruising from the face-lift. I concentrated on the words and let the sound wash around me, hoping it would trigger recognition.

"What about the old biddy who owns the other farm? Is there any way you can lay the rap on her? Most of the Indian crap is on her place, so she has a motive." The woman on the balcony paused, then said, "Fine, fine, fine!"

Ah. So now I knew who lived next door. Marella Taylor.

A wave of anxiety washed over me, leaving me breath-less. Questions began to spin through my mind as though chased by a whirlwind. Who was on the other end of the phone conversation? Marella's father? Highly unlikely she'd be talking to the crime boss in that tone. Brian Kelso? I didn't know much about the lawyer except that Lou Branson had described him as an honest man. But since Willie and I weren't completely sure Lou was an honest woman, we couldn't rely on the information she'd given us.

Most pressing was my concern about why Marella had moved into a condo in my building on my floor when I'd heard nothing about Mrs. Dawson leaving. Obviously, this was no coincidence. And even though I'd not been close to Mrs. Dawson, I should have asked about her at the main office. I mentally kicked myself for not checking on her and hoped nothing bad had happened to a very nice lady.

It was clear, at least to me, that these people were watching me for a specific reason. If Marella had chosen some other place for her recovery, she would have been a lot less vulnerable, especially if Willie and I were the only credible witnesses who could connect her to Wayne Puckett. Why on earth would she want to surface so close to us?

So close to me!

The only thing I could figure was that she wanted to test the effectiveness of the face-lift, hair color, and style as a disguise. Apparently, she didn't realize she would need to work on her voice, tone, and Chicago accent to complete the transformation.

"I haven't talked to her yet," snapped Marella. "The swelling's almost gone, but I still have some bruising. Another few days and I'll knock on her door and see what happens."

Was she talking about me? Did she have any idea how

her voice carried? What kind of idiot would stand out on the balcony and have this conversation? I had an unending list of questions for this woman.

"What do you mean, if she recognizes me?" Marella continued. "Isn't that why Fritz is here?"

The little hairs on the back of my neck lifted like the feathers on an angry rooster's crown. The big guy, Fritz, would definitely like to be useful, probably craved the opportunity. I quietly eased myself off the chaise longue and tiptoed into the living room. My day had changed from light and cheery to dark and lonely. I wanted to close the balcony doors, draw the drapes, and turn on all the lights. There are approximately five days of winter per year when I need to flip on the furnace to chase the chill away. I shivered as the chill now filled the room in spite of the seventy-five-degree air outside.

Inside, I could only hear the background murmur of Marella's voice. Who should I call? I didn't want Willie over here. I might put him in danger. He was almost as much a threat to Marella as I was, which made him just as much of a target. A call to Security or the Boca police would do little more than alert Marella and the big guy that her disguise hadn't worked. To the best of my knowledge, no Florida warrant had been issued for her arrest, and if she'd only been reported missing, well, there's no law against staying out of sight after a face-lift. There'd be no reason to keep her locked up, and Willie and I would become easy targets.

There was only one place I could call to find out what warrants, if any, were outstanding on Marella. As I walked into my bedroom and closed the door, I picked up the cordless phone and reluctantly dialed the Lincoln County Sheriff's office. Sergeant Green put me on hold. While I waited, I rummaged in my dresser drawers for a sweater. After a few minutes I decided the sergeant had forgotten about me, so I hung up and dialed back. Sure enough, Trace Parker had stepped out of the office. I left a message that I had information about Marella, that I thought she'd surfaced in Boca Raton, and would he please call me. Hopefully, Sergeant Green wouldn't forget to deliver the message.

I glanced at my watch and realized it was past four o'clock. Now that I knew the identity of my mysterious neighbor, I felt an even greater urgency to touch base with Security and make sure they understood the potential threat. As much as I hated to walk out the door and risk running into Marella's friend in the hallway, I had to do it. I moved back to the living room and hung up the phone, closed and locked the balcony door, and pulled the drapes.

A careful look through the door's peephole revealed an empty hall, so out I walked into the hallway and locked the door behind me. I scooted to the stairs and rushed out of the building as though there were gremlins behind me. Walking to the condo office made more sense than going into the parking garage. I pulled the sweater off and tied the arms around my waist. The world seemed a lot less menacing in the late-afternoon sun.

The Security Office was unlocked and the sign removed by the time I arrived, so I entered and said, "Hello, is anybody here?"

I heard a door open and close, followed by the sound of footsteps tapping down the tiled hallway. A tall woman wearing a khaki uniform and a badge rounded the corner and stopped abruptly when she saw me.

"I didn't hear you come in," she said.

"I called out."

"I was in the back. Sorry. I'm Fran Millser. What can I do for you?"

I told Fran the complete story. By the time I got to the part about Marella Taylor and her friend taking up residence in Mrs. Dawson's condo, Fran gave me her undivided attention. From time to time she jotted notes on a yellow legal pad. I finished my story and dropped into the chair facing her desk. She sat quietly and stared past my head without making any comment.

"Does this sound too flaky?" I asked. "Do you think I'm overreacting?"

Fran's focus returned to my face. She shook her head and smiled. "No. I was just thinking. Wait here a minute."

She grabbed the legal pad and hustled out of the front office toward the hall. I heard a door open and close. After several minutes the door opened again and I heard the sounds of more footsteps accompanied by the low murmur of voices. Fran came through the doorway, followed by two men. One, a balding, middle-aged but fit-looking guy in a security uniform, the other a nondescript kid in a conservative dark suit, white shirt, and gray tie.

Fran gestured toward the older man. "This is my boss, Ferris Boggs. And this is Damon Falls, FBI. Gentlemen, this is Judge Thorn."

Falls was FBI. I should have known. The love of my life had been very much like Damon Falls in appearance. These guys were supposed to look anonymous. I shook hands with both men and waited while they pulled up chairs and sat down on either side of me. Boggs leaned forward and pulled Fran's legal pad closer. Then he asked me to repeat the whole story, which I did with only minimal impatience. I am an officer of the court, after all, and intimately familiar with interview procedures. When I finished, before any of the others had time to comment, I asked a few questions of my own.

"What's going on here? Do you know who that man is?

What happened to Mrs. Dawson? And what's the FBI doing here?"

Agent Falls raised his hand to stop me. "Judge Thorn, we know who he is. I'm here to find out why Fritz is spending so much time at this complex. He lives in Miami and works as a bodyguard to Vincent Vortinto."

"Vortinto? Vinnie Vortinto?" That name again. Marella had connections to some very tough customers.

"That's the one. Fritz has been his bodyguard and gofer for the last ten years, ever since Vinnie retired to Florida. We have Vortinto under surveillance, so when Fritz's daily schedule changed, we checked it out."

I leaned back and thought about what I'd just heard. There's nothing that could sound a judge's death knell faster than any contact whatsoever with Vinnie Vortinto or anyone associated with him. Were they cooking up a plan to discredit me in case I could implicate Marella in Clay's murder?

"So what's the connection between Vinnie and Marella Taylor?" I asked Agent Falls. "I was told she was from Chicago, related to a family with a shady reputation, and her father's name is Vortinto. But Vinnie's from Jersey, isn't he?"

"We're going to run some checks on the woman. I found out today that Fritz is here because of her. But as far as the Vortinto family is concerned, one brother lives in Chicago and the other operated out of Detroit until he went to prison for income tax evasion. Upon his release, he retired and moved to Florida. That's Vinnie, the man you've heard about. If he's loaned Fritz out to this Marella Taylor, and if she's Aldono's daughter, then Vinnie would be her uncle."

All very interesting, but one word intrigued me more than all the rest put together: *Detroit*.

Little niggling thoughts wormed their way to the surface in the form of questions. I asked the biggest one. "Agent

Falls, do you know any of the companies Vortinto ran in Detroit? Anything in security?"

The FBI man shook his head. "It would be easy enough to find out, though. Do you have a reason for asking?"

"Just curiosity. The sheriff up there in Lincoln County where Marella Taylor's husband was murdered once worked for a security firm in Michigan. There are a couple of odd things in his employment record, so I wondered."

I thought about Fritz again and started to worry about my former neighbor who had mysteriously disappeared. "Do you know anything about Mrs. Dawson?" I asked Falls.

"According to the rental office, she arranged for a sublet to last until the end of the year. She's supposed to return in January. We don't know where she is, but we're trying to find out."

"Do you think I'm in danger?"

"Judge Thorn, I honestly don't know. It can't be a co-incidence that Ms. Taylor is staying here. If she considers you a threat, and if Fritz's job is to protect her, then there could be a reason for concern. Boggs, do you have the manpower to give the judge an escort when she comes and goes from her condo?"

Fran quickly raised her hand. "I can do it. I work a short shift today, and I'm off at six. I could do round-the-clock if necessary."

"I feel silly asking," I said, "when we don't even know if there's a reason."

Fran shrugged. She stood up and walked to a closet behind the desk, unlocked the door, and stepped inside. I heard the jingling of keys and the bang of metal on metal. When she returned, she carried a .38 in a shoulder holster.

I guess she thought there was a reason.

TWENTY-SIX

UNACCUSTOMED TO HAVING a roommate and unwilling to spend hours trying to make conversation with a total stranger, I declined Fran's offer to stay with me in my condo or even in the hallway outside my door. However, I didn't object to having the building under surveillance and didn't particularly care if my neighbors knew someone was watching.

Setting up a schedule with Fran for my comings and goings took little time, especially since I'd planned only one trip out on Sunday. I felt safer knowing I would have company when I entered the garage to get my car. Except for lunch with Willie and Tequila at Boston's in Delray Beach, I didn't plan to leave the condo until I went to the courthouse on Monday morning.

Sunday turned out to be another beautiful day. That was somewhat of a miracle. I would not miss the late-afternoon deluge and I could spend a few more hours on the balcony with my book and a glass of wine. If I finished the Grafton paperback, I'd start right in on the latest Park Ranger adventures of Anna Pigeon. Escapist reading at its best.

At eleven I phoned Willie to make sure he was ready, before I called Fran's cell phone to confirm that she was on her way. No sound of any kind came from my neighbor's apartment. I wondered again about the missing Mrs. Dawson, but shrugged off my nagging concern as I heard

Fran's tap at the door. Minutes later I backed out of my parking spot and headed over to pick up Willie. Fran followed me all the way to the gate and out onto A1A. I knew she'd stay behind me long enough to confirm I wasn't being followed. Even so, I sped through a yellow light with a quick glance in my rearview mirror, and turned right at the next intersection so I wouldn't be visible from the gates. I gave myself a mental pat on the back for being so clever.

Willie stood patiently in front of his building as I drove up. Thank goodness he didn't show signs of agitation or concern, which meant he wasn't having visions or experiences—whatever you want to call them—that involved my welfare. I hesitated before I told him what I knew. Then I decided it didn't matter. He wouldn't believe danger lurked unless he sensed it himself.

"Don't worry, Syl."

Why did I know he'd say that?

"How do you know, Willie? What if they decide to get rid of me? Or set me up in some kind of compromising situation and try to blackmail me? The possibilities are endless. What if they decide…" I stopped. *Why did I say those things?* Maybe I was a lot more scared than I wanted to believe.

"Not a problem, Syl. When Marella Taylor knocks on your door, you do not recognize her. You're nice and friendly. You don't ask questions. She goes away. If I'm approached, I do the same. Simple."

Willie was right. Except…

"What if she asks me about the security coverage? They're sure to notice I'm receiving regular escort service to and from the building."

"You sent someone to prison. He got out. Made threats."

"Yeah. I suppose."

We lapsed into silence. Willie's hands rested motionless in his lap, and he serenely gazed toward the ocean as we drove on to Boston's. I tried to follow his example.

Finding a parking space within a block of the beach didn't happen often, but this time I caught a lucky break. It only took a couple of minutes to walk to the restaurant.

The line was long for the yuppie, upper deck, which didn't bother me because the menu downstairs was much better. Tequila had arrived there ahead of Willie and me, and now paced back and forth on the sidewalk in front of the porch. We were seated almost immediately and had our orders taken within seconds. An easy process when you always order the same thing—in this case, the crabmeat salad sandwich on whole wheat and a Corona.

Tequila ordered the same.

Willie skipped the Corona, of course, but settled on the same sandwich with bottled water. He never ate his chips. I considered that a bonus for me so I never suggested he order a substitute.

I love Boston's. It's my favorite place to kick back and relax, have a leisurely lunch, chat about fun things, and do some serious people-watching. You can look out past the other diners on the porch, across A1A, past the walkers and skaters, beyond the sunbathers, and over the blue-gray waters to the hulking oil tankers or pristine-white cruise ships on the horizon. Small planes trail advertising banners just beyond the shoreline.

Today an occasional motorcyclist roared past. A screaming fire engine forced drivers to swerve and pedestrians to scramble.

Boston's was not all peace and quiet, but it was never dull.

We all watched the steady stream of visitors to the outside shower head across the street—naked kids, nearly naked bathing beauties, and, worst of all, overexposed, potbellied retirees with leathery, sagging, wrinkled skin. All were intent on washing off sand and sea lice in a public ritual often bordering on the obscene. Quite a show.

I shifted my focus to passing traffic, then to a specific driver of a specific car. Fritz. He turned his head long enough to make eye contact with me. Then, with no change of expression, he looked at the street ahead of him. My spine felt as if it had turned to stone.

Tequila eyed a muscular Adonis, who cruised past on inline skates. "Would you look at that," she whispered, never taking her gaze away from the skater's rippling muscles.

I glanced at Willie, but he was watching the waitress who approached with our food. I decided not to say anything.

"What?" Willie turned his head and stared at me.

"Nothing."

"Syl…"

"Fritz just drove by. He saw me."

Tequila must have heard the tension in my voice because she tore her gaze away from those tanned abs and asked, "Who's Fritz?"

The waitress delivered our food just then, so I hesitated, not sure how much I wanted to tell Tequila. With her fiery Latino temperament, she was perfectly capable of charging out to Fritz's car and subjecting him to a rapid-fire piece of her mind. Finally, I gave her a brief summary of the murder case in Illinois and assured her that if there was a connection, the FBI already had everything totally under control. I didn't believe it, but I think I convinced Tequila. She did offer to stay in my condo with me, but I said no-thank-you. I wasn't about to give Fritz another target.

I wish I could say I enjoyed lunch, but truthfully I hardly tasted the food and couldn't stop checking out every car that drove by. With some relief, I finished eating, made contact with Fran, and breathed a lot easier when I found her waiting for me as I drove through the gates.

Back inside my condo, windows and doors secured, alarm turned on, I breathed another sigh of relief. I thought it must feel like that to be agoraphobic.

Several hours later, deeply involved in the next day's docket summary, I jumped and gasped when I heard my doorbell chime. Almost in harmony, the phone began to ring. Already on my way to the door, I let the machine pick up the call while I peered out the peephole. I stepped back in surprise. Trace Parker stared grimly back at me.

"Syl. Pick up the phone. I know you're there." Willie's voice sounded urgent, so without thinking, without any further hesitation, without asking myself why Trace was in Boca Raton and how he got all the way into my condo without a call from Security, I opened the door.

"Trace, this is a surprise. I need to get the phone. Sorry." I opened the door wide and motioned him inside, then hurried to pick up the receiver. Just as I began to speak, my security alarm wailed. I'd forgotten to disarm the damned thing.

"Yes, I'm here. Sorry, Willie, someone was at the door."

"Don't answer it, Syl!"

"Too late. And I forgot to turn off the alarm. Hang on." I rushed back to the number panel and punched in the code. Trace still stood in the open doorway. "Sorry," I said, racing back to the phone.

"Syl, don't say his name. Is it Sheriff Parker?" I turned my back on Trace and lowered my voice. "How did you know that?"

"Hang up now, Syl. I'm calling Security, and then I'm calling the police."

"Why?"

I felt more than heard Trace move across the room and

guessed his intentions even before he took the receiver from my hand and placed it in the cradle.

"What do you think you're doing? That was my brother." Hoping I sounded sufficiently indignant and authoritative, I turned to face Trace with an angry glare. A glimpse of movement in the hallway distracted me. I looked over his shoulder and cringed when I saw the always-lurking Fritz walk through my door.

"Let's go." Trace grabbed my elbow and yanked me toward the hall.

"Wait a minute! What the hell do you think you're doing?"

"Unless you want to be carried out of here unconscious, you'll shut your mouth and do exactly as you're told."

I clamped my mouth shut and walked toward the door, unsuccessfully attempting to jerk my elbow out of Trace's grasp. There would be no opportunity to make a run for it, not with Fritz blocking my way. As Trace pulled the door closed behind us and Fritz moved to take his place at my side, Marella Taylor stepped into the hallway from the neighboring condo.

"Bring her in here. I'm not ready to go yet."

Trace tightened his grip and yanked my arm as he shoved me through Marella's open door. I tried my best to look like an angry judge, no great challenge since I felt like spitting nails. Why had I let Trace inside? How could I have been so stupid? Didn't I have enough clues from the database search to know he wasn't what he seemed? And leaving a message for him, for God's sake. Telling him I thought Marella was in Boca.

What the hell was I thinking?

When Trace loosened his grip, I whirled around—just in time to see Marella snake her arm around Trace's waist. He bent his head toward her and I swear he sniffed her hair.

That really pissed me off. Not to mention embarrassed and humiliated me. Damn, back in Illinois I'd flirted with the skunk. If he started nuzzling her neck, I'd deck him. Guns or no guns. And Marella, too.

"Sit down over there!" Trace motioned toward the elegant, pale cream love seat that formed one side of a conversation area. A quick glance around the room confirmed the furniture and accessories belonged to the missing Edna Dawson.

I sat, one could almost say perched, on the edge of the love seat, ready to bolt if the opportunity arose—meaning if Fritz were to move from his current position between me and the door.

When Trace and Marella walked out of the living room into what I presumed was Mrs. Dawson's bedroom, I guessed she needed help with her packing. Were they going to drag me along with them? Would they use me as a hostage to get past the security guards? Would the police respond quickly to Willie's 9-1-1 call?

I imagined walking out of the building and finding barricades, police cars, a SWAT team. What would the cops do if one of these assholes had pointed a gun at my head? For that matter, what would *I* do? I felt the creeping prickly sensation of sweat oozing from my forehead. With a quick swipe of my hand, I smeared the moisture into my hairline, convinced I'd look braver and tougher if I wasn't dripping with perspiration.

Within minutes, Trace and Marella reentered the living room. He carried two large soft-sided bags. Marella pulled a smaller carry-on with wheels. He leaned over, dropped the two bags on the floor, and said, "What's in here, for God's sake? Fritz, you have to carry these bags. They're heavy as hell and I have to take care of her."

They all looked at me and frowned.

I tried not to cringe. Anytime I'd heard the phrase "take care of her" in regard to criminal behavior, it didn't mean "bring her chocolates and a glass of champagne." I kept my gaze on Fritz, hoping he would march over to pick up the luggage before Trace crossed to the door, but he didn't. Obviously, the big thug wasn't as stupid as he looked.

"Over here," Trace snapped.

Since he looked directly at me when he barked his order, I took it personally and decided not to obey. If I refused to move, maybe I could delay the inevitable as well as give guards and officers plenty of time to react to Willie's phone calls.

"Not until you tell me what's going on. I already know about the IAD investigation in Chicago, Trace. I reported you to the FBI." Trying to look smug, I sat back and stretched out my legs, crossing them at the ankles. Next, I did my best to look tough and brave, even though my guts had turned to jelly.

Marella regarded me thoughtfully, then went for the bait, the arrogant little bitch. "You and that dim-witted brother of yours are the only people standing in my way," she said. "If you think I want to spend the rest of my life in hiding because you can link me to that idiot Wayne Puckett, you're crazy. You're a dead woman."

"We don't have time for this," Trace said. "Get over here, Sylvia."

"Wait! Did Wayne kill Clay? Why would he do that?"

"Don't say anything else!" Trace shouted at Marella. *Good!*

"Oh, what does it matter? She won't be talking to anyone."

Stupid as well as arrogant, I thought. No one in their right mind really believes that old cliché. But unless Trace physically restrained her, or taped her mouth shut, I had a feeling she'd confess. She *wanted* to confess. Or boast. Or both.

She turned to me and said, "I had a deal to sell the land to my father and I was supposed to make sure Clay didn't do anything to mess it up. But when my dear husband decided he'd sue me, in order to take the farm for some crazy nature thing, I told Daddy and he said we had to take care of the 'problem.'"

"So you did it, didn't you?"

She didn't say anything, just aimed a sly, cruel glare in my direction.

"Did Wayne help?" I asked, figuring I could stall a little longer. "He won't protect you," I said, as if I knew exactly what I was talking about.

She smirked. "He's dead, Judge. Got the picture?"

"Shut up, Marella. Enough," Trace snapped.

Suddenly he was a man of few words. He didn't seem anything like the person who'd given me so much information over the phone. Why had he done that? Maybe he was staying in touch to see if I'd figured out who my new neighbor was?

He stabbed his finger at me. "Get up! Now!"

Defiantly, I stayed seated. Somehow, I managed to stop myself from shrinking away when Trace stomped over to the love seat and grabbed my wrist. He jerked me up from the couch and dragged me toward the door, which Fritz had opened before stepping back into the room to get the luggage.

Trace still had his gaze on me as he tried to pull me out of the apartment.

I braced my shoulder against the doorjamb in an effort to keep myself inside the room. At the same time, I worked to pry his fingers loose.

Tightening his grip on my wrist, he yanked me into the

hall, and was immediately tackled by two officers in SWAT gear.

I fell forward on top of the now-restrained Sheriff Trace Parker, and "accidentally" rammed my right knee firmly into his crotch.

He let out a yell and dropped my wrist.

Fran hurried forward to help me to my feet.

I stood up, ready to rat on Fritz and Marella, but found the black-clad officers already herding the handcuffed culprits out of the condo.

Security guards, uniforms, and three men whose caps and jackets sported the yellow FBI logo swarmed into Marella's apartment.

Agent Falls delivered a salute as he passed.

Willie stepped out of my condo, retrieved Marella's purse from the hallway floor, and handed it to Falls. "If there's a cell phone in this," Willie said, "it could be Clay Taylor's. It might have voice mail or something." Then he gave me a knowing grin before retreating into my condo.

As Falls walked over to join Fran and me, he said, "Judge Thorn, glad to see you're okay."

"Agent Falls, you can't imagine how happy I am to see you again. I wasn't sure how this would end."

"We were in a meeting with security and some others when your brother called. Seems Fritz managed to track you to Boston's, despite all our precautions, and we were concerned. We wanted to haul him in for questioning while we tucked you away somewhere safe, but then Ms. Taylor called the security gate. She said to put Sheriff Parker on the list as a visitor. At that point we knew we had a problem."

"I guess I got lucky with the timing of that meeting."

"Definitely."

"I still don't understand everything. What happened to Wayne Puckett? Marella said he was dead. Did Lou

Branson and that lawyer, Brian Kelso, have anything to do with Wayne's murder?"

I stopped when I realized the questions would go on for a long time. Since I'd already concluded that Wayne and Marella were in cahoots, the sheriff's involvement put a nasty question mark right in the middle of my clever solution.

"We know quite a bit," Falls said. "Why don't you go to your apartment with Fran and let me finish up with my men. I'll join you in a few minutes and tell you what I can."

TWENTY-SEVEN

FRAN TRAILED ME into my apartment, leaving the door to the hallway open. I followed the aroma of fresh-brewed coffee into the kitchen, and gave my brother an appreciative grin. Both Fran and I fueled our over-taxed stress levels with caffeine, while Willie pulled a bottle of water out of the refrigerator and retired to the balcony. I knew the jolt guaranteed me a long sleepless night, but that coffee sure did taste good. We sat in silence, waiting, for nearly fifteen minutes before we heard voices in the hall.

A lone pelican glided past the balcony, but Willie didn't notice. He focused his attention on the entrance as he looked through the balcony's sliding door with a surprised expression. Agent Falls was ushering two other men, neither one familiar, into my apartment.

The two extra men were introduced as Brett Ravlin of the FBI, and attorney Brian Kelso of Sangamon City. *Brian Kelso? Why would Brian Kelso be in Boca Raton?*

Ravlin was one of those agents who seemed to belong in a dark gray suit with a white shirt, plain gray tie, shiny black shoes, and dark glasses. He looked over fifty, old school I would guess. As he shook my hand, he stuffed his sunglasses in his jacket pocket. A frown creased his forehead.

"Thorn," he mused. "I knew an agent named Thorn. Andrew. He taught a class at Quantico for a while. Any relation?"

This doesn't happen very often, but when it does, it

throws me completely off balance. Over twenty-five years ago, and I still have trouble coping when unexpectedly confronted with memories of Andy.

Willie stepped through the glass doors and moved toward the three men. "Andrew Thorn and my sister were married. You do know he died in an automobile accident?" Without waiting for Ravlin's response, Willie turned to Brian Kelso. "What are you doing here? Are you under arrest?"

Good old Willie. Diplomacy is not one of his strong points.

To Kelso's credit, he chuckled. "You know, I wondered the same thing about you when I saw you at the Sangamon County Building. I didn't know you were Judge Thorn's brother."

Willie relaxed and moderated his tone. "What are you doing here, then?"

"He's been working with me," said Ravlin. "Brian came across some information in another case that he thought might have a connection to Clay Taylor's murder. Since Parker was involved, it seemed appropriate to talk to the FBI."

"What information?" I asked.

"Two things, actually. The Native American Council he represents plans to file for an injunction against sales or land-use conversions in Lincoln County. They want the whole region surveyed for evidence of burial grounds or sites of archaeological interest."

"And the other thing?"

Brian Kelso said, "I attended a meeting in Chicago about a month before Clay's disappearance. While talking to some other attorneys in the hotel lobby, I saw Marella Taylor enter from the street, followed by an older man and his bodyguard. One of the lawyers cautioned me not to stare, and then identified the older guy as Aldono Vortinto, Vinnie Vortinto's younger brother and Marella Taylor's father. Imagine my shock at seeing our sheriff jump up from a chair and approach the group, shake Vortinto's hand, and put his arm around Marella's waist. I turned my back and prayed no one saw me."

"So then you called the FBI?" Willie asked.

"Not right away. I didn't have a reason to point a finger at anyone. I knew that Marella was married, but her relationship with Parker was really none of my business. Parker was consorting with shady characters, but, for all I knew, he could have been working on a case. However, once Marella disappeared, I became suspicious and contacted the feds."

Ravlin picked up the story. "There were things Brian couldn't discuss with us because Louise Branson was his client, but we were able to piece a lot of the land-use puzzle together by using our own surveillance methods. Nobody gave us a good motive for Clay Taylor's murder until you two identified the prairie grass test plots and the Kickapoo artifacts. Evidence that Mr. Taylor was taking soil samples completed the picture. Until then, we thought the murder was performed to eliminate a jealous husband. With the new facts, we wanted to know who was on-site the day Mr. Taylor went to the farm, and who would understand the situation well enough to recognize the threat."

"So the clues pointed to Wayne Puckett or Lou Branson," I said.

"Right," Brian Kelso said. "But Wayne worked on the two properties most of the time and lived out there as well, while Lou Branson spent most of her weekdays in town. Only on weekends did she stay around the farm, riding and gardening. Since Clay disappeared on a weekday, Wayne became the primary suspect. The FBI approached Lou and asked her to wear a wire when she talked to the sheriff, or to Puckett."

"Wait!" I exclaimed. "You mean Lou was wearing a

wire when Wayne and Marella shoved us into the root cellar?"

"Yes," Ravlin said. "She had it on when she went into the county building. And when she drove back to the farm to tend to her horse, she left her blouse on under her coveralls, so she didn't pull off the wire—"

"And you let us sit down there in the cellar?"

"Well…" He shifted his weight and cleared his throat. "Actually, we didn't follow her out to the farm. We expected the vet to be there, so we planned to wait a couple of hours and then go out."

"Marella and Wayne put Lou in the cellar with me. Would they have killed her, too?"

"I think so. They couldn't let her go because she knew you were in trouble. She would have reported it to the sheriff. They never expected you to escape."

"And later, when Willie and I were at Lou Branson's farm, where were you? We didn't notice anyone around."

"We were parked across Route 10 at the entrance to a neighbor's field. We had a few tense moments when Wayne Puckett caught up with you and your brother by the ditch."

I thought about other events that had occurred Saturday evening. "The cars that came roaring up the road just as Willie and I took off with Marella…was that you?"

"Unfortunately, no," said Ravlin. "Those were Vortinto's people. Mrs. Taylor's father came down to Sangamon City to finalize the land deal, but realized she could be charged with her husband's murder, despite the sheriff's efforts to divert suspicion. Since Vortinto had ordered the hit and knew there was a witness to the murder, he switched his efforts to finding and eliminating Wayne Puckett. Vortinto's people were searching for Puckett when they stumbled across Mrs. Taylor's car. If they had turned west from the farm, instead of east, they would have run into the FBI. Thanks to the wire on Ms. Branson, we picked up Puckett as he pulled out of the Taylor field, onto the road. Then we off-loaded the bales and took them to a secure site where they could be taken apart and examined by experts. We left the truck at the church with a smashed windshield and the door hanging open. Then we fed false information back to Sheriff Parker about blood samples we said we'd taken from the truck cab."

"Blood samples," I repeated, my mind reeling.

Ravlin nodded. "We also made sure Puckett understood how lucky he was that we arrived first. We wanted Sheriff Parker to think Puckett was dead, but we wanted Puckett to think Vortinto's people were still looking for him. Sheriff Parker apparently took us at our word and never checked with Vortinto. Later, Vortinto caught up with his daughter at the hospital and whisked her out of town."

"So you have Wayne in custody," I said, "and Trace and Marella think he's dead. But he definitely witnessed the murder. And Marella killed Clay."

"Yep," Ravlin said. "After she hit her husband with the spade, she took off, leaving Puckett to clean up after her. Since he wanted to move up in the world and get a job with the Vortinto organization, he did as he was told. He still had the bloody spade and tarp in his pickup truck when we caught him, so he knew he'd be charged with murder. As a result, he became very talkative. He also gave us the name of the driver who stole the flatbed truck, the man who helped him transfer the bales from the farm shed. Although this guy didn't know much about the murders, he owned and drove the equipment they used to pile more field trash on top of Clay Taylor's body. He'll be a useful witness."

"Crazy," I said. "Did Wayne tell you Marella was in Florida?"

Kelso shook his head. "Wayne didn't know. The plan didn't unfold until after he was in custody."

"Why were you already here when they tried to kidnap me?"

"We've had Sheriff Parker under surveillance 24/7," Ravlin said. "His office phone is bugged. When you called to tell him about Mrs. Taylor living next door, it was a big break. He'd been in touch with her, but hadn't used his office phone or his cell phone. Maybe a pay phone. After your call, he moved fast to make his travel arrangements and, luckily, did it from his office. I booked a flight right away and asked Brian to come along because he knew Mrs. Taylor well enough to identify her. I'd seen her a couple of times, but only at a distance, and before the surgery, of course."

"So the phone call I made put my life at risk, but saved my life all at the same time."

"What about Stoney Morris?" Willie wasn't going to forget the deputy who'd been responsible for his overnight stay at the county hospital. "Why was Morris killed, Agent Ravlin? Did Wayne Puckett kill him?"

"According to Puckett, Stoney Morris wasn't real bright, which is probably one of the reasons why Sheriff Parker kept him on the payroll. Someone like Morris would follow instructions without asking questions. Wayne Puckett strung Deputy Morris along with promises of future employment with the Vortinto organization, and Morris fell for it. However, he was upset when Puckett berated him and threatened him after Judge Thorn escaped from the shed, and he jumped Puckett in a rage. Puckett hit Morris hard enough to knock him out again. Then Puckett called Sheriff Parker for instructions. Puckett says Sheriff Parker ordered him to get rid of Stoney Morris and dump the body."

"By then," I said, "Trace wanted to eliminate anyone else who might expose his connection to Marella and the Vortintos. I guess Wayne wouldn't have lasted too much longer, either."

"Right," said Agent Falls. "One thing we haven't figured out is why they chose your neighbor's apartment to hide Marella Taylor. It seems unnecessarily risky."

Kelso and I started to talk at the same time. He motioned for me to continue.

"I think they wanted to test the effects of her plastic surgery. When Willie and I saw her in Illinois that Saturday night, she threatened us with a gun, and earlier that day she'd been armed and in the company of Wayne Puckett, so we were witnesses to her possible involvement in the murders. They thought if we couldn't see through her disguise, then she could adopt a new identity and move about freely with no chance of being spotted by cops."

"I guess you messed that up by recognizing her voice," Ravlin said.

Agent Falls pulled two airline envelopes from his pocket. "I think you're right about the identity change. Mrs. Taylor had these in her purse." He flipped one open and pulled out the ticket. "One first-class ticket from Miami to San Juan, Puerto Rico, for Marissa Fortello. She also had a passport, birth certificate, credit cards, and a driver's license in the same name."

"What about the other ticket?" I asked. "Did Trace also have a new identity?"

Falls opened up the second envelope and turned it upside down. Nothing fell out. "Sheriff Parker may have thought he was going to San Juan, but so far we haven't found a second ticket."

Maybe he wasn't part of Marella's future plans, I thought. "Well, Trace doesn't have the advantage of the disguise, so he'd be a hindrance and a potential threat, especially if Marella wasn't as enamored of Trace as he was of her. Maybe Fritz was supposed to take care of that loose end."

"I have one more question," Willie said. "What's the big mystery about Trace Parker's family? He told us his wife died of cancer, but Sylvia found out later they're divorced. Apparently she's still alive?"

"She's alive. I think he wanted to pull the wool over your sister's eyes and get some sympathy," Kelso said. "As long as you saw him as a nice guy and didn't get suspicious, he could let you go back to Florida. His wife divorced him in Michigan and retained custody of their daughter. There's also eight years unaccounted for on the sheriff's résumé. He left the security firm in 1984 but didn't go to Illinois until 1992. We're sure he stayed in Michigan, but the FBI is still trying to find out what he was doing there."

"Trace worked for two different security firms while he lived in Michigan," I said. "He was employed at the second firm right up until he took the job in Sangamon City. I'll bet you anything the second company is owned by Aldono Vortinto. And that could explain how Trace hooked up with Marella." I retrieved the note I'd left by my computer monitor and handed it to Falls.

Fran spoke up for the first time, sparing me the need to dwell any further on my own gullibility. "Agent Falls, is there any danger now to Judge Thorn and her brother? Mrs. Taylor's father hasn't been arrested, has he? And what about the uncle? Didn't you say that guy Fritz, who stayed here, worked for Vinnie?"

"I honestly don't know. I can't see Vinnie getting involved any further. He's already claimed Fritz left his employ and won't be coming back. And the FBI took Aldono into custody yesterday afternoon, based on Wayne

Puckett's statement. Unfortunately, Puckett's testimony is hearsay so we may not have anything that will stick. As for him being a threat, I can't see it. We have the FBI tapes, we're all witnesses to the attempted abduction, and we have Wayne Puckett on ice. There wouldn't be much point in sending anyone after Judge Thorn. You might want to put some extra security on until after Mrs. Taylor's trial, but even that may be overkill…well, poor choice of words. But I don't think there's anything to worry about."

Everyone left shortly thereafter, including Willie, who had braved the busy streets of Boca Raton on his bicycle in order to get to my condo as quickly as possible. I had plenty of time to muse about the strange sequence of events that had turned Willie's innocent vacation into a dangerous experience for both of us.

I thought back to the attraction I'd felt for the old school friend who'd become Sangamon County's sheriff. That brought a blush to my cheeks. You'd think I was old enough to know better. I hoped Willie never brought it up.

Wiser and, hopefully, safer than anytime since returning to Florida, I could now look forward to leaving my condo each day.

SHORTLY AFTER THE FIRST of the year, as I stood on my balcony on a sunny, warm weekend morning, I heard sounds of activity from next door. It was the first time in the last two rainy weeks I'd been able to open my apartment to the fresh air. Putting all caution aside, I decided to find out who was in the apartment. So I knocked on Mrs. Dawson's door and found myself face-to-face with the petite grande dame herself.

"Hello, my dear. You must have heard me banging my

luggage around, trying to put things away. Could you help me lift my bag up onto the closet shelf?"

With a sigh of relief, I entered Mrs. Dawson's apartment and happily stayed for tea while she told me a long and fascinating story about the unexpected prize she'd won in a contest she didn't remember entering. Her travel agent had confirmed the legitimacy of the tickets and reservations, she related, so how could she turn down a wonderful guided tour of Europe, even on such short notice?

"And I met such a lovely man at the Trevi Fountain," she confided with a girlish giggle. She sighed and gazed wistfully into the distance before clearing her throat and changing the subject.

As I left, I promised to come again to see all her pictures when they were developed, and to meet the "lovely man" who had called her just last evening to see if she'd arrived home safely. Edna Dawson's travels put a few ideas in my head. I pictured myself in Rome, or Paris, or Nice, and imagined a tall distinguished fellow walking toward…no, roaring toward me on his motorbike. Maybe he'd be a bit younger than I—okay, quite a bit younger than I.

I returned to my apartment and plopped down in front of my computer. The red and orange graphics of my screensaver bounced around in joyful abandon while I watched.

The whole murder business and the threat which had followed me home were over now. I should be feeling safe, secure, happy to be free of the anxiety which had plagued me for so many weeks. But way down deep, my gut kept telling me not to relax. Was this what post-traumatic stress felt like? Or did my subconscious know something my practical mind hadn't figured out?

I put my fingers on the keyboard, connected to the Internet, and traveled to the French Riviera.

TWENTY-EIGHT

MY INVITATION TO meet Edna Dawson's new friend and look at her pictures came sooner than I had anticipated. But I was grateful for the diversion, especially since my week had been full of unpleasant cases involving young offenders who had little desire for rehabilitation, interspersed with tedious and mind-numbing homeowner association disputes, which had erupted into an escalating series of retaliatory acts that defied the imagination.

Defecating on the lawn of a neighbor's three-million-dollar estate because the owner's poodle had escaped from its leash and urinated on the rare orchid growing by the defecator's pool was only *one* of the less imaginative examples.

Edna's excited voice on my answering machine apologized for giving me such short notice. She claimed she would understand if I could not come, but cocktails would be at seven and dinner at eight, please no formal dress, and, oh, yes, it would be Saturday, the next evening, and she would be so happy if I could be there, and, by the way, all her pictures were developed and they were wonderful.

I wouldn't miss this dinner for the world, for I counted on enough inspiration and encouragement to bolster my own travel plans. When I tapped at Edna's door at seven-fifteen the next evening, I wore a simple black sheath with a short skirt. Draped across my shoulders was a delicate black-and-white crocheted shawl. My black sandals were strappy flats, designed as much for comfort as for elegance.

There were at least twenty people milling about, a few chatting on the balcony, a couple perched on the edge of one of Edna's gorgeous sofas. I flashed back briefly to my defiant attempt to disobey Trace Parker's demand to get up from the couch, but shook off the memory.

I intended to have fun.

Edna pulled me into the room and handed me off to a striking young woman named Pamela, who promptly led me to the kitchen where a well-stocked bar took up most of a marble-topped island. I made myself a gin and tonic, spiked a couple of olives with a red toothpick, and edged through the guests, who were smiling and speaking as I passed by. As I looked for someone I knew, I wondered which older fellow had taken up with my neighbor in Rome.

Two women on the balcony were trying to persuade a wandering pelican to come closer. The bird watched them, occasionally dropping his head so his enormous bill rested on his breast. All he needed was a pair of glasses and he'd look like a pompous professor. Totally engrossed in the pelican's lazy perusal of humans at play, I jumped when Edna's bubbly voice, trilling an octave higher than usual, broke through my thoughts.

"Oh, there you are, Sylvia. I want you to meet my handsome Italian."

I turned, prepared to shake hands by switching the drink to my left hand and extending my right hand.

"My dear, this is Vincent." Edna looked at the man and grinned. "Vincent, this is my neighbor, Judge Thorn."

It was too late to pull back my hand. Vincent Vortinto had already taken it in a two-handed grip that looked gentle and friendly. But I felt as though I'd thrust my hand into the tight confines of a sink disposal and couldn't jerk it free. All I could do was pray no one flipped the switch to ON before I'd extricated myself.

In my heart I knew I was screwed. I tugged gently, but Vortinto didn't let go. Finally, raising my eyes to return Vortinto's gaze, I forced my mouth up at the corners and mumbled, "So nice to meet you."

I didn't want to embarrass Edna in front of all her friends, but no way could I stay at her party with this man in attendance.

"You two can chat," she said. "I need to check on dinner. Help yourselves if you need a refill. You look flushed, Sylvia. Are you okay?"

"I'm fine. A little warm. Maybe I'll go out on the balcony."

"You do that. Take care of her, Vincent."

Edna bustled away as I mentally listed the excuses I could make later to explain my speedy departure.

"Could you please give me my hand back?" No longer making the effort to smile, I straightened my shoulders and raised my chin, thinking haughty might get Vincent to back off. I probably looked more like my head was about to explode, which wouldn't have been far from the truth.

Instead of releasing his grip, however, Vincent Vortinto leaned forward and whispered his bourbon-scented words in my face. "Aldono and Marella send their best, Judge Thorn."

"Judge Thorn! Over here!"

When the male voice called out, pure reflex action jerked my head to the left to see who had called my name and—*oh, no*—who would see my hand still firmly in Vortinto's possession.

The answer registered at the same instant the flashbulb clouded my vision. All of South Florida would see my handshake. Maybe the whole country would see. I shut my eyes and watched tiny black bugs with shiny yellow skins wander across the backs of my eyelids. When I raised my right hand to rub my eyes, I realized Vortinto had finally let go.

As my vision returned to normal, the little bugs began to rain downward like black and yellow confetti. I could see the tops of people's heads and then, finally, the rest of their bodies, unfolding the same way photographs load on my computer. I frantically searched the room for the man with the camera, planning to assault him and destroy his property if that's what it took.

He was gone. It was over. The black and yellow confetti represented my life and my career, and there would be no need for a sink disposal to get rid of the pieces.

Somehow, I moved my numb body into the kitchen and set my glass on the counter, explained to Edna that I wasn't feeling well, and returned to the comforting silence of my own condo. The black dress went back into the closet, the shoes to their slot in the shoe rack, everything else in the hamper.

A hot shower, lavender body lotion, warm pajamas, and my thick terry robe—what else would I need except for comfort food?

I cut an apple into wedges and placed the wedges on a large plate with a scoop of caramel sauce and another scoop of chunky peanut butter. Armed with a plastic spoon and an old-fashioned glass filled with Sauvignon Blanc, I sat down in my favorite chair, propped my feet on the footstool, and sampled a tart, crisp apple wedge coated with caramel. The book I'd been reading lay on the table, but the subject matter, true crime, didn't seem to satisfy my needs at the moment. I picked up the TV remote and began to flip from channel to channel, looking for something that would make me laugh. The best thing I could find was an old black-and-white Road show with Bing Crosby, Bob Hope, and Dorothy Lamour.

When the movie ended, and I'd used my plastic spoon to scrape up the remaining sauce and peanut butter, I placed my plate in the dishwasher and poured another glass of wine. Before I sat down, I pulled the drapes across the balcony doors and set my security alarm. With the lights and television off, there remained only the green glow from the alarm control panel and a tiny red light on the answering machine.

The evening had clearly been a setup. Edna's trip had been arranged by Vincent Vortinto to help his niece keep tabs on me while she recovered from her face-lift. When he decided to catch up with Edna at the Trevi Fountain, it could have been insurance to keep her traveling, or maybe he'd thought the contact with her would be potentially useful.

Only later would he decide to wage his vendetta in such a blatant manner. I suppose I should have been counting my blessings. Vortinto could have hired someone to execute a more permanent ending to my story.

Willie and my parents would need to be warned. Since my brother had accompanied them to Orlando for the weekend, nothing more could be done until they returned on Monday. Unless Willie started receiving the bad vibes which I no doubt sent out in waves, he wouldn't call until they were home.

With that thought, the phone rang.

"Judge Thorn. I'm glad you're home," said Agent Falls. "Vincent Vortinto is inside your complex and may be inside your building."

"I know. He's having dinner in Edna Dawson's apartment. I was just there."

"What happened?"

"A photographer took pictures of Vortinto standing close, my hand in his. Before I could object, or even react,

the photographer disappeared. My reputation is compromised. Gee, I can't wait to see tomorrow's newspaper."
I'd been droning until I slipped into sarcasm.

"Judge Thorn, I'm so sorry. We'll be nearby until Vortinto leaves. You're not going out?"

"No. I won't be going out."

"Could we meet tomorrow? Breakfast?"

"Come over here, please. Anytime after eight. Bring pastries, lots of them."

This baby FBI agent chuckled, as if he thought I was joking.

"I mean it, Agent Falls. You'd better show up with two cheese Danishes and a bear claw or you're not getting inside this apartment."

I slammed the receiver down, grabbed my glass, and went back for one more refill. The sobbing started before the tears came, and by the time I finished, I was drained. The pathetic self-pity disappeared, however, replaced by cold, calculating outrage. Vincent Vortinto wasn't going to mess with me or my family again. Maybe Agent Falls would be helpful, but my own Yankee ingenuity remained my weapon of choice.

Time to do a little homework. The more information I had, the better prepared I'd be for my meeting with Falls. Still carrying the now-tepid glass of wine, I hurried to my computer, fired it up, and connected to the Internet. As I logged into the database, I realized I would soon be losing access to that system, so I needed to gather as much information as I could.

I sat back a moment, thinking. I'd been worrying about how to explain my sudden departure to Edna Dawson, but what if she wasn't the innocent little old lady she appeared to be? When I entered her name and address, the returned data answered my question and made me feel like an idiot for believing her Trevi Fountain story. The brief entry gave one alias, Anna Vortinto, and listed Aldono and Vincent as her brothers.

Anna Vortinto had one conviction for running a house of prostitution which she tried to pass off as a motel.

She had served three years in prison before securing her parole.

Unbelievable. I'd heard so many stories about the risk of making friends with your neighbors in South Florida, but I'd never had firsthand experience.

I returned to the query screen and entered Vincent Vortinto's name. The program chugged away for several minutes, then returned a whole page of clickable date entries. I foresaw an all-nighter ahead of me, and I needed help.

It took a little over ten minutes to make a pot of full-strength coffee and to gather legal pads, pens, index cards, and a can of mixed nuts. I clicked on the first date entry, 1944–1950, and started to read.

TWENTY-NINE

I BECAME CONSCIOUS of a persistent tapping on my door. Forcing my eyelids open, I tried to figure out where I was. The darkened room eventually came into focus. I'd fallen asleep curled up on the sofa with a soft, crocheted afghan bunched around my shoulders and my bare feet tucked under a plush throw pillow.

The last thing I remembered was the decision I had made at four in the morning—to take a fifteen-minute nap. If I read my watch correctly, it was now eight-fifteen. Agent Falls had probably been waiting for a quarter of an hour. Hopefully, he hadn't eaten my pastries.

Pulling my robe around me, I staggered toward the door. At the same time, I tried to remember if I'd turned off the coffeepot. I wanted *fresh* caffeine, and a decanter of burned sludge would piss me off big-time. A quick peek through my door's spy hole confirmed young Falls—first name Damon—standing in the hall. He must have heard me rustling around near the door because he looked back at the peephole and held up his right hand, which clutched the bakery sack. I could also see the stack of newspapers he had balanced on his left shoulder.

I disengaged the security alarm and let him in, snatching the bag out of his hand and heading for the kitchen without a smile or greeting. The coffeepot was off, and an inch of water sat in the bottom of the decanter. I thanked the goddess for the favor, wondering how she'd managed to extend such a gift to someone whose karma was obviously in the toilet.

"Good morning," Damon ventured as he closed my door and flipped the lock. He carried the newspapers to the table, opened the balcony drapes, returned to the table, and pulled the paper sections apart, separating the Sunday ads and sorting through the main sections.

As I made a super-strength pot of coffee, I watched him out of the corner of my eye, noting his tidy sorting procedure. His appearance and confidence and silence didn't escape my notice, either.

I touched my hair, wondering how bad I looked, then dropped my hand, disgusted with myself. Agent Damon Falls was a kid. Well, relative to me, anyway. I checked him over again. He hadn't shaved, but his hair was wet, so I figured he'd either been running or had recently showered. Jeans, running shoes, and a gray sweatshirt that said BADGERS on the front. An aqua Dolphins baseball cap turned with the bill to the back. Definitely a kid.

"I have the *Miami Herald, Sun-Sentinel, Boca Raton News,* and *Palm Beach Post,*" he said. "Sit down and look through them. I'll pour the coffee when it's done."

I gave him a dirty look for telling me what to do, pulled two mugs out of the cupboard and set them by the pot, carried my sack of pastries to the table, then sat down and devoured my bear claw.

"The sections are sorted." Ignoring my antisocial behavior, he cleared his throat and pointed to each pile in turn, identifying front page, local news, business, and sports.

I shoved the goodies sack aside and pulled the front-page sections over, beginning with the Boca paper and ending with the *Miami Herald.* Happy to find I'd been spared the indignity of a front-page story, I checked the local sections. Sometime after I started, I noticed a cup of coffee had magically appeared in front of me. By the time I'd finished drinking three mugs of coffee and knocked off one cheese Danish, I'd completed my search.

Damon sat quietly across from me, nursing his coffee and watching my every move. He'd apparently had no trouble finding his way around the kitchen. The sugar bowl, a teaspoon and a container of cream sat on the table. His coffee was pale beige.

I leaned back in my chair and rubbed my hand over my face, the crumbs from my feeding frenzy spilling onto the terry-cloth loops of my robe. "Why?" I said. "Why isn't it there?"

Damon didn't answer.

I jumped up, entered the kitchen, and refilled my cup. I rinsed out the decanter and threw away the old grounds. After a moment's debate with myself, I started another pot of coffee. Then I slowly paced back and forth, thinking while I waited.

Finally, I returned to the dining table. Damon, silent, watched me. I was sure he knew something but wanted me to figure it out.

"He plans to hold it over my head, doesn't he? Use it to get something he wants."

Damon nodded, but still didn't speak.

There must be something more, I thought. The hours of reading I'd done the night before—studying Vortinto's criminal record and his short prison stays and his huge list of known associates—hadn't yielded a clue. Or else the clues hadn't penetrated the foggy exhaustion that followed the encounter in Edna Dawson/Anna Vortinto's apartment.

I shut my eyes and tried to remember.

Wait a minute! My eyes popped open and I glared at the

man who sat across from me. He didn't know I'd spent the evening reading Vortinto's history. What had I overlooked?

Vortinto, Vortinto, I thought.

Nothing.

What else?

Suddenly, I jumped up and hurried to my desk and yanked my briefcase off the floor. I fumbled the combination on the tiny lock twice before the case snapped open and I reached in to pull out my copy of the dockets for the current and following months.

I found the answer on my calendar, just two weeks away. A kid, with a snotty attitude and a well-known lawyer with dubious credentials, had been charged with a hit-and-run. The rich, powerful victim was very much alive, and determined to nail the kid. She also had an attorney with impeccable credentials.

And the name of the punk was Donny Dawson.

Like hell it was! I'd bet my last cheese Danish the kid's real name was Aldono Vortinto, Jr.—Marella's brother. Or maybe Aldono Vortinto III—Marella's nephew.

I hadn't given a thought to researching the rest of the family, not that I'd really had the time, considering the amount of information I'd waded through just looking at Vincent's history.

"Did you already know this?" I asked as I thrust the schedule into Damon Falls's hand.

He glanced at the papers and then placed them on the table. "Sure."

"Why the hell didn't you tell me?"

He shrugged. "Because I don't know what you should do. I thought maybe if you got there on your own, you'd see a way out."

"You mean a way to get Vincent Vortinto out of my life forever?"

"Yes. You can't do what he wants you to do, which is to make sure Donny Dawson never goes to jail. At the same time, you can't refuse without jeopardizing your job. And possibly the safety of yourself and your family. I think that's what they call being between a rock and a hard place."

I rolled my eyes at his less-than-clever observation.

Neither of us spoke for several minutes, then Damon said, "With your background in the FBI, your security clearance, your knowledge of the law—"

"Damn it, Falls, I'm too old and too smart to get sucked into undercover work."

He gave another nonchalant shrug as he pushed his chair back from the table and stood. He pulled a business card from his jeans pocket and tossed it on the table. "You know best, Judge Thorn. If there's anything else I can do, call me."

Mouth agape, I watched my only safe and secure connection to the outside world turn his back on me and stride briskly to the door. He turned briefly to suggest I reset my security code and lock the door. Then he left.

Hell, I didn't need him. And I sure as hell didn't need the FBI. Working for Vortinto would be more lucrative and probably less dangerous.

I walked to the door and peered through the peephole, hoping, just a little, that Damon would be lurking in the hall, waiting for me to call him back.

He wasn't there.

It wouldn't have mattered, I assured myself. With the door locked and the security code reset, I relaxed and wandered into the kitchen. I grabbed a fresh cup of coffee and returned to the table where my last Danish waited for me.

Seated so that I could stare out through the balcony

doors, I let my mind free-fall through my options. The obvious and least desirable ones came first.

If I did what Vortinto wanted and found a way to keep his delinquent relative out of jail, the threat of exposure would go away.

Sure! For about ten minutes!

There would always be another task, then another. And even if the threat disappeared, there was nothing in my up-bringing, education, or life history that would ever let me cooperate with a crime family that dealt in drugs, prosti-tution, fraud—and the list went on and on.

Working with the FBI undercover to nail Vortinto for bribery was tempting, but I knew it wouldn't end there. The FBI would get me in so deep, my whole family would qualify for the witness protection program.

I could bring my dilemma to the chief judge of the 15th circuit, although, if I did, it would lead to a fairly predictable result. A stickler for the rules and a rigid enforcer of procedure and appearance, Judge Blue would force me out without a moment's thought and never suffer one second of conscience in the process. It would be called a resignation, of course, probably due to ill health or the desire to follow other pursuits. And what could Vincent Vortinto do? He could still pay me back by releasing the picture and spreading stories of an association between us. Sabotage any future plans, without a doubt.

The pelicans were back, a flock of three cruising along the canal. I pictured them reaching their destination and plopping onto the water, where they would bob up and down on gentle ripples.

It would be nice to fly away from my problem. There were no money constraints. Andy's life insurance and my divorce payoff had left me financially secure.

Stupid idea. I would never bail out and leave my family to face Vortinto's vengeance.

Suddenly, I nodded. The answer had been clear all along. When I considered the stubborn nature of my family, our independence and our loyalty, I knew there was only one thing to do.

THIRTY

SUNDAY PROMISED TO BE a long and lonely day, I thought, as I realized what I'd ignored up to this moment.

Thank goodness my parents and Willie would not return from Orlando until Monday evening.

Maybe my friend Tequila Picon was home! I dialed her number but sighed in frustration when her answering machine announced, "Don' want to talk now. Leave message. Maybe I call you back."

Would Fran be on duty in the Security office? I decided it was worth a try, but I struck out again. Mr. Boggs said that Fran had scheduled a couple of vacation days and would return Monday. When he asked if he could do anything for me, I thanked him, said no, and hung up.

As I wandered toward the glass doors of the balcony, I wistfully considered the pale streaks of white cloud against the light blue sky. I thought of the soothing sound of tiny waves washing over the sand…and suddenly realized what I'd done.

Confining myself to my condo, in a sense building my own prison, was not the way I intended to live my life.

Within five minutes I'd thrown my robe on the bed and dressed in sweatpants, T-shirt, and running shoes. I turned off the coffeepot, grabbed money, driver's license, and keys out of my purse, and pulled a small bottle of water from the refrigerator.

The drive to Delray Beach was short, the hike along the

water long and peaceful, like a meditation, and the blissful lunch at Boston's had surely been spiked with tranquility and flavored with contentment.

With a sense of resolve and relief, I returned to my condo. I reminded myself again that life must be lived to the fullest; that an overabundance of safety and security makes us weak and complacent, and that risk and loss can make us strong.

Monday's heavy court schedule kept me busy until five, leaving me plenty of time to change clothes before driving to the airport in West Palm Beach. My folks and Willie were expected on the Orlando-West Palm shuttle at seven.

Willie, of course, immediately wanted to know what was wrong, while my mother predictably asked if I'd had any fun over the weekend.

"Kristina, stop, leave Sylvia alone." My father hugged me while Willie raised one eyebrow and watched as though he could read my thoughts.

"Later, Willie," I said. "Let's get out of here, first."

My reticent father and the temporarily subdued Willie sat back in silence as I drove to my parent's retirement community apartment. The quiet, however, did not deter my mother, who wanted to update me on Epcot's new attractions, the wonderful Norwegian buffet they'd enjoyed, and the exorbitant prices charged for everything, even though she'd loved every minute of the trip.

That made it even more difficult for me to tell my family what had happened over the weekend and what I wanted to do about it. I said that my plan of action could place them all in danger, but I needn't have worried. We sat around the table and everyone listened, their faces reflecting first dismay, then indignation, finally resignation.

"How dare that man threaten a Grisseljon?" my mother said. "Especially a judge."

"Well, Mom, he hasn't exactly threatened anyone yet."

"But the threat is implied."

"Yes, I think so. And the FBI agent seemed to think so, too."

"You didn't consider the FBI offer?" asked my dad.

He was a great fan of novels of national and international intrigue. I'm sure he thought I'd make a wonderful agent, involved in exciting cases which he could experience vicariously through my stories.

"Dad, that's not an option."

He shrugged and pursed his lips, and I wondered if his formerly high level of rational thinking had slipped. But he reached forward and patted my hand as he assured me he only wanted to make sure I'd thoroughly considered all of my options.

Since my parents had made an equally drastic life change when they retired, and were thrilled with the choices they'd made, they would not hesitate to support my decision. All three of us turned to Willie, waiting for the words of wisdom we knew he was dying to share.

He cleared his throat and shifted his position so his elbows rested on the table. "Are you sure this is what you want to do, Syl?"

"Absolutely."

"You know, of course—"

"I know, Willie. You told me so. I've heard it a thousand times."

"Only good will come of this, Syl. I feel it."

That was good enough for me. "Okay, guys. Be ready first thing in the morning. I'll call before I leave my condo. Come on, Willie, I'll drop you off."

Willie remained thoughtful during the twenty minutes it took to return him to his Boca apartment. When I stopped the car to let him out, he said, "It will be fine. I can help, you know."

"Do what?"

"I mean, after."

"Ah. Yes, there is that."

Once again, Willie left me with something to think about. However, I needed to put the problem aside until after I'd dealt with the immediate situation. I was certain that Tuesday would prove to be a busy and very stressful day.

When I arrived back at my condo, I was greeted by the flashing red light on my answering machine.

"Hey, Judge, you hung up without leavin' a message!" Tequila shouted. "Why you do that? Then I have to call that star-six-nine thing and then call you back and you still not there. At least I leave a message."

Her hang-up was pretty loud, too.

Tak must have had a bad day, so I decided to wait a little longer to return her call. I didn't think she'd care for my plan of action, and figured she'd offer to contact a hit man for me. Or offer to do Vortinto in all by herself. Tak knows no fear, and she had her own code of ethics which didn't always conform to the legal system's definition of right and wrong.

Most reasonable people would wonder how it happened that a woman who'd advanced to the lofty position of circuit court judge would become close friends with a wild woman like Tequila Picon. Frankly, I would have trouble explaining the relationship myself, unless I admitted that in my heart and soul I was Tak's gringo twin. If only those damned Norwegian genes wouldn't keep getting in my way.

Rest and relaxation were much more appealing than the prospect of listening to Tak screech at me for making big decisions without consulting her. She would consider this crisis no more earthshaking than the bad haircut which had triggered our first verbal exchange, and she would offer her opinions as well as instructions without hesitation. Once again, I decided the conversation could wait.

It was ten o'clock, plenty of time to formulate my plan for the next day, watch the news, and maybe try to lose myself in one of the novels I'd picked up at the grocery store. I walked into the kitchen, heated a cup of water in the microwave, dropped in an orange spice tea bag, and carried the hot drink, a legal-sized pad, and my book selection to the living room. I started with the pad. Soon a list of checked and starred items filled the first page. I spent the next twenty minutes reading the list over and over until I could recite each item without hesitation.

After tossing the pad into my briefcase, then returning to the kitchen for another cup of tea, I switched on the TV and checked the top headlines and the weather.

By twenty after eleven, I was curled in the corner of the couch with the new paperback open on my lap. By eleven forty-five I realized I'd absorbed nothing I'd read and would have to start over when my mind was ready to focus.

Afraid I wouldn't be able to sleep and worried that fatigue would interfere with my ability to communicate clearly, I stared at the ceiling in my bedroom, where the minutes ticked from the clever clock that displayed the time wherever I aimed its tiny projector. I saw the hour turn from twelve fifty-nine to one. Then nothing more until the alarm jarred me awake at six o'clock, after a deep, dreamless sleep.

THIRTY-ONE

SINCE I HAD to pick up Willie in Boca, and our parents in Deerfield Beach, each at their respective apartments, I scrambled to leave my place by seven-thirty.

Our destination was Judge Blue's office in West Palm Beach. By the time everyone was gathered and we were on I-95 headed north, rush-hour traffic controlled our speed. Even so, we made it by nine, thanks to a remarkable absence of accidents and construction slowdowns.

I knew walking into Judge Blue's office without an appointment wasn't going to make him a happy man. But since he rarely smiled anyway, what did it matter? The firestorm I was about to ignite would make a little unscheduled meeting seem like a spark from a cigarette lighter.

When we entered the judge's reception area, my family sat down and I approached Margaret, who had been Blue's inhospitable assistant for the last ten years. Her eyes wide with shock, her brow furrowed in alarm, she pulled her calendar forward and read the day's schedule, even flipping a page or two into the future to see if she'd missed something.

"No, you won't find me on there," I assured her. "We have an emergency, Margaret. And the first thing I need you to do is call my court assistant and tell him I won't be in for the rest of the week, and that he should postpone the schedule until you get back to him."

Margaret turned into a pillar of salt. Her skin faded to

a pasty white and the only part of her body that moved was the corner of her eye where a tiny twitch appeared.

My mother walked up beside me and whispered, "Do you think she's okay?"

"She'll be fine." I knew that to be true because I'd seen this before. "She's only temporarily paralyzed. Happens with any extraordinary event. Any moment now, she'll recover."

Mom gave Margaret another doubtful glance, and seemed relieved to see a little color return to Margaret's cheeks and the focus return to her eyes as she said, "You're not playing a prank?"

Did the woman honestly believe I'd try to pull a fast one on Judge Blue so I could have a few days off?

"No," I said. "This is a very serious matter."

"I'll make the call right now. Shall I tell Judge Blue you're here? He doesn't have anyone in his office at the moment." She looked down at the appointment book. "He's not expecting anyone until ten."

"Maybe that would be best." I straightened my shoulders and waited, praying the next few hours would pass by quickly and that I would forget the pain as quickly as a young mother is said to forget about the trauma of childbirth. Of course, I'd never believed that, so I didn't have high expectations.

Before I had time to pursue that line of thought, Margaret returned and invited me into the chief judge's office. I motioned my team to follow, startling the now totally confused assistant. We filed into Blue's inner sanctum and waited until he acknowledged our presence with a glare, then waved us into the chairs lined up in front of his desk.

"You don't have an appointment," he said, staring at me. "And I know you have cases before your court today. What the Sam Hill is this all about?"

It took me a full hour to tell my story, starting with the

call that summoned me from Florida to Illinois to assist Willie. I have to give Blue a lot of credit. He gave me his full attention, even jotted down a few notes as I spoke. When he saw I'd finished, he reviewed his scribbles and asked a few questions, which I answered as thoroughly as I could. Then he sat back in silent contemplation.

"Are you sure this is what you want to do?" he asked.

"I think it's best."

He looked at my dad and mom, then at Willie. "And the three of you support her decision? In spite of the risks?"

All three nodded yes, but only my dad spoke. "None of us are willing to compromise our principles, nor are we willing to run like scared rabbits. This is the right thing to do."

"Okay. First things first." Judge Blue pressed the button on his phone and told Margaret to find a court reporter as fast as possible. He also told her to find the highest level prosecutor from the district attorney's office.

I sighed, a strong sense of relief slowly absorbing the tension in my neck and shoulders. Events would now move beyond my control, and the only tasks ahead of me involved telling and retelling the story, and then finally announcing the method we'd chosen to resolve the dilemma.

It would be a long day.

After five hours of recorded testimony, a thirty-minute break to wolf down the sandwich and chips ordered by the now fully functional Margaret, and a couple of short coffee and restroom breaks, we were all ready for the final scene. Margaret had made the arrangements shortly after lunch, and everything was set up outside on the courthouse steps. The press conference had been called for ten after six—a good time for live coverage.

I hoped Vincent Vortinto was sitting in front of his television with a strong drink in his hand. I also hoped he'd get a roaring case of indigestion so he wouldn't enjoy his dinner.

When I stepped outside to face the microphones and the local reporters, I was accompanied by a support group that had grown from three to fourteen. Judge Blue spoke first, describing in general terms why the press conference had been called and praising my integrity, honesty, and sense of ethical responsibility.

I moved confidently to the podium, buoyed by Judge Blue's praise and his strong support, ignoring the fact I'd given him the easy way out.

The reporters liked me, a sentiment I didn't always return but usually pretended to, and they made the conference easier by listening respectfully during the twenty minutes it took to give an abbreviated version of my story. The biggest difference in the telling, of course, was that I spoke to the press now, and had to be much more careful of slander. Hard to believe slander could be an issue when discussing a family of criminals and ex-cons.

"I recently attended a social event at the apartment of my next-door neighbor," I said, after wading through the involved tale of murder and deceit in Illinois that had followed me back home to Boca. "At the party, a photographer took my picture, just as I was introduced to another guest, Mr. Vincent Vortinto. The photograph will show my hand in Mr. Vortinto's hand, and our heads bent toward each other as he greeted me. There has been no further discussion between Mr. Vortinto and myself concerning this photograph, and I have not been approached in any way by any person on any related matter.

"However, as Judge Blue explained, his court is above reproach and has never faced a scandal involving the appearance of impropriety, the violation of professional ethics, or the dismissal of a judge for illegal actions of any kind. It is our intention to make sure it does not become an issue now.

"I am currently involved in two situations involving members of Mr. Vortinto's family. The district attorney's office spent the day with me, my family, Judge Blue, and a court reporter. The details of every incident related to the Illinois murder case and all subsequent events have been recorded, signed, notarized, and copies are now on their way to the FBI and to the Illinois authorities, who will be prosecuting the murder case.

"It is, therefore, in the best interest of the court, and in the best interests of me and my family, for me to resign. I want to thank Judge Blue for helping me accomplish so much in such a short amount of time, and for standing with me during this announcement. I will not be answering any questions at this time. Thank you."

The attorney from the D.A.'s office came forward and spoke briefly to the reporters, giving me a chance to edge toward the building. From there I could get to the parking garage by taking the elevator down to the basement level.

The reporters were fooled for a couple of minutes, until they realized they weren't getting any information of substance, but by then it was too late. I had gathered my family around me, exchanged one more handshake with Judge Blue, and escaped into the waiting elevator.

I grinned at the trusty Margaret who'd propped open the doors, but by the time I'd turned around to say thanks, she was gone.

Everyone was tired and no one wanted to talk. I dropped Mom, Dad, and Willie off at their respective apartments, with promises to call. Then I headed home.

Did I feel angry? Resentful? Depressed?

The truth was, I felt I'd been given a gift.

My biggest task now would be to decide what to do next. So far, my only solid plan involved lunch at Boston's with Tequila Picon, currently scheduled for the next day.

By then, Tak would have read the papers and would be in rare form.

She'd probably have my new life plan down on paper!

TAK STROLLED ONTO the restaurant's downstairs porch, spotted me sitting at an end table with my first Corona already half-consumed, and waved as she hurried inside to the bar to grab her own beer.

Upon her return, she tossed her newspaper on the table. "The crap you find in the *Sun-Sentinel* these days," she muttered. "Did you read about the bitch with all those dogs? Starvin' them! How could someone do that? You tell me, Syl, how somethin' like that happen in this country."

Almost immediately, I realized she'd called me "Syl" instead of "Judge." But by a mutual and unspoken agreement, neither of us brought the subject up. We didn't have to. When we were halfway through our sandwiches, with our chairs arranged so we could ignore the other restaurant patrons and, instead, watch the beach scenes across the street, we heard someone move a chair very close to our table. We both turned to see who'd invaded our space.

Vincent Vortinto. What a surprise.

"Well, the former Judge Thorn," he said. "Imagine running into you here."

"Who is this man, Syl? Do you know him?"

I could practically see the hairs standing up on the back of Tak's neck. She already knew about this man, and exactly what he was doing.

"Don't worry, Tak," I said. "Mr. Vortinto won't be staying long."

He nodded. "Only a moment. I wanted to tell you how much I admire cleverness, Ms. Thorn. You must be an excellent chess player."

"No, Mr. Vortinto. I don't play chess at all."

"I think you should. You would be very good. Perhaps you'll let me teach you."

It was the final straw for Tak. And it didn't sit too well with me, either. Both of us stood, forcing Vortinto to stand, too, or look incredibly rude.

"Not bloody likely," I muttered.

"Bye-bye now," Tak added.

"Ladies. Until another time." Vortinto tilted his head in the suggestion of a mannerly bow. Then he walked stiffly away.

"He try again, Syl, you know?"

"I know." I sat down, picked up my sandwich, and took a huge bite. "Look over there," I mumbled through a mouthful of food. When I realized Tak hadn't understood me, I pointed toward the beach.

She turned to look, then sat back in her chair and watched the tall blond guy shed his street clothes and toss them into his car. He now wore red briefs, which may or may not have been official swimwear. He reached into his car, pulled out a tube of cream, and applied it to his already pink shoulders and arms. Finally, he pulled out a large beach towel, slammed his car door shut, and sauntered toward the water.

Tak's chuckle was barely perceptible, but I heard it. We always laughed at the winter tourists who were foolish enough to go into the water. When they came out, they were often blue and shivering violently.

I took a swallow of beer, then another bite of my sandwich. Life was great. I had everything I needed to survive. Only one small dilemma niggled at me. What to do with the rest of my life? *Later!* For now, it was enough to be at Boston's, enjoying every moment with Tak.

I lifted my empty beer bottle and held up two fingers, signaling the waitress to bring us another round.